How to Slay a Lion

A sweet small town rom-com

Jen Carpenter

Cover Design by Ally Haney at @allyhaney.myportfolio.com.

To Neil: My love, my muse, and my partner in all things impossible.

A note from the Author

To capture the small-town vibe and reflect the complexity of a large family, having a wide cast was essential.

For your enjoyment and ease, I've included a comprehensive cast list at the end of the novel. Below are the most frequently appearing characters:

Amelia May Anderson, Librarian

Lucas Chernov, Oldest son and Head Contractor at Noil Construction

Nemean (Neme), Newfoundland Dog

Grandpoppy, Amelia's Grandfather

Andrei Chernov, Second oldest son and works at Chernov Realty

Baba (Babushka), Lucas's Grandmother

Mikey Edgewood, Library Patron

Sandy, Library Board Member, Patron, Grandmother of Mikey

Simon, Retired police officer with speedometer
Magnolia Grace, Lawyer
Mitchell Ricks, Noil Construction CEO
Kim Ricks, Daughter of Mitchell and ex-fiancé of Lucas
Mayor Davis, Mayor of Herasburg
Marcus Mettle, Library Director

This story contains mild, light-hearted references to conflict, delivered with a comedic touch. Cancer and a degenerative disease are discussed in brief. Themes include family dynamics, small-town life, and forgiveness.

How to Slay a Lion

A sweet small town rom-com

Jen Carpenter

Chapter One

Amelia

As the town librarian, I know better than to break the law—but I'm about to do it anyway.

I scan for escape routes—the dense forest, towering vines, and abundant ivy at the end of the immaculate driveway will do.

I twist my shoulders, reversing the car with a delicate foot on the brake pedal. If I ease into stop just right, the squealing of my back wheel won't give me away.

In the backseat, Nemean, my trusted decade-old Newfoundland dog, whines.

"Don't worry, boy," I whisper. "We'll find it."

I slip the car into park and open the back door, "The library needs us, now more than ever," I remind him.

Lucas—the oldest Chernov son and a head contractor trying to demolish the 110-year-old town library building—has a document that threatens the library.

He is staying at his childhood home, the Chernov mansion. I know my irrational amygdala is driving right now, but I don't care.

I have to destroy that document—the manila envelope must die.

Earlier that day, my years of refined eavesdropping librarian skills became imperative. The Chernov brothers had met outside the library building, took some photos of the building, and gave Lucas a manila envelope.

"This should be the ticket to convince any doubter on the city council why demolishing the library is best for the town," Lucas's brother Nikola said.

Lucas waved the envelope, "The library building has to go."

Lucas's words felt like a knife twisting in the middle of my booklover of a heart. Little does he know, I'd do anything to protect Lionstone Library—like breaking the law.

All day, thoughts swirl of Lucas having evidence to persuade the town that the library must be pushed down, pulverized, and demolished—for slimy, lucrative, disgusting modern apartments.

A heist is the only answer, I repeat to myself. All I know is that the manila envelope is the wrecking ball to the walls of my home away from home—the town library. He has it, and I have to destroy it.

Becoming *The Terminator*—just for tonight, is essential for our town.

The car door light flickers; Nemean whines as his entire body lumbers out of the back seat. "Shhhh," I say, "Neme, it's a brilliant idea. You'll see." I swat at a few of his long orange hairs floating in the car and realize several are my reddish strands.

"This will be quick." I close the door with two hands.

I even reason that not knowing exactly what is in the envelope will work in my favor—I rehearse my statement to Judge Clements if I get caught: "Your honor, I'm so sorry." I'd flip my frizzy hair over my shoulders and bat my eyelashes at him, "I didn't actually know what I was destroying, honestly; can you blame me? I was trying to save our town from another dark age and from the *Chernov Brothers*."

Lucas Chernov deserves this, to be robbed; seriously, what type of contractor announces to his hometown that he intends to demolish the library to build apartments?

The Chernov mansion is in sight; soft lighting up the long driveway pulls me in, and the warble of the frogs bolsters my confidence.

Neme—who watched all the rom-com DVDs from the library with me and always waits his turn to lick my spoon for our favorite pistachio ice cream—has gone most places with me since Mom died. Bringing him along wasn't the wisest move tonight, but having him always helps. If I ran into any of the Chernov men who tried to attack me, Nemean would scare them away by his sheer size. But if I'm being honest, life seems a little more bearable if I can reach out and touch him—I need his reassurance, especially as I break the law.

My legs reach long as I use my stealth strides along their property and around the back. I'm sly—I'm Robin Hood; Chernovs are filthy rich and don't need some mangy new apartments.

I know the Chernov mansion well enough; Dimitri, the fourth Chernov son, dated my best friend in high school, and I was the dependable third wheel. There are ten blasted Chernov brothers—*ten*—from four different women.

I hoped my odds of running into Lucas were high when I went to their home as a high schooler.

I can admit to myself now, because I'm in the sunset of my twenties, that my twitterpation for Lucas in high school is the most one-sided feeling I've ever experienced—maybe my undeniable curiosity about Lucas helped me mourn Mom somehow? To this day, I'm proud that I asked him out when I finally did run into him.

I, Amelia May Anderson, high school queen of frizz and taped-together glasses, asked him out. His senior voice said no, and my freshman eyes cried for a week—he taught me my first hard-learned lesson of the dating pecking order: Beautiful men with money have wings and can fly high up in the sky and have the pick of the flock.

And I was a penguin—the frumpy kind with a lion's mane for hair. I had Lasik eye surgery a few years back, so that helped, but my hair was much longer, almost to my waist, and just as frizzy.

It doesn't matter now that he was the first and longest crush I'd ever experienced; Lucas was the one person who was threatening my proverbial child—the library.

My feet slide across the cut grass, passing the fountain and the edging with perfect shrubs—his window is open.

The screen pops off with one quick push. "Wait here, boy," I whisper. He whines and looks behind us, out into the yard and the forest beyond, like he drew the shorter stick.

"I need you to warn me if anyone comes, okay?" He pants with his tongue hanging out.

Legs bent tight, I slip through the window.

In high school, one of Lucas's many younger brothers somehow deactivated the alarm system for this window so we could sneak in and out without their tycoon father, Mr. Zolton Chernov, catching us. Lucas was always gone. I assumed he used the non-alarm window and attended every party in town, breaking every freshman girl's heart he got his hands on.

My feet search for the ground, but it's too far down, so I slip off the window sill. A long wooden leg twists up my landing—my hands are quick, and I stabilize a three-legged lamp I almost sent to its death.

No alarm blaring. I lower my shoulders, allowing my heart more room to hammer against my ribs. A whirling white noise machine doesn't hide the loud inhale and exhale of snores—the nightlight from the hall lights up the room just enough, and I cover my mouth.

A pink robe hangs on the back door. Intricate blanket designs hang on the wall. Tiny Russian nesting dolls cover the bookshelf, and dentures are on the nightstand. I look at the bed; a bundle of curlers, grey hair, and a giant pink mask with clipart eyeballs look back at me.

The small lump of blankets goes up and down like a reinflating balloon.

This is *not* Lucas's room anymore.

I instantly reach back to slip out the window, but I freeze—I've made it this far—aborting my mission right as I got my foot in the door would be counterproductive. *The fate of the library depends on this*; I pinch my eyes tight.

Manila envelop, that's what I came to destroy.

My feet face the room and are soft against the inch-thick carpet as I escape the room, and the hallway is as wide as I remember. My chest heaves as I rationalize that Lucas's room has to be close by.

My hand twists the door handle of the closest room, and it cracks open. Hallway light spills across the dark room—the manila envelope lies on a desk several steps into the room.

I walk heel to toe, heel to toe, and extend my arm.

The slim envelope fits nicely in my hand like it knows its fate. I can hear it say, "Amelia, thank you for rescuing me from this evil man. Let's get out of here, and I'll happily live in the library's shredder until you recycle me. I promise to live a better purpose in my next life."

Heel to toe, I'm back out of the room.

That's when a loud crash freezes my body, and the envelope slips from my hand—I cover my face at my lack of foresight. I've left the window open, and the sound of those giant landing paws; I know them anywhere.

I open the older woman's door again and tense every limb. *Please still be sleeping and breathing.*

"Neme," I hiss, "what are you doing, boy?" I speak more with my hands. My dog turns his head like he was asking me the same thing. He walks toward me, and I look at the sleeping body in the bed; she doesn't move an inch. Neme starts to breathe heavily, letting some giant drool stream from his mouth to the ground.

I crouch down and wipe the drool with my sleeve; it smears like egg whites.

I stand up and roll up my sleeve, hiding Neme's slobber, and we make it back to the hallway, and my hands reach back down for the envelope, only to hear the faint cock of a gun.

"Don't......move," a solid male voice.

Lucas.

One room off. One step away. *I'm so close.*

The envelope lay between us.

"Hi.....eh," I stand tall and bite my lower lip, "I don't want to get shot," I say, trying to look innocent.

My big eyes scan the gun. It looks like a Nerf gun but has an extended short barrel and an orange tip.

I take a deep breath—it's a salt gun. I remember his brothers shooting each other with salt around the mansion every time I visited.

My scan extends to him and I cringe.

Red and green flannel pajamas cover him with large lettering, *Want to hear a pizza Christmas joke?* with a small picture of a cheese pizza wearing a Christmas hat. *Never mind, it's too cheesy.* I press my lips tight.

His shirt isn't buttoned up all the way, and I jerk my eyes to the envelope.

"It's not even Halloween yet—it's too early for Christmas flannel," I say.

"I said don't move...or talk."

"I'm pretty sure you only said, 'Don't move,'" I clarify.

He points to my hands as if he wants me to hold them out in front like in the movies. I don't owe him anything—except for a lamp.

"Are you wearing a cat mask?"

I rip it off my face. Bye-bye, Robin Hood—mask disguise failed.

My shoulders sag; after this, I'd go on a long drive and evaluate some of my life decisions.

But I was, *oh so close...*

"Do you break into homes regularly wearing Halloween masks?" He scowls at me, "Or am I special?"

The only thing I can think of to say is, "Are you going to report me?"

If I can stall him, maybe Neme can do something, work his magic.

"It depends," he says, stepping closer to me with the nozzle. "Why are you in my house?" He takes in my black clothes. "I don't have any overdue books. Is this how serious you take library fines?"

I think for a moment, "Yes, actually." I swallow hard, "I haunt all patrons who have overdue practices, like you." I move my hand before him, pretending to hypnotize him, like drawing out a demon.

He frowns, "That's impossible; I don't check out books."

I hold a hand to my chest, taking offense. "You should try it sometime," I say before I pounce forward and snatch the envelope.

My body twists to run as I hear the click and a pop of the gun.

A salt ball hits my collarbone—a piercing sting radiates through my chest. I whimper. My right hand covers the injury sight—a direct hit to bare skin no less—only a devil's henchman would strike so bold.

I scowl, but I feel Neme's wet lips on my fingers as he pulls the envelope out of my left hand.

Lucas steps back, just now noticing the giant dog standing in the hallway, "You brought a lion into my house?" His tone cracks at the end.

I smile.

"Say hello to my Nemean." He's chewing on the envelope like it's the expensive bully sticks that he loves.

"He's destroying my envelope!?" his face bunches up, and I'm glad Neme scares him. I place my hands on my hips, "He won't swallow it. Not yet, at least."

He shakes his head, bends down, and waves Neme to come close, "Come here, boy. Come here, lion."

Neme—like the worst dog in the world—walks right over to Lucas, wags his tail, and drops the envelope down on the ground at his feet. His tongue flaps out, and a pool of drool piles up on the envelope, seeping into the teeth holes he left behind.

Lucas frowns.

I smile.

And Neme begins to lick up the salt trail between us.

"Get out," Lucas growls.

I move fast, leave the hallway, pass through the clipart eye mask room, and jump out the window. I turn around to watch Neme jump out, too—like a trained lion jumping through a hoop.

Jogging to my car, I note lessons learned on this once-in-a-lifetime break-in excursion. Number one, Lucas has a unique taste in PJs.

Number two, from now on, giving an illegal idea at least 36 hours to marinate so I can think of all the possible things that could go wrong will be a valuable practice.

I finger my new welt as I decide on the third and most prominent cementing fact of my quasi-failed heist: Lucas is a horrible person.

I can see my car in clear view now, but my mouth drops as blue and red lights reflect through the trees along the roadway up to the mansion.

Could alarm systems be silent?

Brilliant, just brilliant, Amelia.

I duck down and veer toward the forest, "Neme, follow me, boy. We can't drive away fast enough; they might see us."

Neme runs close by my legs as we escape into the safety of the foliage. Several police cars pull into the Chernov mansion driveway.

We're safe for now.

I have Neme with me; no bears can get me, and my nerves keep us running toward home.

Lucas wouldn't turn me in, or would he? He shot me...

But I can't help tugging a slight smile across my face; we didn't destroy the document entirely, but how Lucas reacted—was priceless.

We messed up his plan.

We've tampered enough with whatever evidence was in the envelope, enough so to save the library, hopefully.

We did it—a laugh escapes my lips.

Neme, my trusted sidekick, did well, and I now know what Neme needs more in his life.

Salt.

Lucas

I hear wheels turn into the driveway, and the flashing blue and red lights turn off when they park.

Good night; how in all the small towns is anyone supposed to get any sleep here?

She probably wouldn't have broken in if she knew she was being recorded; every move she made outside the window was caught on camera.

I pull my phone out and click on the app connected to our new high-tech security system. I can zoom in and see her Catwoman mask.

I smile—she's ridiculous.

I'm not the least bit threatened by her, contrary to her regular hate mail titled "To Lucas, the library killer. I hate you," which she started sending me several months earlier when I proposed rezoning the library lot. She's an old friend of Dimitri's, and I do actually remember making her cry a long time ago, which I really shouldn't have felt bad about.

I make most women cry.

Dimitri had figured out how to sneak out of my old room window years ago without triggering the old system; she probably knows that.

I rewatch the video—did she talk to her dog like he was in on it?

She's after the library deed; I'm confident of it. I thought I saw her spying on us earlier today when my brothers handed me the notarized library deed, enclosed in a manila envelope—proof of ownership of the library building and the lot.

I fill my cheeks with air and blow out a large breath. If that's her objective, she's the worst burglar I've ever met.

Amelia failed.

I'm going to destroy the library, which she illogically believes is hers, but I don't want to throw her in jail, too. Dad would have—my jaw clamps hard at that thought.

She doesn't deserve to be punished; maybe taught a lesson of some kind, yes. She's ultimately harmless. Turning her in wouldn't fix the crunched manila envelope now.

My finger hovers over the delete button on her security camera footage—the app is handy, but I slip the proof of her law-breaking acts back inside my pocket.

I walk up to the window; the officers only use their lights, with no sirens. If their sirens had been blaring, the whole town would have jumped out of bed to drive by and see what was going on.

My socks slide me to the front door before a knock comes.

"Mr. Chernov," the officer wears a mustache...with a mullet? I'm too tired to make a snide remark. The short man's uniform is crisp and stiff; he stands as tall as my shoulder, and I don't recognize him.

"We were notified by your security system team that there was a break-in."

I give him one brisk nod. "False alarm, officer," I cross my arms, trying to look annoyed.

"We noticed an older Corolla parked just down the corner from here. Would you like us to investigate who the owner is?"

I shake my head. "No. You're interrupting my beauty sleep." My face stays straight, emotionless, as I point out toward all the cars. "A phone call next time will do."

He nods, "I-I'm sorry, Mr. Chernov." His mustache juts out with every word. "We just wanted to make sure everyone was safe."

This is the safest town along the Appalachian Trail, thanks to our diligent police officers. They're a small SWAT team at every city event. I'm glad we have them—just not in my driveway in the middle of the night.

"I'm certain you're keeping all the thieves at bay."

He stands slightly taller at that: "Thank you, Sir Mr. Chernov. You're a valued citizen, and we care about your family's safety. We'll take off if nothing else is left for us to check out." He turns to go but stops when he reaches the edge of the expansive covered porch. "What tripped the alarm?"

"A raccoon." I've seen those critters out in the tree house.

He nods. "Good system you've got there then. I'll tell Bob, your security team rep, how well it worked. See you at the town meeting?"

I don't even care who Bob is; and of course. He knows about the town meeting, and I imagine he doesn't want to miss the show the town meeting will be.

And Amelia thinks she's winning right now.

I pull my hand over my face, step inside, stick out my hand, and wave, hoping to make the officer leave faster.

"I'll be there," I say and close the door before he can say goodbye.

He's new—anyone else would have known whose car that was in a heartbeat. Despite the trouble she's bringing to me, I hope Amelia makes it home safe with her drool puddle of a sidekick.

I'm starting to enjoy my hate mail.

In all seriousness, that woman needs a social life. A real one. Outside of the library. Pushing it over could be the best thing for Amelia; she'd be forced to move on and try new things. I don't know much about her, other than that she's ridiculous, doodles on her hate mail, uses scented markers, lives with her grandfather, and now—is my problem.

Because she destroyed the wrong envelope.

I turn off the hallway lights and return downstairs; Baba is still out cold. Our Babushka sleeps through everything, but a break-in? My brothers, Dim and Nik, sleep out in the guest house. Andrei has his place in town, and I feel knots in my stomach, knowing she's alone in this house while Mom is gone.

But I can't let myself get involved.

I don't plan on staying a single day longer than I have to, so I focus on pushing the feeling out. I flip on my bedroom light and pick up the wadded manila envelope I left on the desk.

I wiped off most of the sticky saliva right after she left, but the damage was done.

I drop into my bed, and it creaks as I lean over to my nightstand, open the drawer, and pull out the *other* manila envelope—the actual library deed, the envelope she clearly thought she was destroying.

She didn't notice the Chernov seal on the envelope she'd grabbed.

I drop both envelopes down on the desk against the wall. One envelope is now wrinkled from liquid, smells like salmon bites, has holes, and is crumpled. The other is as flat as the floor.

My sigh is so deep that it pulls my shoulders back to my bed. My brothers are going to kill me—I'm glad I put the library deed document somewhere safe, but it seems pointless now.

My fingers ran through my hair several times, trying to turn back the clock thirty minutes earlier when I placed the manila envelope from our deceased father—his will and all the additional instructions that our lawyer promised would come—somewhere safer.

I have no idea how I will explain this to all nine brothers. How am I supposed to know that the local librarian with a giant lion-looking dog would try to eat our inheritance documentation in my room at the stroke of midnight?

Dad was a billionaire, so his will instructions were worth much more than a library.

The library deed—the document Amelia was after—I'd procured only as a safety net, proof to the town, and a reminder to the city council who owned the library.

And so, it is with the Fates—the Chernov Brothers waited a year for our inheritance, and within fifteen seconds, everything changed.

I shake my head.

I was getting ahead of myself, and if I opened the soggy, half-eaten envelope to see the damage, the seal would be broken. It was a miracle the seal didn't pop off from dog teeth punctures.

I wouldn't do that to my brothers—we needed to be together when Dad's wishes were opened and read, with the lawyer present.

Amelia caught me off guard, and I'd happily admit I didn't like the idea of including another beautiful woman in the Chernov drama. Whether she wanted it or not, she's now involved.

So I pull out my phone, open the security app, and press delete on the video that captures Amelia in the act of failing.

Tomorrow will tell, and I genuinely think there is no way her dog actually ruined what was inside. At least, that's what I convince myself so sleep will come.

My final blurry thought before dozing off—*we need a louder alarm system.*

Chapter Two

Lucas

I roll over and hit my alarm clock like it's a whack-a-mole—today is the one-year anniversary of Dad's death; I've been waiting for this day since his funeral.

Magnolia Grace, our family lawyer, shared shortly after Dad's death, "Three hundred and sixty-five days is when you'll have access to your father's will."

It won't help to be irritated today—last night's break-in led to a crap-shot attempt at sleep. A simple manila envelope sealed shut with the Chernov seal—I don't know how Dad orchestrated it all—was delivered to the mansion yesterday. Baba, here alone, signed for the delivery, and the sender's address was the actual post office—a dead end.

A year dead, and his instructions *finally* show up.

And a dog ate them.

My nails scratch my head, and I flex my feet out with a big bear yawn—*I have the right to be irritated today*. She'd come for the library deed—a Hail Mary attempt to save the library.

I've returned to my hometown for two meetings today—Dad's estate allocation and a will reading at the lawyer's office this afternoon with all my brothers and half-brothers. Then, the town meeting tonight to get the rezoning passed.

Big day. Today, I'll learn how to split my inheritance ten ways.

Dad was full-blooded Russian; everything was about family—and his secret power was making everything impossible for others around him—like making his family wait an *entire year* for his will, freezing all his assets.

And the fatuous break-in from Amelia Anderson last night? It spread my frosty attitude all through my dreams and agitated my balled-up nerves: A man only makes you wait for that type of information if he wants to mess with you.

I rub my eyes and throw off my royal blue sheets. The air is crisp, and my room is empty except for a desk against the wall, a lamp, and a small nightstand.

I see the sky begin to lighten up with the sunrise. Dad was up at 4 a.m. daily when he was alive and swam laps in the pool out back. Now, the still pool sprays out the reflection of the clouds—white and sporadic—and it's stunning. It could have been calming and peace-provoking, but not today.

As a 32-year-old bachelor, the oldest son of the late Zolton Chernov, I don't want to be tied to my father even by one thread of his shoestring. I own a smattering of apartments and rental properties; my sizable assets are coming together nicely—I don't need Dad's money or his legacy.

I try to loosen my jaw and envision leaving the town as soon as I square everything away for the new town apartments, and in the same breath, the pain of Kim floods me.

When I return to Richmond, Virginia, for work, I'll begin cleaning out my townhouse so that I can rent it out. It feels too much like Kim. I'll find a new apartment to fix up and rent or sell for profit. Even with Amelia's break-in, being here feels only an inch more bearable than being in Richmond.

Andrei warned me several days before I arrived, "Don't mention your breakup with Kim to Baba; she'll give you the whole cursed thing."

"Curse?" I asked.

He laughed, "Trust me, you don't want to know."

I won't mention anything to Baba, Dimitry, Vincent, Nikola, or any of my other half-brothers.

I slip off my pajamas and put on my running clothes. I tie up my shoes and stand tall. I need to get this project underway and rezoned. The promotion is my ticket of proof—a Chernov could be successful outside of Dad's shadow. Having office doors touching those of my brothers is a version of a life I swore off five years ago. I scratch my stomach and know why I'd never return to Chernov Brothers Realty—I'm a coward.

Our family company wants new apartments along the main street of my hometown of Herasburg, Virginia. Noil Construction—the company I've been working for since I broke my ties with Dad—won the bid for the work. My brothers really came through and picked our bid. And I'm the perfect liaison for Noil Construction and Chernov Brothers Realty for this project.

"Thanks to you, we've secured this bid. Now get the land rezoned, and I'll promote you as my partner," my boss Mitchell said two weeks ago. "Lucas, before November fifth, you hear. My promotion offer is only good for this year."

It's the first of September. Moving up so quickly in a company demonstrates that I don't need Dad, and all my brothers will get off my back about why I'm not returning to the family company—after I secure my promotion with Noil, I can live in peace.

I step into the hallway and crack Baba's door; she's gone. When I moved out years ago, she liked my bedroom best of all. "The sun rises from the east, and I want to see it when it sets, not rises. It matches my mood better."

Matryoshka dolls and some of the blankets she had brought from Russia when she immigrated decorate the walls and shelves, and our mid-century modern ranch-style mansion has windows in every room—Baba's window doesn't look damaged. I'm surprised Amelia didn't break the lamp that jarred me awake.

I close her bedroom door, and head for the staircase upstairs to the kitchen.

Hot cakes and fried eggs tickle the back of my throat—my mouth waters.

I jog up the stairs into the kitchen and grab a plate, "You're up early," I say to Baba.

Cottage cheese pancakes and fried eggs are a specialty of Babushka's—a traditional Russian breakfast I never get sick of.

"I am," she says, flipping the pancake; she never burns them, always golden to perfection.

Baba took Dad's death like a soldier. She let us all weep on her shoulder, especially Mom. Mom had been scheduled to be back today, but Dad's estate in Russia was old as a turtle and wasn't wrapping up nicely. She said, "It's complicated, but I've got it covered," when we talked yesterday. "I'm sorry, I won't be back in time for the meeting with Miss Grace. I'll get to the bottom of this and be there in no time."

Baba takes my plate. "It's nice to see that you still like my cooking," she says in her Russian accent, making it sound like an insult.

"I've always loved your cooking."

"Fancy restaurants in Richmond would have tainted you, spoiled you too much." She gives me a double scoop of eggs; they aren't runny or firm, but they have a unique in-between texture that your tongue can chew.

"Baba, you are my favorite cottage cheese pancake cook."

"Good. Now eat. I have questions."

I sigh. I've fallen right into her trap of *let me feed you so I can pepper you with all my questions.* I should have plugged my nose up, but I can't say no to Baba, so I sit down, letting my elbows rest on the cold white quartz. I stuff my face, and I don't make eye contact.

"You know... Kim is nice."

I choke and chug some orange juice, "Don't lie."

Kim is anything but nice; no one loves Kim—she's a gold digger, and everyone saw it before I did.

Baba curses in Russian under her breath. "I have been doing some thinking..." she leans against the quartz.

I failed at both things that matter most to her—weddings and babies.

Baba smiles a little. "Our family is cursed..." She says matter-of-factly, like she's pulling the words out of a family book passed down for generations.

"I think I know where you're going with this," I say, hoping that would speed up the conversation.

"I've not told you this before. I tell you, you are cursed!" Her big eyes don't match her short frame. She's emphatic, too, like she's about to talk about her Kartoshka recipe.

"Lucas, it's not your fault that each woman you are engaged to calls it off. It's just not."

I fold my arms and use my tongue to dig the doughy pancake out of my teeth. I don't know how Baba thinks blaming my relationship skills on a curse will help me feel better.

It does the opposite—I'm like an old banana peel, browning by the day. I broke it off with Kim, and I wouldn't tell my family that part of the story.

"Who told you my engagement was off?" Which one of my brothers snitched? Vincent or Dimitry? Andrei would never.

"Just look at you, scowling even in the morning."

"I always scowl," I say.

She touches my forehead, "Not this deep, though." Her thick finger pushes down into my forehead.

I scowl deeper.

"As the oldest grandson," she says, placing her wrinkle-splotched hand on my shoulder now and looks into my eyes, "I know you've always felt pressure. But I know whose fault it is." She starts patting me like I am her lap dog, Anya.

I arch my eyebrows up high. "Whose fault is it?" I'm curious now, who could she blame?

Dad, a first-generation immigrant from Russia, created several companies and forged the way to bring his mother, our Baba, to America—he never blamed anyone for anything. He just twisted their arm, pushed their face to the ground, and jammed an elbow into their kidney; his methods were controversial. And he taught all ten of his sons the same thing, especially me. Needless to say, Baba could use some exciting tactics herself sometimes.

"I believe it's the Fates."

I roll my eyes.

"The Fates have cursed our family," she repeats herself.

"And..." I say.

"I believe it's your father. He's done something."

I bark out a laugh—I think she has forgotten that Father had done something to everyone; the whole town practically stayed away or scattered like swimming minnows anytime a member of our family entered the room.

Chernovs are like sharks in the shallow waters of a small southern town, each large and burly. We all look like Dad, too—successful, wealthy, heartbreakers—all seem to be spun into the fabric of our DNA.

Dad had either dated most girls in town or broken their hearts; he'd divorced four times, and the romantics in town counted on us to be the local live soap opera. My mom, who was his first wife—and his last before he died—yes, he married her twice, with three marriages in between—seemed to cope with Dad's shenanigans eerily well.

But no one else did.

"Baba, I am just here to help with the next phases of the development."

Baba moves her hand from my shoulder and motions for me to follow her to the moss-green chair. Baba said it reminded her of sleeping on the ground during the Soviet Era in Russia. She never talks about anything from her past; neither did Dad. All extended family is lost to us; it's like the bottle of fermented sardines in the back of the cupboard—it never gets opened.

Baba sits down and leans back as the springs snap like bones.

"You know the company I work for won the bid to build the apartments," I say. Baba nods, and I pull a wooden chair across the white carpet.

"We've picked a prime location for the downtown apartments."

She cuts in. "No, I did not know." She frowns. "You and your brothers will stir up a beehive if you put those tall buildings along Magnus Avenue. Please tell me that's not the prime location."

My lips pinch tight. "Don't you think the city will love the additional foot traffic and a new building downtown? We'll take down one that's falling apart. A handful of buildings are breaking all kinds of safety hazard regulations."

She waves her finger, "Find a different spot. You will aggravate your curse."

I sigh. "Go on..." I submit, "How has Dad offended the Fates?"

Like the answers are ready on her tongue before I even ask, she rubs her chin, pushing three long white hairs side to side, "I'm sure it started with him. And now look at you all. Handsome, strong men, none of you can keep a girl!"

I agree.

Dad forbade girlfriends. "They will distract your young minds too much," he'd preached. Some of my brothers had girlfriends behind Dad's back—others of us, like me—listened and didn't know how to act around girls until our late 20s. "Your duty to the family is here, to your mother and brothers, to grow the business, and then you will have your pick of women."

We all remain bachelors to this day.

Baba looks at me, eyebrows drawn. "You are getting old."

"Baba, the curse—" I now wonder how deep my scowl is really getting.

"I married and had a son by the time I was eighteen years old. It's the best part of my life. I want that for you, too, Lucas." She takes a deep breath and rests her arms on her chair.

"You must begin healing our family." She shakes her crooked finger at me. "You have to start undoing the curse."

"And what does this curse entail?" I flare my nostrils.

"Labors." She closes her eyes. "Ten labors. One for each of you." She nods her head.

Baba is one of the strongest souls I know.

But she also believes in everything—and I forget to school my face, and I cringe. Any fairy tale, myth, fortune cookie, afternoon infomercial, or archaic omen feeds her ideas.

She was illogically loyal and consistent to everyone in her life, and it was an unspoken family rule: Baba could believe whatever she wanted to, and we'd accept.

"I'm not up to date on curses, Baba. What labors are you talking about?"

Baba smiles. "Hercules, of course." She points her finger at our family photo on the wall. "You and your brothers must complete Hercules's ten labors. There's one for each of you. Lucas, every time I think about it, my scar hurts."

I look down, mouthing her words, and can't stifle my laugh.

"Baba, you are watching too much television."

She swats the air. "You can judge me after you give me grandbabies."

I wipe the smirk off my face—Andrei warned me about this.

"You cannot judge me—my scar tingles," she points to her arm. "You start mending your relationship with the town. Perform the first Hercules labor so you can start breaking the curse."

She stops rocking, and I reach out and hold her hand, keeping my face as serious as stone.

"And what is this labor that I must do?" I ask.

"Slay a lion."

Chapter Three

Amelia

I reach for the leash, reminding myself why I became a librarian—reading, relationships, and for Mom.

Since I was eight, I have daydreamed about falling in love in a library. And helping others fall in love with reading? Finding new books for patrons to try? Organizing books?

Like boiling soup to my heart.

I want to relive my memories with Mom at the library, which is another reason why it can't be demolished. So yes, I reason with myself; all my choices last night were justified in principle—getting to walk to work today because I'm a terrible thief who left her car at the crime scene is a natural side effect.

"Neme," I call.

He stretches off the couch beside the low-humming TV and walks toward me. Grandpoppy's chair is reclined back, and his stomach is moving up and down. I clip onto Neme's collar. "It's story time today, boy."

Neme always attends story time with the children at the library.

I grab a frozen lunch out of the freezer, fill my tumbler with hot water, and pour in two more packs of dark hot chocolate mix than I usually do—it's a four-pack type of day. I boil some malt-o-meal for Grandpoppy, scoop it into his favorite daisy-designed bowl, and set it next to the newspaper.

My hand touches the garage doorknob when I hear Grandpoppy's low, scratchy voice: "Milly?"

I lean around the corner. "Yes, Grandpoppy?"

"It's rather early for your run today, isn't it?" He adjusts his eyes.

"I'm walking to work today; I just have some extra stuff...on my mind that I wanted to walk off."

Grandpoppy nods. "Can you watch The Mystery of Potato Cellar with me tonight?"

"It's the meeting tonight. Can we raincheck?"

He blinks. "It's tonight?"

"It is." I can't look at him, so I fumble with Neme's leash. Grandpoppy knows that if the library dies, it'd be like watching a part of Mom die all over again for me.

He nods his head. "You'll do great, Pumpkin."

I have planned to defend the library at the city meeting since the proposed rezoning. Sadly, I've been so nettled up lately that I haven't had time for Potato Cellars. My fingers press down on the salt welt on my collarbone. I'll face Lucas Chernov again tonight—

"I love you." Grandpoppy interrupts my circling thoughts.

"I love you, Grandpoppy. Don't wait up for me. Breakfast is on the table." I step to his side, kiss his bald scalp, and lift the minky blanket around his chest.

He smiles and fiddles with the remote. "That I can promise," he says, flipping the channels to reruns of Xena: Warrior Princess and Hercules.

Neme whines and tugs me to the door. We slip out, and the fresh mist of Herasburg licks me up. I'm glad I tossed on my scarf—the pre-autumn morning shivers up my spine, and I know honing my happy thoughts about our town would ease the shadow of guilt I feel for everything right now.

Herasburg, nestled along the Blue Ridge Mountains, has quaint sidewalks, friendly flavors of all types of penny candy, and the best seasonal ice cream a small town could ever keep in stock—I bite my lip.

I swear all the old buildings—sinking foundations, falling rain gutters with weeds growing out of them, and crumbling bricks—stay around to protect the town's charm and hide it from anyone passing through.

We have a Christmas parade in the cold temperatures—the bank passes out free hot cocoa while the mayor turns on the town Christmas tree lights. Hashtag heartwarming. In the summer, everyone who is anyone gets a swim pass—cannonball competitions always end in blood. Still, the bonding is real, even after some teen single-handedly snaps the 45-year-old diving board in half like a long garden carrot last year. When a high school team wins state, the entire fire department escorts the bus through town—sirens blaze, everyone comes to Magnus Avenue and cheers. On Halloween—my personal favorite—all the businesses close early, the employees and owners dress up, and everyone passes out candy to the kids.

Herasburg is heaven on earth—with one minor flaw: My fellow citizens are about to let one of the best buildings in town be plucked off Magnus Avenue.

But tonight, I will show them the light.

Neme starts to jog a little. "Slow down, boy," I say. My hot cocoa keeps shooting out of the straw—every third step, I extend my arm out to help save my shirt. My hair—long, thick, red, and curly—like a confused mop, is in a tight ponytail on top of my head; I don't want my hair to wear my hot chocolate, not today.

During craft time last month, Charlie tugged on my leg. "Look! It's you's hair, Miss Milly." He pointed to his craft, which consisted of the biggest pompoms we had in the craft box with taped feathers on them.

Great.

A voice cuts through the air, "See if you can hit thirteen today, Pumpkin."

Simon's underarm skin flaps like his Southern accent as he waves at me. Simon, a retired officer who still suits up daily in his uniform from 50 years ago, has sat next to a small solar-powered speedometer by his house every day since he retired—which was ever since I could remember.

Magnus Avenue wouldn't be the same without his faded blue lawn chair, tin can, and a trail of sunflower shells. I'm sure the police station pays him under the table—he heckles speeding cars along Magnus Avenue like an angry mama bird.

My jog is about four miles per hour, or that's usually what the speed display reads when I run by on a morning jog. I try to move a little faster, but it doesn't change.

"I'm going to work, not jog—"

"Come on, today is the thirteenth."

His daily goal is to get the date to appear on the speed display. He's law-abiding, but the only days he lets speeding slip is the last week of the month to see how many speeds he can match with the date.

"I'm on a streak, Pumpkin. Can you help me out?" He turns and spits the seeds out, missing his tin can.

I slow down as I pass him. I'm late to work and don't have time for this.

"Fine," I say impulsively.

He smiles big, and a black-and-white striped shell falls onto his chin.

I set down my purse and hot chocolate. Neme tugs on the leash as if he knows how late we are, and I drop the leash and watch Neme run over to Simon, hoping he'll forgive me. I jog back, giving myself a good runway.

"Here goes to the thirteenth," I mutter as I try to run fast.

Simon's hand goes up to Neme's head, "Good boy," as Neme licks the shell off his chin.

Salt—I reason.

I begin running and push myself; my long legs stretch to nine miles per hour; that won't do.

He smiles, nods, and pets Neme again like he has been doing it all day long—Neme sits like a statue, his eyes following me. I jog back farther. I need a head start, and I roll my sleeves up. I push myself this time; the speed display blinks eleven.

His laugh is low and raspy, and he points back for me to try again.

I force my cheeks not to smile, "It's not a touchdown, Simon. I didn't even make it to thirteen."

Neme leaves Simon's side and runs to where I started. He gets a little too far away, "Neme!" I yell. Neme picks up his usual pace. The speed display blinks thirteen, and then he curves off to the sidewalk back to Simon's yard, back to his side, and licks Simon's fingers again.

I blink.

"Neme, you deserve a biscuit, boy," Simon says like he's talking to a baby. "Come by tomorrow, and I'll get you a fresh one," Simon scratches Neme under his chin.

My chest feels slightly lighter as I grab my mug and purse and sip my hot chocolate again. "Neme, let's go, boy."

I start to jog over to the leash but the gopher hole in the grass snags my foot; my entire body weight compresses against my left ankle with a pop sound.

My drink slips; Niagara Falls is reenacted in all directions.

My tendons snap back as the pain throbs up my leg like wasp venom, and I suck in air as Neme jogs toward me.

I'm not going to cry in front of Simon. But then I look down, and my shirt looks like a canvas after the children have finger-painted it.

I lift my ankle, and I feel the blood drain out of my face.

"You okay?" Simon asks.

I turn away, blinking rapidly. "Yeah, no big deal; I'll walk it off," I say, my voice cracking. I bend down and pick up my hot cocoa again, putting slight pressure on my foot.

"Come back tomorrow, Pumpkin! And bring my favorite lion with you."

He's not a lion. "Neme," I whisper. He's there by my side, tongue out within an instant.

"I can't make any promises, Simon," I try to say a little louder.

Neme lets out one bark like a goodbye and walks beside me, his leash dragging along the sidewalk, my leg brushing against his body.

I take a deep breath as I wipe my cheeks—if I need to get a sprained ankle, I'm glad it happened now and not during my escape last night—I force a happy expression, the tears following my smile wrinkles.

We are three blocks from the library when a car slows down and pulls up beside me. I use the back of my hand to wipe my face and nose again.

"Car in the shop today?" I know that voice.

"I'm late, Lucas," I say, but I don't know if I'm indignant or more humiliated when he sees me limping.

I want him to go away, to leave town and never come back.

"You looked nicer last night in all black." He takes his sunglasses off.

I scowl and say the words that come to my mind first, "I-I'm sorry."

He pretends to be genuine. "What for?" His arm bends outside his window, black sunglasses spinning in his hand. His blue shirt is crisp, his arm muscles defined even through his shirt, and his hair looks like every strand obeys his every whim.

I swallow and hope my hot chocolate stains hide some of the grease and homemade gel shine in my hair.

"I wasn't myself last night." I say it, there, that should appease him.

He eases the car along the road, checking his rear-view mirror. "Oh, that's a shame," he says.

"How can you think my apologizing is a shame?"

He watches Neme walk slow for me, leash still dragging. "I was curious to see what you would have done with the envelope."

I clench my fist. "Burn it," I say under my breath.

He cups his hand over his ear. "I think you just admitted to your crimes of breaking in. Are you a thief and a pyromaniac?"

My shoulders slump down. "I'm sorry, I," my eyes stick to the sidewalk as I muster a seed of humility, my limp getting worse. "What I did was wrong. I said I'm sorry."

He nods his head. "Good. I was hoping you felt bad," he says, reaching into the back of his black car—it matches his soul.

He holds up a crisp manila envelope.

"Because that will make persuading everyone in the meeting tonight so much easier with the deed document."

My mouth drops open.

"I thought..." I close my mouth and open it again. But then I cover it with my hand—my tears bubbling up again, and his smile is slime to me.

"You had another copy?"

He shakes his head coolly, "You destroyed the wrong manila envelope."

I feel my neck tendons tighten. *Typical. I fail even at stealing.*

"I will say I'm impressed with your eagerness to get inside my bedroom."

My hand and jaw drop.

He smiles down at the envelope, his lips extending deeper. He turns up his music, pushes on his sunglasses, and drives, I swear, at thirteen miles per hour.

Exactly what I'm incapable of.

My hot, salty tears fall. *I hate him, I really do.*

When I was seventeen, my best friend showed up on my doorstep—a Newfoundland puppy. I named him Nemean, after a mythological lion—a library namesake. Two gargoyle-like lion statues out front of the library have held up well over the years, and the town decided to name the library after the statues and not the city: Lionstone Library.

Naturally, as a young girl, I named the statues Gertrude the Grand and Bartholomew the Boastful (Gert and Bart for short). My mother would blow them kisses when we walked by and say, "They are the guardians of the library."

When I saw Neme for the first time, and he looked almost like a lion cub, I knew I had to name him Nemean.

He'll be eleven on his next birthday, and I can't believe he doesn't act his age.

His whines bounce off the cracked walls and the uneven ceiling as he hoists himself up and stares out the window, looking for the usual story time kids to show up.

It's been several hours since my incident with Lucas—Tylenol and a few strategically placed stickers on my shirt make it look like I decided to be the craft example for the day—I could work with that.

I have taken my hair out of a bun, blending in most of the dried hot chocolate. I take a deep breath and blow some frizzy hair out of my face.

Rezoning hasn't been passed yet.

Lucas Chernov became my primary target months ago. When I left the bank, Katie Dale, a teller at the bank just down the road, confirmed everything; he was behind the rezoning.

Now that he's here, I wonder if I had the wrong address for my hate mail.

"They're coming, promise." I say to Neme as I pick up the nonfiction book on the browsing cart and walk past the circulation desk, the kids' room, my homemade sign that reads *pothole* where the floor divots, right before the nonfiction section. The nonfiction shelf here always seemed to be added later, like the non-fiction bookshelf was an afterthought.

A faint muffle of wheels turning reaches me, and my ears perk up—someone is approaching the first door into the entrance walkway of the library before noon.

"Positions," I holler out.

I limp to the air freshener and crank it up. The vanilla covers up the hint of mildew in the air. It gives Mr. Mettle, my boss, a headache, so I use it sparingly, only when patrons are around. I then pop open the library's two biggest books, and the smell of freshly opened books fills the air.

I use my hands to calm down my frizz, and I pull my stained and stickered shirt tight; when I let go, some of the wrinkles bounce back in.

I try limping less as I make it to the front door and open it.

Neme walks to the middle of the entrance and lays down, waiting to see who I'll let in—just like I trained him to.

"Hi, Sandy, welcome!" I open the door for her walker; her bag drapes loose on her arm. She's one of my favorite patrons over 70, who reads western romance books like they're water.

"Amelia, it's great to see you too," she says. Her dark glasses have a little lip on all sides, keeping most light out.

"No Mikey?" I ask. Her grandson is one of my regular patrons who also seems to leave me with a smile.

She points to her bag. "He's with a friend today, honey. I'll bring him by later."

Her bag has two books.

"You finished that one fast," I say. I love that she still reads, even as her eyesight slips.

"We both thought I could handle small print; we were wrong." Her gray teeth poke out of her dry lips.

"Let's go see what large print we have, shall we?" I know exactly how many large print books we have; I personally defended the budget item to purchase thirty large-print westerns for one of our patrons when I first started working here—freshly out of grad school. And Sandy has almost read the entire section.

I hear someone run up to the doors, and pop both open.

"Miss Milly?" I look down. Charlie's shoes don't match again. "Is it story time yet?"

Charlie's mom walks in, out of breath. "Charlie Roo! I told you to wait at the door for me, honey!" She barks.

I squint my eyes at Charlie. "You know I'd never start without you." I wink at him. He winks back, closing both of his eyes.

I smile. "Go on, now. Make it right with your mama so she'll bring you next week, too."

"Yes, ma'am."

Charlie walks back to the door. I can't hear the mumbled interaction, but I see Charlie walk back out of the library with his mama, passing several copies of the flyers I'd hung all around town.

They're for a raffle on Halloween, and I want to squeeze in as many Halloween books as I can to help promote the raffle I'm hosting that'll happen on that day. I'd made posters and hung them up all around town—I'd eaten Cup of Noodles for an entire month to afford prizes for the raffle. It was an idea I had shortly after I found out Lucas wanted to rezone the lot—citizens needed to come to the library so they could love it as much as I did.

Sign up for a card or check out a book to get an entry into a drawing for BIG prizes! I hope everyone can see it, and I hope it will help with the library's patron count.

"Velcome to the vibrary, Charlie!" I say in my Dracula voice. I step out from behind the counter, straighten one of the flyers.

"Today vee vill be vreading about Georgie the Goblin and Van the Vampire!" I add my best vampire laugh for effect.

Charlie covers his mouth as he giggles, and Neme greets him with slobbery kisses. I can't help but laugh—it bounces my frizz mop up and down. I lead him into the children's area.

The twins and Evee tumble in with their guardians.

"Miss Milly!" Evee's arms go wide, and she clamps tight around one of my legs.

"Evee! You made it!" I hide my cringe and lower my body to the ground. "Find your circle!"

Mine is orange. I knew I'd be testing my ankle limits if I had to get up and off the ground, but I do it anyway.

Their eyes widen, bodies sway like chattering birds, never leaving their spot as I turn the pages, and it's moments like this when all the children laugh or bend forward as I read the story in my best vampire accent, that I'm reminded, even if I'm a failure—I'll do anything to keep the library open, I'd keep trying—even if it's just for these four children.

And for Mom.

Chapter Four

Lucas

They're late again—I flex my hands, irritation from yesterday snowballing into today; my conversation with Baba has spun a web in my mind all morning.

She's watching too much TV.

Maybe I could bring her with me to some of my meetings? No. She'd slap hands and tell people how to eat their food.

Maybe I should have brought her along today? No. She would have lectured me on my frowning too much.

I pull out my phone and text.

Me: *You're late.*

I send it to Andrei, Nikola, and Dimitry, my three full biological brothers.

I'm about to see all my half-brothers at our meeting with the lawyer in one hour, and we planned to take a few more photos of the library for the town meeting tonight. There were a few more shots I wanted to get—and low and beheld; they are standing me up again.

Dim: *We stopped for some breakfast. Be there in five mins.*

It's 11:45 am.

I flare my nostrils.

I don't want to waste my time; November fifth is less than three months away, and it's the back that I need more photos of. So I loop around the building and look up to the second and third floors on this side.

I see a mannequin? No, that's not right, so I squint now and definitely see a mannequin holding up a map—it's dressed like it was mugged by Goodwill—blue pants, button-up brown shirt with pockets, and a jacket adorned with sailboats. A stuffed animal is right behind its arm, carrying a book in its mouth.

This town is so weird.

It only briefly distracts me from the crumbling bricks, the rain gutters jutting out several inches from the roofline, and multiple cracked windows. As I round the back corner of the building, I look down at the foundation. It sinks six inches more than the rest of the foundation.

I smile.

I read the complaint in city notes from past public hearings, including the store manager next door—the flooding that happened in the narrow alleyway affected him, too; the gradient to the street is off.

Zooming in, I document everything. The cracks reach up from the foundation to the roofline like a cracked pot. I've seen worse, but as a public library? No. It's unacceptable.

I'm glad I didn't stick around in this town; it's just too... cracked.

There are no windows along the entire back corner on the main level, which is strange, but it means no windows are cracked, and no moisture can get in that portion of the building.

Maybe it's where the restrooms are on the inside?

As the future CEO of Noil Construction, I'll live by one motto: All cracked pots are never worth salvaging.

This mantra makes my chest swell.

When I get back to the front, I take a step inside. I haven't gotten my fill of the librarian for the day yet—Amelia needs to be taught a lesson that doesn't involve incarceration.

I don't care what anyone thinks of me here, not anymore, but I can't hide who I am here—all my brothers and I fit the Chernov mold—darker complexions, strong eyebrows, and striking facial features—and I look like Dad.

One thing about small towns that Hallmark never tells you is that they remember. They remember when you drop your shorts to pee at the city carnival. They remember your crooked smile before you had braces. And they remember the final touchdown you fumbled at the high school state championship game and worst of all—they remember your father.

My phone pings.

Nikola: *Go read a book and get some ideas on how to slay a lion.*

I roll my eyes. Both Andrei and Dimitry laugh at the text.

I like mythology but am not familiar with all of Hercules' labors or his back story.

Me: ***Not funny.***

Me: ***It could be funny if you weren't late.***

Andrei: *Just be glad you didn't have to watch all the Hercules reruns with her. When we're done, we'll meet you at Magnolia's office.*

I slip my phone into my pocket and push through the first glass door. I look up in the foyer and don't see any cobwebs in the building; I see no peeling paint...but it doesn't take long to find structural concerns.

The entire ceiling slants from one side to the next, the carpet is missing in several spots, and I'm sure I feel like I'm sliding downhill as I take more steps into the building.

My gaze lands on her, though. A circle of children surrounds her. She talks like a vampire, and she wears fake fangs.

I press away a smile and try to find the mythology section; she did say that I should check out more books...maybe I could use this as an opportunity to point out to her how slanted the building is.

It's broken. The whole thing.

Her eyes follow me to the bookshelf, and I slip my hands into my pockets, giving off a carefree air. I can see out the windows, and the view will be perfect for apartments; from this corner, with more windows, it would be panoramic. It would change the flavor of our quiet main street. This sleepy library will have its final resting place soon.

Nobody really wants to come to a small town near the Blue Ridge Parkway to get books. They come here to hike. To ride their bikes. To be outdoors. Not be stuck inside, under yellow, fluorescent lights, in a decrepit building with an old stuffed mannequin with bad taste attempting to haunt you to read books.

Plus, the other library one town over has live bunny rabbits the kids can hold and care for. Stuffed mannequins versus fluffy snuggles? There's no competition.

I finger the poster on the shelf—they're impossible to miss—hundreds of them hang on every shelf or wall and all around town.

Someone needs to block printing rights to whoever wasted this much paper. 'Check out a book and enter to win prizes.' I shake my head; this initiative is two years too late. The public hearing is tonight, and our company has already set a demolition date; we're that certain.

I click my tongue and pull down a few to see the section that might have a book on ancient Greek mythology.

I find a graphic novel and flip through to find the right page. I dog-ear one that I'll come back to. It's about Zeus, Hera, and a curse.

In ancient Greece, the mighty hero Hercules was burdened by twelve Herculean labors, a punishment inflicted upon him by the Gods.

Baba is already wrong. There are 12 labors and 10 of us. *These were meant to test Hercules's strength, courage, and determination. As he undertook these impossible feats, he discovered his capabilities and the importance of unity, humility, and self-discovery.*

Maybe that's what Baba wants me to know. Dad had several wives, too. Is that another connection that she's reasoning? I flip the pages as they outline each labor Hercules had to complete.

One - Slay the Nemean Lion.

I don't see that happening in a million years.

Two - Slay the Nine-Headed Lernaean Hydra.

Yikes, sorry, Andrei.

Three - Capture the Golden Hind of Artemis.

Nikola would get a kick out of that.

Four - Capture the Erymanthian Boar.

I laugh; Dimitry deserves that task.

Five - Clean the Augean Stables.

I cover my mouth as I laugh louder. Atticus would die.

Six - Slay the Stymphalian Birds.

I sigh. Interesting, Anton would hate that.

Seven - Capture the Cretan Bull.

There's no way Max could capture a bull.

Eight - Steal the Mares of Diomedes.

Yes, if anyone could steal something, it would be Vincent.

Nine - Obtain the Girdle of Hippolyta.

Sounds important; Apollo would be down.

Ten - Obtain the Cattle of the Monster Geryon.

A monster? Remington wasn't the adventure type. Maybe I'm wrong?

Eleven - Steal the Apples of the Hesperides.

Twelve - Capture Cerberus, the Three-Headed Dog.

I chuckle. Baba had me worried for nothing, and I want to find the page again, so I bend a different page this time, which lists all the labors. I could google it, too. Maybe I should warn all my brothers; they could dodge Baba better than me. I can't even imagine—

"Lucas!"

A voice and hands come out of nowhere.

I jump up, toss the book, and tumble backward as I try to reach out for a shelf, anything really, but all I can reach is fur?

Oh. My. Hair.

Despite my efforts, I fall hard, pulling down the body connected to the hair.

The librarian.

She falls right on top of me like I'm the best well-placed cushion in the entire world. I can't breathe as I try to pull my hand out of her hair.

"Ohh no!" She yelps and tries to push herself up, placing her hands on my chest. My eyes are wide, and my face is turning red.

"I'm a-so s-sorry!" Her eyes meet mine, and I can see her cheeks blossom a deeper red than her hair. She pushes up, bracing her hands on the side of my body this time. My hand is still stuck in her hair.

I try to breathe out but can't even turn my voice on—no air yet. She stays bent at the waist as my arm extends up over my head.

She fans my face. "I-I never meant to make you fall," she says.

I swallow air. "What," I squeak out, "were you doing?"

She bites her lip. I look into her green eyes with golden specks.

I begin to tug on my hand. "Oh, owe, ouchie." She cringes.

"I'll just—"

"Hold still," she says. I don't trust myself to stand up without pulling her hair, so I watch as she touches my hand and tugs her hair clear of my large fingers. Her hair is loaded up with some kind of gel.

I swallow more air in, my diaphragm remembering how to work.

"Egg whites," she says.

"Excuse me?" I feel her move my hand down and place it on my chest, her eyes resting on my hand.

"I tried using egg whites in my hair yesterday..."

I squint and stare at her hair, watching her mouth move.

"I mean, not all the time; I hear it can help with the frizz...but I can't get around the frizz entirely. I usually don't use any product, but I wanted to start trying something new because Charlie Roo thinks I have feathers sticking out of my head, but then I didn't want to leave Grandpoppy alone any longer when we were shopping." She meets my eyes again. "I'm rambling." she extends her hand down to me.

I take it and hoist myself up using a backhand to brace myself against the harder-than-cement ground.

"I guess an apology is in store for..." she gestures with her free hand toward the book.

I haven't let go of her hand yet. Amelia Anderson. I'm rather shocked at how different she looks up this close. She's taller, fuller, her face more defined, and much more hair—her eyes hook mine, and I can't pull free.

When the silence becomes awkward, she pulls her hand away, and I rub my hands on the back of my jeans. "I guess I can forgive you for startling me," I say.

She blinks. "Me?" she shakes her head. "I was trying to catch you in the act."

I bend beside her and pick up the book. "What are you talking about?"

She plays with her earlobe and sweeps her gaze up to mine. "I meant you needed to apologize to me." She looks down at the book. "And the book."

She plucks the book from my hand.

"You can't be serious," I say.

She opens the page that I bent and flips the corner back up to make it flat.

"Mr. Chernov," she says.

"Lucas," I blurt out. I'm not my Dad. She knows my name, so formality is unnecessary.

She pauses—not in a *I'm nice and I'm shy and want to give a good first impression* type of pause. It's a pause of a mean cat who's about to pounce. She zeroes her glare at me, squares up her stance, and bends her knees.

The book has flipped a switch.

"This is library property," she says. She looks like she's getting ready to pull my ear and kick me out. "Bending pages is... wrong, okay? Our funding can't cover replacing books right now... felonies like this can't be tolerated here."

I lift an eyebrow at her. "Libraries can always afford to buy books." I can't believe she knocked the wind out of me, got her egg whites on my hand, and now is fussing over the fact that I just bent a page or two in a children's book. "And a felony? Really?" I cross my arms and tilt my head.

She extends her neck like she hasn't planned her speech beyond this point. She actually expects me to apologize immediately. Her face turns red again, starting from her neck, reaching her ears, then to her cheeks.

Is this what growing claws looks like?

"You must not visit libraries often, Lucaaas." She extends my name like it hurts her to say it. She lifts the book up and wiggles it in front of my face, "Why are you reading this?" she asks.

Maybe she'll loosen up if she knows the truth.

"For Baba."

"For your grandmother?" Her lips twitch, and I catch myself staring. "Let me get this straight. You go read and vandalize a middle-grade graphic novel just because your 'Baba' told you too?"

"Yes, well no. Baba believes that our family is cursed." I shake my head. "But more importantly, I should ask *you*. Tell me, Amelia, what could *vandalism* look like?" I say.

"I guess it depends on your definition of vandalism." She doesn't even look guilty as she shifts her weight and limps a little.

"You're going to make me pay for this book?" I ask.

She pops out the word. "Absolutely. Felonies cost."

I bark a laugh; she's got to be kidding me—who in their right mind calls bending books a felony?

She turns, flipping her hair like a whip. "Follow me," she says.

I follow her to the front desk, and my hand has undoubtedly messed up her hair—I try to keep my face relaxed; I don't want her to think I'm laughing at her, which is absolutely what I would be doing.

"Is this how you treat everyone in the library?" I ask as she limps around the front desk. She seems to be ignoring me now. "Fresh, just like the smell in this place." I plug my nose.

"An eye for an eye—" She doesn't take her eyes off me while she pulls something up on the computer.

"You quote the Bible the day after you are caught in the act of a felony." This lady has some lessons to learn in life.

She swallows. "Minor lapse of judgment. At least I'm not as sinful as you." She lowers her voice. "I know what you are."

"And what is that?" I lean in a little closer, letting my eyes flash to her lopsided hair, and feel disappointed she's wearing a scarf—covering up my salt shot from last night.

Without blinking, she lifts her chin and takes a deep breath before she opens her mouth. "You're a killer. A library killer."

I arch my eyebrows, and the sides of my mouth pull down knowingly, and I can't help it—I laugh.

She crunches up her nose, and I'm sure I see steam come out of her ears. But then I hear the door, and she paints on a smile, limps away, and doesn't look back at me.

I'll have to add enraged librarians to the list of bizarrely entertaining spectacles that are best avoided. With her hair seeming to crackle with static electricity, she's practically a fire hazard waiting to happen.

I didn't notice earlier that her dog had walked out of the children's area and sat in the middle of the foyer.

"James!" she says. "How are you today?"

I follow her, and she's ignoring me now—this could be good. She fist bumps the man, plastered with tattoos, starting at his fingertips and clawing to his neck. Maybe this was a past boyfriend? But then they would be hugging right now.

"James, did you get the job?" Amelia asks.

"Milly." He shakes his head and looks down, "I'm so sorry to disappoint you. No, I didn't. That's why I'm back."

She nods, frowns, and places her hand on his shoulder. She points through me and sidesteps around me as they both start to walk to the computer wall—correction, where an archaic monitor lives along the east wall like a Jurassic boulder. When she fires it up, it sounds like an entire AC system is online.

"Their loss," she says, nodding her head. "What job are you applying for next?" Amelia pulls out the chair for him. The man pulls out his wallet and removes a card. I squint; maybe he's a cousin?

"Several. I'm emailing my resume to all the available positions today." Amelia crosses her arms and blocks me from James—like he's a hidden prize, and I'm the bull she's trying to deflect.

"Like always, you can have as many timed sessions as you need." She beeps the card in, unlocking the screen. "James..." She puts her hand on the back of the chair. "Don't tell me you had some of your uncles moonshine before your interview?"

He cringes.

Amelia shakes her head and crosses her arms. "James, you've got to get yourself cleaned up. Your son needs you to keep a job down."

His shoulders sag, and he traces a tattoo on his arm with his finger. He nods. "You're not wrong, Milly."

She kneels beside him and speaks quieter; I can't hear her.

James smiles. "Milly, you are the best thing about this town. I'll wait for the email." He leans over and gives her a quick peck on the cheek. Those cheeks turn red on cue this time—not a cousin.

She pats him on the back. "If there is anything I can help you do, you know I'm here for you."

James smiles wide. "I know, Milly. You're the best."

The man turns to the computer, and Amelia walks toward the door—I follow.

She waits until I'm close enough to reach out and touch. "I don't think you should come back," she whispers, folding her arms as I stop behind her. I'm not sure who she's talking to.

I whisper, "Me?" and point to my chest.

She rolls her eyes. "I just don't want you to scare the children."

I muffle this laugh and finally let myself take her in—she's serious. Brown splatter shirt with stickers everywhere, scarf-wrapped neck, worn-out flats, fitted pants, vibrant hair everywhere, especially where my hand has been, and green eyes that pierce—slice, really.

"I'm serious," she says, wrapping her arms around herself.

"I'm not a villain," I say.

She sends me lightning bolts with her eyes, "You are to me."

I feel my phone vibrate and take it out—it's the alarm for the meeting with the lawyer and my brothers. I swallow and nod my head. I walk backward, and the dog walks up to me as I turn around and wink.

"I guess our feelings are mutual." I hear her suck in a loud, high-pitched breath as I walk out of the library. If I've learned anything in the last twenty-four hours, Amelia is a passionate creature, and maybe her life is just as lousy as mine. That doesn't stop the thought that I'd like to do everything I can to ruffle her to the core; I'd get the chance tonight in front of the entire town, no less.

I fully intend to return the library to the dust that it is.

Maybe, just maybe, I *am* a villain.

Chapter Five

Lucas

I'm the first to arrive—the lawyer's office is wedged between two newly renovated storefronts along Magnus Avenue. The large conference table is on the second floor, facing a picture window with an unobstructed view of the Blue Ridge Mountains.

It's an expensive view—I drink it up.

My fingers drum against the table, my heart pounding in rhythm—I sit down on the loveseat near the window and then try the leather couch. Next, I try the swivel chair at the tall table along the wall.

There is no sign of my brothers, but I can see the top of the library, and Amelia's red face makes me smile.

Amelia is fuming at me.

"Mr. Chernov," a mousey voice interrupts the silent room. I jump, knocking over a candle decor on the table. The secretary points to the sidebar full of fresh fruit, snacks, sodas, and juices, bordered by elaborate spider plants and full-shaped hostas.

"We're good," I nod.

"We'll wait until each one of your brothers has arrived," she says, tugging on her blazer.

Dad had several months to get everything in order—pancreatic cancer has no mercy, especially at stage four. His meticulous ways paid off, and he always had his will and trust funds adjusted every time a new boy was born.

Sweat pools in my lower back; whatever is in that envelope will be well thought out. No one has seen his will; I know he can strategize, but I hope his posthumous instructions don't take it to an entirely new level.

"It's a unique one," our family lawyer, Magnolia Grace, said several weeks after Dad died. She's become one of Andrei's new best friend since I'd left.

"I am bound by law to follow it exactly," she said, lifting an envelope high at a family meeting in her office the week Dad died. "You don't have access to anything until one year after his death." She took a deep breath and put the envelope with the instructions on her desk.

She'd practiced law for three years, and my brothers buried her with questions. Finally, she raised her voice. "Chernovs!" We all stopped yelling and listened to her. "That's all that was in here. I know nothing else. Till next year," she'd said.

I texted Magnolia Grace earlier this week when the envelope arrived. She gave me a thumbs-up and said, "Bring it on Wednesday."

I pull the envelope from the bag I brought and pull my hand down my face.

I don't want to feel manipulated by a dead man.

So I walk to the window again, too nervous to text and harass my brothers to make it on time—but I see several cars pull up and Chernovs pour into the building. Remington and Apollo are the two youngest of the ten. They cruise down 21st Street on some electric skateboard. The high school is right in town.

I rub my hands together and blow into them. Mom helped coordinate with everyone except herself to be here for this meeting. I find it ironic that she can't make it. I hope she can get home soon.

Andrei helps Baba out of the car. Max pulls up on his Harley.

The entire building leans and moans as the Chernov brothers walk up the steps and into the conference room.

I hear Vincent holler up the step.

"Lucas, hot shot show-off, wanted the secretary all to himself."

I could punch him; she's half my age. I'm surprised he's only been suspended twice in high school for his sharp tongue.

Everyone comes in and sits around the table.

Nikola and Andrei, my two brothers closest to me in age, sit on both sides of me; Andrei's jaw is tight, and I smell stomach acid on Nik.

"Atticus, what are you wearing?" I ask, raising one of my eyebrows. He's the middle brother, number five, and I long ago stopped trying to figure him out.

He looks down and says, "A workout suit."

I shake my head. "Att, not the right space for a speedo."

He shrugs his shoulders and bends his head under the table.

"Atticus, we are all wearing pants, like normal people," Nikola says in a monotone voice rubbing his eyes.

"I think it could help with the stress," Apollo says, defending Atticus.

"The extra airflow is the way to go. I can trade with anyone." He points to several of my brothers.

Vincent speaks out again, he's brother number eight in the lineup and a twenty-year-old who knows it all. "Lucas looks like his pants are too tight. He's going to have an accident, or he's going to pop his neck artery."

My brothers make bathroom jokes at all ages; I had forgotten that.

I hate that I have Dad's similar mad artery. His was in his forehead. I guess a neck artery is less noticeable. If I wear a turtleneck, it's covered.

I rub my face. "I'm not trading pants with anyone."

The secretary comes up with a platter of tortilla chips and salsa. She tries hard not to look at my pants, but she fails, and my brothers snicker. I don't make eye contact with her.

Magnolia Grace, the lawyer, walks in—everyone looks at her except Andrei. She keeps her gaze on me as she fiddles with a ring on her finger. Her fit figure adds to her demanding presence.

"We have the next set of instructions," she says, right down to business. Her firm exploded overnight because of her reputation for being down-to-business.

She points to the sad, crumbled envelope on the table.

"Did you put it through the wash?" Vincent asks, his hair almost covering his eyes.

"No. A dog ate it," I say.

A few of my brothers laugh. "Mom will be back soon to help with your dog-eating laundry issues," Vincent says.

Andrei steps in. "Vincent, let's get the instructions, and then you can be gone." Andrei is moody, and it doesn't fit him. But everyone seems to agree—the nerves in the room are overwhelming.

Except for aired-out Atticus—and Remington, the carefree youngest brother, who is on his phone.

"Pull it out," Dimitry says.

I pop the seal, and my lungs release as I pull out the letter. It's doubled up inside another envelope with a seal.

I use the back of my hand to wipe my forehead.

The second envelope looks much better. The outer manila envelope took most of the beating. My fingers start to shake as I reach for the letter opener. One tooth hole made it through the actual letter that I can see—my neck artery pulses as I use the letter opener to ease up the dark, waxy Chernov crest.

My heartbeat is in my ears.

I pull out the letter. My thumb flips open the tri-folded paper, and my eyes scan the contents. The hole made it through four spots on the letter: three in the margin and one over a word.

One word is no big deal, I reason.

My palms sweat, making the envelope slip. Dim jumps up to get it—I hold up my hands for them to back off; I pick it up, toss the envelope on the table, and clear my throat:

Dear Lucas and all my sons,

I hope this letter finds you well. As you know, life can be unpredictable, and there are things I wish I could have shared with you in person.

There are even more things I wish I'd never said. That is why I want to make sure each of you knows about my most important projects—I hardly shared them with anyone. I had only begun most of these projects before the news came.

Others I've nurtured like a child.

If you accept, your inheritance will include large projects I believe in and the funding to get you started.

These aren't easy projects; they are the hardest ones I've ever undertaken. It's not what you think, and trust me. It's worth your time.

When you turn eighteen, you can access your passcode or inheritance box. The catch is that it won't be given to you.

You have to find it.

Lucas is the only exception; I'm giving him the passcode freely—I've put you through enough already.

Your box contains a manila envelope for your brother and a letter I wrote for you.

Some boxes might bend the rules a little, but for the most part, once you find your passcode or your inheritance box, you should have collected all the necessary pieces for your inheritance.

The manila envelopes will give you clues that lead you directly to your physical box (anywhere is game, by the way) or to a passcode. If you receive or find your passcode, go to the bank, which will open a safe with your inheritance box.

Your inheritance will be outlined in your personal box.

Andrei, your first clue is inside Lucas's inheritance box. Nikola, yours is inside Andrei's, and so on. This chain is a built-in system to ensure you all help each other get your inheritance.

If someone gives up, every younger sibling goes without an inheritance. And I repeat, this is your inheritance. You don't get one if you don't find your box or code. Lastly, they're all relatively close in monetary value—I've tried to make it equal but different.

Except for one.

Lucas, you have a passcode, which means your box is stored safely in a locked box at the town bank.

Please nurture your projects. You will learn about me and will help others along the way—accept this journey with an open heart.

Near the end, I didn't have time to correct many wrongs. But if you are still living and breathing, I still have time. I don't want you to live the rest of your life holding resentment because of me. I believe in each project you will inherit, just like I believe in you.

I want you to embrace your potential.

Find your inheritance box—your future wealth depends upon it.

Work together—and to keep your attention—I've made it difficult.

Remember, it's never too late to discover what you're capable of.

Zolton Chernov

Passcode: Re_____e

I hold the letter up and look through the hole between the letters of the passcode, "Re_____e." My eye peeks through, and I can see Atticus.

When the letter slips out of my hand the second time, I don't bend down to pick it up—the boom of chaos that erupts freezes me to the chair.

Amelia Anderson's dog has eaten my inheritance passcode.

I sink into my seat at Amora Comida; hot corn tortillas, lime juice, and grilled chicken hang on my clothes every visit. Luna Prosa approaches the table, "If it isn't the oldest Chernov in the flesh! What can I get for you, Mr. Chernov? It's been ages."

Her dark eyes are level with mine despite my low booth seat. I don't make eye contact. "I know it's been a minute."

Since the meeting an hour ago, my phone has been vibrating nonstop. The silence button screams at me, and my thumb fumbles toward the small switch when a call comes through. It's

Mitchell Ricks, and the contact title, The Big Boss, flashes on the screen. I hold up my finger to Luna, and she nods and leaves.

I feel numb, but know this might be an important call, so I swipe answer. Mitchell communicating outside of email means only one thing: He's nervous about tonight's meeting.

"Lucas, my number one, how are you?"

I steady my breath. "About to eat, and you?"

"Never better, never better. I just wanted to see if the engineer is still heading to the library today?"

"As far as I know. I'll follow up right now."

"Fantastic, fantastic, fantastic." He says things in three when he is juiced up over a deal. "Also, good luck at the meeting tonight! Let me know if you need backup. You know those town meetings are my specialty."

"One of many," I say, scowling at the menu. He laughs, and I motion Luna back.

"Take care," he says, and I end the call to start texting the engineer.

Having the engineer today will make it full, but having his thoughts before the meeting could go a long way, though; I shoot off a quick text to the engineer to confirm our meeting time.

My speech and handout are full of real-time statistics and data points. I feel prepared for tonight, but until now, I wasn't expecting Dad to slice in and take over my life again. And I think I might actually hate Amelia right now, too.

I'll take it out on her during my speech tonight; tearing her to shreds would be inadequate payback for ruining my inheritance.

My eyes close, and my fingers pinch my forehead.

He pits me against all my brothers, and he knows exactly what he is doing—forcing lessons on me even after he dies. I won't go for it, the inheritance box hunt, the passcode, none of it.

Could he just stop haunting me?

As if on cue, Andrei walks in the door. "Two chicken enchiladas with a side of red rice," I say, pretending to scan the menu to avoid eye contact.

My face turns to stone as Andrei pulls up a chair—Luna reads my face and practically runs from the table.

"Drew," I say. They haven't even given me twelve hours before they send him in—Andrei is one year younger than me, and my best friend since the day I could walk.

"I know Dad is asking a lot—"

I cut him off. "Don't you see how it's all a game to him? Even after he is dead, he's still trying to manipulate me with his games. I just can't, Drew."

He nods his head. "I get it." He places his hands on the table. "An engineer was headed to the library today, correct?"

I check my silenced phone.

> Karol: *I'm so glad you texted. I'm sorry, but I'm in the hospital with my wife. She's had false labor pains. I can't make it back*

in time to start the inspection today. Can we raincheck it for a few days?

A small pain starts to spread through my neck.

Me: *Fine. Stay in touch.*

"Not today," I say.

Drew nods. "Some of my contacts tell me the librarian might be the hardest person to convince, that everyone in town would love to see a new, fresh building on that corner. She's becoming a real barrier."

I take a sip of my water. "She has no decision-making power—her opinion doesn't matter at all," I say.

Drew crosses his arms. "You could go farther with her on your—"

I cut in. "You know I need this contract."

"We could build the apartments somewhere else. Chernov Realty hasn't really considered another location. You could propose other spots," Drew says, his face calmer than earlier.

I shake my head. "And ruin my chance to run Noil Construction? The survey recommends that exact location. I'm not giving up." I shake my head—it's the only thing I have focused on for five years—I have sold my soul to this company to help pay for the falling out I had with Dad. "I can't let it backfire now; I'm so close."

What I'm not saying Andrei reads on my face: The only thing I have accomplished without Dad's influence is this company—I found my job on my own, worked my way up, and now I've secured one of the most significant projects for Noil Construction up to date; building apartments for my brothers—Chernov Brother Realty.

Andrei takes a deep breath. "I know you're still hurting about the way Dad...was," he says, "but Lucas, come on. We've all felt pressure from Dad. We've all had our beef with him. Don't think you are the only one who had a falling out with him. Others have just coped..."—he twists his pinky ring—"differently."

I blink at Drew. I'm not so arrogant as to think it was sunshine and roses for everyone else with Dad, but I do feel like Dad forced me to become him—and I hate him for it.

"You got the most of Dad, even if you weren't happy about it."

My tight jaw rotates a little, chewing on his words.

"Others didn't get that. This could be a way for Dad to...rebuild some of the feelings he neglected." Drew lowers his voice. "It could help some brothers to think of him in a better light." He pushes the saltshaker closer to me. "Think outside your own hurt, Lucas."

He always knows where to punch, and I trust him enough to put down my walls and let him take a swing. "I don't like it, Drew." I hate when I can't anticipate Dad's next move, and this is a new trick he's never ventured into—being dead and still calling the shots. His projects have always made the front page, causing chaos, growth, or lawsuits.

"I need to secure this rezoning project," I gruff and look behind me for the food to come. "I don't have time to play Dad's game."

Drew nods his head. "So I read in your reports. I don't know why Mitchell has you on such a tight timeline. I don't know if it's worth the drama..."

I have a thirty-minute speech ready to go on about this, but before I can speak up, he says, "I'll support you, Lucas. I will vote however you think I should. If, for whatever reason, the brothers vote on a different location for the apartments, I'll give you my vote and convince others to follow if..."

He's good—and I love him despite the acid in my stomach.

"All I ask is that you participate in Dad's games. Help us figure this out. Help get your passcode and box so I can get my letter and clues to pass it along."

He stands up to go. "Don't let Dad die because of your hate."

A sting pricks my chest, and I fist my hands.

"Fine." My neck vein pulses. "Tell Apollo to stop spamming my phone. My time goes to rezoning the land, not the inheritance boxes."

He nods, and I catch a shimmer of hope in his eyes.

"I love you, Lucas. This will be a good thing; I can feel it."

He turns and leaves the table as Luna places the steaming food in front of me. I pop the lid off the hot sauce and drench my plate. I shred the enchiladas and swallow my bubbling feelings, hoping the hot sauce can calm my heat.

It doesn't even come close.

Chapter Six

Amelia

Neme doesn't try to pull me faster, and I'm grateful. My face pinches up with every step; my ankle is officially swollen and warm to the touch. I've been on my feet all day. Mr. Mettle, the Library Director, had me bring boxes of books out to the book exchange display near the library building.

"Let's get rid of all the old books with damage," Mr. Mettle said, no doubt wanting to punish me for being late to work today.

"That's most the books..." I protested.

He just pointed and had me start on the far end of the library. I made judgment calls with one eye closed. I filled the exchange box, hoping the books found lovely new homes.

With all the extra steps, my legs ache, and I don't have time to get my car or change into something presentable—a replica of a two-year-old splattering paint canvas sweater will have to do. I'll make it look like I meant to wear this shirt—in honor of the children.

I press the stickers tighter; yes, it could buy the library sympathy votes.

My speech is as good as gold. Rosabell, an avid reader, loyal library patron, and standing five-year winner of our local Scrabble competition, helped me write it—she's fantastic with words.

I fill my ribcage with a deep breath—do a few setbacks get me down?

No.

My determination could fuel a small expedition to Middle Earth.

I know he'll be there, Lucas, and he has what he needs to win over the council, committee, and audience. That thought rests between my cheek and back molar, prime for infection.

I can do this, I repeat to myself.

The pastel pinks and light tangerine clouds from the sun setting don't even distract me or tempt my eyes as the day wraps up. Enjoying sunsets again could be a pastime after I save the library.

Neme looks at my limping leg. The kids played hard with him today. During their pretend playtime, he was a bear, a stuffed animal, and a butler. I am not surprised anymore at how well he plays along. My heart melts; he is so good with kids. They giggle whenever he licks their faces.

I love Neme.

"It wasn't worth it," I say, "if that's what you're trying to fish out of me. I'll let you be the first to try getting the number Simon wants next time. Are you happy now?"

He sticks his tongue out and starts to pant.

"Good, it's settled."

Town hall parking spills over to the street, and I focus on the floor as I walk through the front door into the main entrance, replaying my speech.

But the yelp fills my ears before the cold liquid splashes into my hands.

"Oh, my cracker days!" Betty Sue, the recorder for all the town meetings, southern drawl is wide and tight. "Milly May, are you okay? I'm so sorry, honey!"

I step into the utilities office without thinking and grab a roll of paper towels. The neon yellow liquid bubbles on the floor by both of us. It'll take a minute to clean up, and I feel my night wilting like thin, soggy paper towels.

"No one told me the newspaper reporter was coming to be here tonight, honey." She looks down at her pants. "I needed to get fresh air before we started. Please, heaven above the earth, tell me that doesn't look like what I think it looks like?" her hand pushes on her cheek.

My eyes go to her white pants.

Yes, Mountain Dew on white pants indeed looks like she got a little *too* nervous.

"Oh, Betty Sue," I wince.

She starts breathing heavily and swatting her hand around her face. "Don't cry, don't cry," she says. Her thick eyeliner coat with a lash wisp at her crease will leave a streak.

"Here," I say, pulling my oversized scarf off my neck, "use it as a belt."

She is slow to reach for the scarf—her eyes take in my shirt and dance across my welt for the briefest moments.

"Oh, honey, your day looks as smashing as mine. Are you sure?"

She wraps the scarf around her waist and ties the knot at her navel. The thick sides cover most of the spill.

Her face relaxes.

"I'm sure," the words come out smooth.

This is going to be a disaster.

Neme licks fast; he's never had Mountain Dew before; it makes the rest of clean up go fast.

I ask George, the nice officer standing at the entrance of the large meeting room, to hold Neme's leash while I go into the courtroom.

He nods his head. "Anything for you, Pumpkin." I blush because that nickname never stops spreading despite how I style my hair.

Betty Sue is dabbing her eyes, and I lean against the wall and say, "You're going to do a wonderful job. No one looks under the recorder's table. You'll be okay. Stay sitting down no matter what."

I sound convincing—fantastic practice.

"Oh, Milly, I feel bad." She gestures to my shirt.

"It's okay, Betty Sue," I say. "I wasn't paying attention to where I was going. I'm sorry as much as you are."

We hear someone holler, "Quiet down, quiet down."

I gulp and enter the room; it's a standing room only. All seats are taken, so I scan the audience like a fox in a field. Lucas is sitting in the front row with several other men dressed as nicely as he is.

Even the back of his head looks combed in a mean way.

I slip in along the back wall—Mayor Davis begins the meeting, and they vote on several items. It gives me time to study my opponent: freshly cut hair, pressed clothes, and I can smell his confidence from here—I scowl.

Finally, the Mayor opens the floor to the public—and Lucas is the first to stand. He is at the podium in two long strides—it's along the left wall, and everyone turns to see him.

Before he looks at the Mayor, his eyes search the crowd. When his eyes meet mine, he smirks, takes a deep breath, and starts his speech.

My stomach tightens.

"Ladies and gentlemen, distinguished members of the Planning and Zoning Committee, Mayor Davis, City Council, and fellow residents of our beloved town." He winks at me, and I don't breathe. He then spreads his gaze across the audience.

I look to my neighbors to make sure they aren't looking at my flaming hot red tamale cheeks—it's nature's way of making sure the world knows you can't hide a single thing you feel.

"One of my team members is passing out the main points I will touch on today. Please see the handout for specific data charts, specifically statistics from nearby towns similar to our population size within 100 miles of here."

Does he have a handout? I fill my cheeks with air and hold it like a chipmunk. I slip around the back and see a seat close to the front, on the edge. I hunch over, limp to it, and take one of the packets being passed around.

It's titled "A Vision for Progress: Transforming Our Community Through New Apartments."

Lucas pauses momentarily, letting the packets get dispersed before diving in.

My hand starts to crumple the packet, and I hold the rest of the pile on my lap until the person behind me taps my shoulder.

"I stand before you today not to oppose the values our library embodies but to propose a vision for progress and transformation that I believe can better serve our community. Like many others, our town is amid growth and change, and we must adapt to the evolving needs of our residents."

He looks like he has practiced his hand motions in a mirror, and I can't push down the bile tickling the back of my throat.

"First and foremost, I want to emphasize the pressing need for affordable and accessible housing in our town. As we all know, the demand for housing has been steadily increasing nationally."

I scan the crowd—people are flipping the pages; others are listening and nodding.

No, no, no.

"By constructing apartments in place of the library, we can address this urgent need head-on."

He steps out around the podium and finds my gaze again, and I'm mad at how fit and neat his entire presentation is.

"Our library, while cherished..."—he lets his eyes linger on me; he studies my shirt before he turns and looks at the council— "occupies valuable real estate in the heart of our town. We must consider the economic potential of this prime location."

He walks back to the podium and grabs the cursed manila envelope.

"Here is proof of who has ownership of the building and land. I'll pass it around." He hands the envelope to the first council member by the podium. "By repurposing this space for apartments, we can provide much-needed housing and stimulate economic growth. New residents infused in the heart of town would increase local foot traffic." He lifts his arms "Who doesn't want more money?"

All the important people sitting up front seem to be nodding their heads.

"I understand the concerns about losing a community resource."

No, he really has no idea. Is this the part where I can interject? I bite my tongue hard. Not yet.

"But we must remember that libraries are not the only places where knowledge and community can thrive."

Oh no, he didn't. Where would a place for the community be? There are so many more moving parts that he is sidestepping, but the audience looks like they are eating pudding out of his hand. My face turns fever-hot as he reads through statistics, community projection charts, and local needs.

"In conclusion, I urge you all to consider this proposal as an opportunity for positive change and growth in our town. Our library has served us well, but it is time to reimagine our community's future. By constructing apartments, we can address the housing crisis, boost our local economy, and ensure a prosperous future for generations to come. I believe in the resilience and adaptability of our community, and I trust that, together, we can embrace this vision for progress. Thank you for your time and consideration."

His final words are clipped with several audience members applauding.

"No applauding," Mayor Davis speaks into the mic. "We want everyone to feel equally listened to on all sides."

Lucas gathers his papers on the podium and freezes with the cheapest smile as the reporter flashes his camera.

I'm too distracted watching him shake people's hands as he makes his way back to his seat that several other men line up at the podium, which starts to boil venom in my stomach. I don't hear a word anyone else says as I shoot flaming ice stares at Lucas.

When the mic finally opens again, I stand up and walk past him. Instead of slightly bumping his shoulder, I twist my hurt ankle and catch his sleeve as I fall forward.

In a quick turn and twist, he is there.

He catches me and looks down into my face with a smile.

"It's easy to fall for me," he whispers into my ear, "and in front of everyone, you are bold." He looks at my lips. "But now's not the time for you to break a leg."

I fight his tight embrace, and he nearly drops me.

He lifts me back up, and I straighten out my stained shirt and pinch my nose, trying to get his clean soap and cologne out of my nose.

I step toward the microphone and take a moment to pause. My eyes close for the briefest of breaths, then they pop open, find Lucas, and give him more stares.

His eyes linger on my collarbone, on his welt—good, I can use sympathy from the bully. I straighten my shoulders, elevate myself above my greasy hair, welt, and hot cocoa splatters, and focus on Lucas Chernov.

"Ladies and gentlemen of our beloved community" —*pause for effect, let arms hang loose at sides*—"I'm not someone armed with numbers and statistics, but as a humble patron and librarian of Lionstone Library—it means the world to me. I-I have something more profound to share with you all."

Make eye contact with the audience. "Our library is not just a building filled with books; it's a place where people from all walks of life seek solace, knowledge, and connection. I've witnessed the power of this library in countless ways, ways that numbers can't quantify. Hidden treasures and even...love can be found—"

"She's just the librarian; she's tainted!" someone yells out, and my next words get stuck in my throat.

Another woman from the back chimes in. "Jimmy, shut it! You didn't interrupt any of the prattling men. That ain't respecting freedom of women's speech." The woman stands and points at Jimmy—now I see him.

I don't like Jimmy.

Mayor Davis cuts in. "That's enough, let's ge—" Jimmy stands up and starts letting the colorful rainbow of words fly out between his lips. I see a mom cover a child's ears, and my mouth drops open as several other library patrons pop up like baby aspen trees to defend my speech.

A prick forms behind my eyes, and my tongue feels like a cotton ball—I haven't even made it past my introduction.

My eyes float to Lucas as the police step in and escort Jimmy out of the room. His lips are in a straight line, and his face is unreadable.

Mayor Davis clears his throat. "I apologize, Amelia, for that interruption. Do you have anything more?"

I do, but my paper is shaking now. The crowd is loud, still in commotion, and no one is looking at me. Being wise, I cut right to my ending.

"So, as we contemplate the future," my voice cracks, "let's not just focus on the bricks and mortar. Let's remember the lives it touches, the dreams it nurtures, and the bonds it strengthens. Let's honor the heart and soul of our library, for it's not just a place; it's a part of us. Thank you." I say wobbly. If I can sit down, maybe I can get through this meeting without crying.

The Mayor speaks up. "I know this might be a little unorthodox, but I ask Lucas and Amelia to approach the council box."

Lucas walks, and I limp. The crowd is getting noisier as some try to look out the window to see if Jimmy is getting arrested.

"For the sake of safety and peace, I have a recommendation for you both." His voice is quiet.

Lucas nods.

"I'm listening," I say.

His eyes dip down to my shirt and then my collarbone welt. One eyebrow goes up.

"Do you have a boyfriend I don't know about?" Mayor Davis often stops by the library to say hi, and he had a good relationship with Mom before she passed.

His eyes sparkle a little.

My hand flies to my neck. "No, no," I stammer.

Lucas smiles. "By the looks of your mark, one would think a doting lover visits you regularly."

I imagine him growing horns.

He crosses his arms. "He's a lucky guy," he says.

I bore my eyes into him; the nerve.

The Mayor clears his throat—it breaks our trance.

"I called you up here for an idea that just struck me. A majority of the library board members are here tonight. I'm an ex-officio member, and I'd like to recommend both of you as temporary board members to perhaps oversee the library through this transition." He rubs his chin. "If you two can model teamwork, it will help the community." He points to several citizens who are now talking at the window, watching Jimmy's showdown with the police force.

"I believe that you both want what is best for our town. You both seem to know what you're about."

He looks into our eyes. "Join the board. Write up a proposal together, and I'll do all I can to see it through. I'd love to see what you both could come up with if you're on the same team."

Lucas nods as if he doesn't hesitate at all, but I have so many questions.

I can see Clyde, the executive director of the library board and regular visitor of the library, nod his head.

"We can make it official right now. We have a quorum here—"

A man clears his throat, sitting by the Mayor. "Mayor Davis, now is not the time or place. This is a public hearing."

Against my better judgment, I nod my head, too. I won't let Lucas be on any board over the library without me defending it.

"You are right," the Mayor says in a louder voice. "We are out of time tonight to hear from the public. The meeting is adjourned. Excuse my unusual tangent. If you're a library board member, will you stay momentarily?"

Some of the audience members clear, but most people stick around to see the rest of the show.

Mayor Davis points to us. "I'd like to recommend a nomination to the library board: Lucas Chernov and Amelia Anderson. They could be ex-officio members to help create a strategic plan for the library's transition."

I know most of the board members, but some look unfamiliar.

The mayor continues, "We have a retreat coming up that's hosted by the state's southern region. Many city officials can't attend, so we've asked the library board to take up our extra reservations. We hope they can use that time to create a strategic plan that we'll hear about in the next public meeting. Tonight was just the first step in the strategic planning process."

A woman sticks up her cane. "I second that," she says.

Someone else jumps in. "All in favor?"

Then I hear a smattering of ayes.

Clyde, the director speaks up, "Actually, it's not in our bylaws to have to vote in ex-officio members—they don't have voting rights, but good job everyone. Way to practice proper non-profit etiquette."

The mayor nods and continues. "The retreat goes on all week, but the board will go up only for the weekend. It will be ideal for you both to create a plan on the retreat together and present it to the board."

Several other board members stand up and walk toward where we are standing.

Clyde taps Lucas's shoulder. "I recommend you and Amelia help collect library data." He shakes his finger at Lucas. "You, young man, have some impressive data in your packet. I think it's only fair if we try our best to collect data for the library, too. To help strengthen our strategic plan."

The prune-hand lady nods her head. "That sounds only fair."

They have another impromptu vote, and in a matter of moments, we are given the task of collecting data for the library by *whatever means are most logical.* They agree in unison.

Maybe I did such a terrible job they tricked Lucas into helping me? Is this the best thing or the worst thing that has happened?

He leans over to me as we walk back to our seats. "I know you've been pining to spend more time with me," he says.

I swallow. I have thought about him every moment this week, just not in nice ways. My cheeks puff out.

"Pining is not the right word," I say.

His lips twitch. "I'll be coming to see you first thing..." He scratches his head. "Data collection takes time; you better get used to me in the library."

I leave his side in a limp and squeeze through the crowded hallways. Neme and the officer are waiting for me outside.

If I hurry, I can get a head start to my car, still hiding near the mansion, before the crowd starts leaving.

I have lots to think about as the weight of the day crushes my shoulders and reaches around my throbbing ankle.

Chapter Seven

Amelia

Magnus Avenue feels three times longer than it should, but the forest surrounding Herasburg gives off clean air with a hint of fresh leaves and water droplets from the river. The sun is long gone and no moon is out, and the humidity is too thick for early fall. I shiver, despite my stickiness, and hug my chest.

Maybe I should have asked for a ride. Uber? No, no. Too poor. Maybe Carrie would drive forty-five minutes from her university to bring me the last two miles? That's what friends do, right?

Honestly, I've made it farther than expected as the stream of cars comes down the street. My path scoots a little off the sidewalk into the small gravel pieces as my rhythmic limp crunches against the rocks.

The light from the snow-globe lamp posts can't illuminate my tear-stained cheeks for the drivers passing to see. My mind imagines the citizens at the meeting driving by shouting, "Better luck next time!" or "Bless your heart, Pumpkin...you're so cute for trying." Any Southern woman over the age of forty would say, "You're a hot mess boiling like an egg on the asphalt; your speech was a disaster." At least they would be honest with me.

He had a handout. He had statistics. He had a team. His shirt was clean, starched even, with no cut corners ironing. I can tell when someone lifts their arm; boom! Armpit wrinkles—corners cut, sloppy. Not him; perfect hair, form, and straight shirt, every inch of his upper body. I only look to find his weakness, like scouting out a predator.

My shoulders feel stones forming, and my stomach rumbles. "Come on, Amelia," I say, trying to stop my downward spiral. My eyes close for the briefest of moments, letting the night air tickle my nose hairs. My hand finds my pocket as I exhale a worn-out sigh and take out my phone, flipping it off silent.

Carrie, I'll call her so I don't look so destitute as everyone drives by.

Maybe she is in town visiting, and she will save my ankle.

"Hi!" I fake happy.

"Did you single-handedly save the library? I cannot wait to hear—"

"No." I don't even know where to begin.

"Oh, Milly, I'm sure it's not as bad as that. Besides, I know the best thing to cheer you up!"

My fingers clench the phone tighter.

"I found the perfect guy for you! You know eight months is not getting any closer."

I moan, pull my phone from my head, and almost throw it across the sidewalk. I don't have the energy to focus on finding a date right now.

"I heard that moan," she says.

It's not that I don't remember agreeing to double with her fiancé and his family visiting out of town, like a bazillion days away; it's the date part.

"Can't I just come alone? I can be silent or just the quiet observer. I really don't have time to find a date."

She pauses and makes a throat-clearing sound.

"I could just bring Neme?" I spit out.

My eyes take him in; his tongue is dripping drool next to my throbbing ankle—it pools up between the small rocks.

Just my type.

"Mil, come on. I need someone there with me; I don't want to face my future mother-in-law alone. We finalize the reservations at the end of the year. I have to know by then."

I twist my face and wrinkle my nose.

"You know that doesn't sound like you think it does. You will have to learn to get along with your in-laws eventually."

"You promised, Mil, and I will learn, but just not until after the wedding next summer."

I let my sigh blow into my phone. "If I don't have someone picked out by Christmas, I'll go with whomever you pick." My voice cracks, and the tiredness seeps through the microphone.

"You're the best. I'll have this mystery man on backup! You're the most dependable friend in the entire world! I'll call you back soon. Aaron is calling me right now on the other line."

I slip my phone inside my pocket, and the trail of cars continues to pass.

That was counterproductive.

I make it to Griffin Lane. Five more blocks with a large hill to go. My foot drags, plowing the gravel with my shoe now. A car slows, gravel popping underneath the tires—my legs walk faster, and the engine turns off. Someone steps out, and he clears his throat.

I hold up my hand. "I can't."

"You can't what?" Lucas asks.

"Why are you talking to me?" I cross one of my arms over my elbow. I keep walking, and the wind blows some of the first falling leaves. The wind tosses my hair into my face and open mouth.

"Is it against some rule you have?" he asks.

My stomach growls, and my arms tighten around my waist. He can't see my cheeks, so I pull my hair out of my mouth and pat it against my cheeks like a shield.

"Like bending a piece of paper?" he asks.

I shake my head. "Most people who come into the library know some of the unwritten rules of the library."

"It looks like I need a lesson or two."

I grunt. "Way more than a lesson or two." My eyes stay glued to my dragging toes.

Zolton wasn't a nice person, and most of his boys were the same. Stubborn, mean, powerful men who use their deep pockets to get exactly what they want, not what is best for the town. I don't want to slip into the trap of thinking he's kind. My shoulders instinctively put more space between us. I look back at him.

"Unwritten rule one: Don't talk to your enemy after a battle," I say.

"I thought you said rule one was don't bend pages in a book?"

I roll my eyes. "Order comes during the editing process."

"Can I make recommendations?" he says as the wind plays with his hair. I hate how good he looks—it's sinful and unfair and tempts me to smile. He must have sold his soul for a hairstyle that looks perfect in the wind. It isn't even influencing me—the small drool in the corner of my mouth is because I am hungry.

I glance down over my clothes and remember that I look like a Monday when it throws up on you. And if I close my eyes and smell my shirt, it kind of smells like it, too. Not Lucas, oh no—his cologne and fresh soap scent glides up my nose as he closes the gap between us.

I take a deep breath—*no, Amelia. No smelling the enemy.*

"We want different things; that's why we shouldn't..." I move my hands between the both of us.

He unbuttons the top button on his shirt and rolls up his sleeves. I keep my gaze nailed to Neme as my mouth suddenly starts to dry up.

He sighs. “I’ve had a very long day.” He keeps to my limping pace. “And from the looks of it, so have you.” He points to my shirt and ankle.

“Well, that makes me feel like a million bucks.”

“Now—” he kicks a gravel piece. We aren’t getting too far from his parked car— “I want something that you want, too.”

“You think we’re similar? I hate to say it, but you are losing your touch, Chernov,” I say.

He smiles. “I am.”

I eye him again. Shoot.

“All my agendas are dried up for the day. Think you could hear me out?”

“Fine. Only to prove you wrong.” I push my hair behind my ear. He is the opposite of me in every way. He has a team. He has resources. He has power. We most certainly don’t want the same things. I want a crisp book page for everyone to enjoy. Is that so hard to believe?

“What I really want is a...Fannie’s Fry burger and milkshake.”

I pause to reject him, but my stomach growls again on cue.

“No strings attached,” he says.

My hands fly to my hair—I need a shower, bed, and Grandpoppy. Plus, I need to get my car. I need Oreos, a box of tissues, and a book. Not people, especially the Lucas kind.

My back hunches over. I want to start over by saying: Hello, hi, I'm Beyond Help. What's your name? A sample of my hot mess up close might give a strike or two against the library.

Pull it together, Amelia. "I don't think that's a g-good idea," I stammer out.

His eyebrow stays up. "Unwritten rule I don't know about?"

"I need to get my car..." I reply. The humiliation of what I did last night slaps me back. "And Grandpoppy."

"Let's get a burger, and I'll drop you off at your car afterward."

"No, I better not. Neme—"

"He's fine to ride in my car, promise." He stops and starts to turn around, walking backward. "Why don't we drop him off at your house so he can keep your grandfather company?"

Not getting a burger with the enemy has to be in the rule book somewhere. I'll add it after tonight. "No, I'm okay. I better make it to my car and get home." I instantly grow a second stomach like an alligator that yells, "Feed me grease!"

He shakes his head. "Amelia, we both had an intense meeting today. I've had two, in fact." He probably charmed everyone at both meetings, "And I don't want to go home yet. I'll be getting a Fannie's Fry meal with or without you." He turns back toward his car.

He deserves to be all alone.

I pull on Neme's leash; he is following Lucas now. "No, boy," I whisper. Neme starts to whine with every step Lucas takes in the opposite direction. "Nemean," I say, "come on, boy." He stops and lays down in the gravel; his legs pop out like he is sinking in anchors. I can't move him when he becomes dead-weight determined.

My fast breath puffs out with a baby growl.

"Promise you won't drive me right to the police station?" I walk toward Lucas. Neme hops up and walks right between us—Neme is conspiring with the dark side; I'll make him sleep on the ground tonight.

Lucas smiles and nods his head once.

I hope Neme sheds extra in his car.

"Did you hurt your ankle during your getaway last night?" he asks.

I swallow. "No." Much less of a noble act. "Not like the break-in did any good anyway," I mumble.

"You like to make things difficult." He looks at the car in front of us. "Especially for me, don't you?"

At his words, I feel a surge of energy, one of my new life purposes or a theme I can hold on to during our future interactions. "Yes," I say with a bright face.

"You made my life very complicated today." His eyes draw back, suspicion no doubt, about my shift in mood. "If I didn't know any better, I'd think you seem proud of that."

I cover my cheeks. "I am a horrible person, aren't I?"

He scratches his cheek. "The verdict is still out, Amelia Anderson."

He reaches around me to open the back car door, and he grazes my arm. Neme hops into the back seat. It looks detailed and sanitized, like an operating room, and some of Neme's hair floats in the air. I smile wider. He reaches for my door handle when I do, and his arm brushes against my bare arm again, where I have pushed up my sweater sleeves.

"Oh, I-I've got it," I say. My skin prickles, and my shoulder jerks my hand, rubbing the point of contact out.

Touching the enemy is another unwritten rule I'll add after tonight.

He opens the car door and nods his head. "Allow me." I hold my head high and meet his gaze. I am on to him—he's being fake nice—so he can tease me out of my book lair and then squash it.

"You could say thank you?" he says.

I press my lips together and slide into his car. He opens his car door and starts the engine, and the crisp black interior—like his heart—encloses us both.

Neme starts to whine, and I turn around to see if he is okay. As much as I want him to barf in the back seat, I don't know if I can handle dog vomit scent right now. Music always seems to settle Neme during car rides, so I lean over and turn the music on.

Neme settles down, and the music feels like an ocean wave on the driest part of the beach. It hits the beat of the day, drowning it out—until it switches to an 80's song with a fast tempo. My hands and waist move to the beat. Lucas looks at me, and his mouth drops open. I can't help but laugh. He probably thinks I am crazy—he wouldn't know happy if it slapped him across the face. He reaches to turn down the music, but I put my fingers on the volume knob first.

He uses the volume controller on his steering wheel, but I twist the knob up. He pushes his button down. I crank the knob up as high as I can, then plug my ears. Operation bother henchman is in full swing, and I laugh as he scrambles to turn it down.

"Amelia, really?" he asks.

I flip my hair to the opposite side.

I am not with a friend or a date; I am with my enemy, and my blood sugar is questionable.

"I don't know what overcame me," I lie.

He mumbles something as a small smirk touches his lips; at least, that's what it looks like when I turn toward him.

"What did you just say?" I ask.

He smiles a little wider. "You're impulsive."

I hold up my hand in defense. "Spontaneous. Fun-loving and bursting with creative energy." I correct him, but I feel tears forming in my eyes again because I know deep down that he's not wrong.

I brush my shoulder; his opinion is dirt to me. He dog-ears books.

"Let's get to the burger place in one piece, okay? I'll feel better after some food," he says.

"I agree." I nod and try to keep my gaze out the window but sneak a few glances at him. This might be as close to the enemy as I'll ever get. I want to get a good look at the man version of Lucas, and I know I can keep to a stealthy five-second stare.

One Mississippi—defined jaw. I've always noticed that part, but his brown eyes look distracted, and he taps his fingers against his leg to the quick music.

I twirl my hair around my finger.

Two Mississippi—his sideburns and nose look cut at a straight edge; his smile sings years of braces. I remember those braces; he used only blue bands.

Three Mississippi—he has some smile eye wrinkles sinking in. I bite my lower lip a little.

Four Mississippi—his flat stomach looks wider than it did ten years ago, and it seems like he is doing the man version of sit-ups now. Or his shirts seem to have grown a half size smaller; both are a possibility.

Five Mississippi—his dress pants fit him nicely; they are not baggy, not tight, and just nice.

I suck in a quick breath. They are the ones telling the lie because he isn't a nice person. He smiles.

Five Mississippi again—he looks like—

"Is this it?"

I jump. He points out the window. "With the...unique mailbox?"

I nod. He pulls up to our tiny one-car garage house. The mailbox has a rusted license plate for a roof, with a small trap door and an old hinge to the side. It's made from reused barn wood and a handle that looks like it came from a secret garden door. I've always loved our mailbox.

I jump out, and Neme jumps through the middle and out my car door. The front room light is on, and I follow Neme in.

"How'd the meeting go?" Grandpoppy looks up from his book.

"Swell." I know what the doctor said about his heart. He doesn't need to worry about my problems. When I moved back in with him right out of graduate school, I decided to keep a stress-free face for him. He lost his wife and daughter already; I won't give him one more ounce of disappointment.

"Oh good!" He reaches for my hand, and I take him up in mine; his warm wrinkles drain some of my stress out. "I'm so proud of you, just like your mom would be."

I pull away, not letting guilt grip where his warmth is. Neme trots to his side, and he pats his head. "I'm going to grab a burger with a friend."

He looks at me through his glasses, his eyes doubling in size. "Good. I'll leave the light on for you. Promise you'll watch our show together this weekend?"

"Always," I say. He smiles and picks up his book again. I round the corner and limp-run to my room. "Focus, focus," I say. Best *I'm undercover to push you and your apartments to a different part of town* outfit. Ready, set, go!

A clean, slightly wrinkled t-shirt, hat, and some jeans ultimately win out. They are the only cleanish clothes I have. I promise myself I'll get to my laundry this weekend as I lace up some high-top shoes; the tight compression helps. Perfume? I don't own any, and I step on that thought the second it pops in. I don't want to smell like BO, that's all. As I do a quick reapplication of deodorant, I put a little on my neck, too.

My fingers find a painkiller in the same drawer, and I swallow it dry. I don't want to get stuck limping in and out of Fannie's Fry.

I kiss Grandpoppy and Neme and step outside. Muffled music plays, and Lucas's mouth moves to the beat; he stops singing the words when I slip in. I sit on my hands and smile out the window as we drive in silence.

Lucas Chernov sings in his car.

He pulls into Fannie's Fry, and I jump out so he doesn't have to get my door. He holds the front door, painted like a cast iron grill, and the grease seeps into my nose like an old friend.

The line is short, and most of the booths are open. Lime green booth seats line the exterior wall. It adds a pop to the vibrant paint covering every surface. The floor and ceiling have globs of tan and brown paint in all shades, with every type of stir fry option on the menu. Food is illustrated on every surface—it's an "in the frying pan" kind of experience. Some of the favorite menu items are wearing off due to foot traffic of selfies. I am glad all my personal favorites are painted on the walls and one on the ceiling.

I order my favorite. "Franko's fish sandwich, please, hold the mayo and pickle."

Sydney nods her head. “Anything else for you, Pumpkin?” Sydney always puts an extra cool whip layer on my milkshakes with an extra cherry. It was a bright spot in my dark months while mourning over Mom.

I don’t dare order a milkshake now; I tend to get a little too creative with cool whip at my fingertips; I reach into my back pocket and pull out a twenty-dollar bill I stuffed in earlier.

“I’ve got it.” Lucas reaches his hand out to Sydney before she puts the twenty bucks in her till. He orders a complicated custom burger with lots of avocado on it.

Say something, “Complicated tastes.” I look at my feet.

Who says that? You could just say, Thank you for buying me dinner, Lucas.

He lifts an eyebrow again. “My Joe’s stacked special with extra avocado is so complicated.” He scratches his jaw. “Do I dare add the pigtail fries?” He looks like he’s contemplating a serious decision.

They aren’t real pigtails; I remember the first time I ordered them—they are the best curly fries in the world. They stop time and make you want to lie down in the mud like a pig.

I shake my head with a smirk. “Pigtail fries? Careful. You’d be making a statement about yourself.”

“Maybe that statement would be that I’m...assertive about my hunger?”

He nods to Sydney as she adds fries to our order.

“Anything on this menu is an option for you—if you need to make an assertive statement, I can support that here, Amelia.”

I try not to roll my eyes, and he keeps his brown eyes on me like he is daring me. I scan the ground to see if anything jumps out at me.

"Fine," I say. "Fannie's deep-fried frog legs, please." Life is too short not to try something new.

His mouth makes an *O* shape. "Feel better?"

Yes, I strangely do—I press my lips together, not giving him an answer.

Fake nice, I remind myself as we walk to a table with our buzzer. The long pendant lighting over each table makes the small-town burger joint feel soft with a slice of home. The sizzle and ding of pans hitting in the back lull us into another silence as we wait for our food. I readjust my *libraries are for lovers* hat; it is tighter than I remember. My greasy hair might reflect the light and blind poor Sydney, so I had better keep it on.

I look like the girl next door who showers every third day and is obsessed with her library. Which is exactly who I am.

They deliver the food, and I start counting car lights that go by as I chew. I don't want to break the silence and see him fake nice anymore. The silent companionship is strange and refreshing in the same bite.

He sips his drink. "How long have you been a librarian?"

I slow my chewing down. "Three years," I say with a full mouth.

Both of his elbows are propped up on the table as he takes large burger bites—he even chews nicely. He doesn't use twelve napkins like I do with the inevitable juice in Fannie's cooking. I need every single one to wipe the juice off my arm and chin, and yes, I dribble on my quasi-clean T-shirt.

I consciously put my fish sandwich down; eating faster won't make the day go away.

"If we are on neutral ground, it's a question for question," I say.

He nods his head. "I can agree to those terms."

"How many years have you worked outside of your family's company?" I ask.

He takes a deep breath. "I'm going on my fifth year." He wipes the corners of his mouth. A-ha, he does need a napkin. He tosses it in my pile close to the window, adding to my mountain.

I try not to watch him chew. "Did you not like working for your dad?" I ask.

He swallows and crosses his arms. "It's complicated." He looks over my shoulder and seems to go blank for a moment.

A small smile goes across my face. "So you didn't like working for your dad?" His face twitches.

"No..." He takes another sip of soda. "You got me. I didn't."

I scratch my chin. "Did your brothers feel the same way?" I think all the Chernov brothers work in that Realty on Magnus Avenue. Success typically means everyone is happy, right? They should have buckets of happiness stored up for several lifetimes.

"Some do. Several worked well with Dad. But we all have had to find ways to..." He looks up at the ceiling, searching for the right word, "Manage Dad."

He sits back against the green booth backing. "How about you and your parents?" he asks.

The questions swing back to me. I look down at my food. "Mom passed when I was in high school. I never knew my dad. Mom was a teen when she had me; he didn't want anything to do with us."

I hate saying that out loud. It reminds me of how alone I am in the world. But then guilt always follows because I have Grandpoppy and Neme. I am not alone—not really.

I learned that saying it quickly makes the sting go away faster. I keep my eyes glued to my mostly eaten fish sandwich; it really hits the spot, extra juicy and all.

The squish of the ketchup bottle makes me look up. He piles the ketchup high onto a plate, almost emptying it. "I thought I had a thing for ketchup...maybe you should get some help," I say. He takes a pigtail fry and draws a circle in the pile, two ears, and a long nose.

"Any guesses?" he asks.

I close one eye and say, "An elephant." He shakes his head. "Nope, try again."

"The trunk is here, the ears are here, and look," I lay two straighter pig fries down on the plate. "It has two curly tusks now."

"Wow," he nods, pulling the plate closer for a second. "I see what you're talking about...but you're wrong."

The lower lighting gives his eyes a soft twinkle. My stomach tightens up. "You sound like you've said that a lot before."

"Hmm?" he asks.

"The 'but you're wrong' statement," I say, picking up the ketchup-slathered fries and stuffing them in my mouth. I watch his eyes, now watching me chew.

I don't like his brown eyes on me. "I guess so. I've heard it a lot."

He points to my chin—I feel my chin and smear the ketchup even more.

"How could you not feel that?" he smiles.

"I did," I lie. "I was just finishing chewing before I cleaned myself up. Is it a panda bear?" I ask. I snag a napkin and clean up my face, and I will my cheeks not to turn pink. I don't care about his opinion, remember?

"No, it's a lion," he says. He dips a pigtail fry and chews it up.

Sydney's hip sways as she takes the last few steps to our table and pushes the fried frog legs between us. They are steaming and covered in a crispy, deep-fried coat. The zigzag shape is easy to imagine leaping. I sniff and readjust myself. I would never eat one of those in a million years.

"Looks tasty." He looks at me with a half-smile, "I can't wait to see how many you leave for me."

I play with my napkin. "I am so full already. I think I ordered them—"

He raises an eye. "*Impulsively*?"

I shake my head no. "Actually, they are the best texture. And the protein? Heaven above, you can't go wrong. Seeing how you've been gone for so long, I was doing you a favor. I just wanted to remind you of how delicious our small-town diner is and remind you of the charm of our local cuisine." I bat my eyes. "I ordered them for you."

"You are a thoughtful woman." He fingers one of the legs, he pinches the tip, and it crumples a little.

I gag.

"You know what they say?" I glare deep into those murderous brown eyes. His view zeroes in, and the diner melts away as we hold our stare.

I swallow—his eye twitches.

He pushes the plate closer to me, and I keep my lips pressed tight.

"The locals show the way."

I blurt out, "That is not a saying at all."

"Of course, it is. If you go somewhere new, the locals treat you to their favorite dish, and they taste it first to make sure it's up to...hops."

I press my lips tight. "I trust Fannie with all my heart. Her legs are divine."

He breaks our staring trance, and he blinks, laughing out loud.

"I will notify Fannie before we leave."

I smile, too; his full-chested laugh changes the air in the entire restaurant.

He taps his finger along the plate. "I dare you."

Oh no—I hate dares with a passion—they apply to every part of my vanity. I am the person in the room who jumps up and down without even knowing what the dare is.

I bite my tongue.

"I dare you to eat an entire frog leg, and I will..." He holds up his hand like he won't accept any of my suggestions. "I will get a library card."

I suck in air, releasing my tongue, and let my jaw pop open. "Don't tempt me."

He smiles wide. "Glad I know the way to your impulsive little heart."

I shake my head—he is dangerous.

"You will check out at least one book, too," I add and poke at one of the legs. It rolls over, and I cringe.

He laughs again.

He pulls the plate back. "I don't know if I can do that." He furrows his brows.

I pull the plate back to me, and a few legs slosh off the plate—I gulp.

"Doing hard things is good for the character," I say. "I'll eat one leg." I reach out and pick up the smallest leg I can find. "You get a card and one book."

He nods.

I move one leg to my lips. I close my eyes—I will not vomit. Or I will, at least, hold it until I get home.

It crunches—something pops. I close my eyes tighter, tighter, and I wave my hand at my face as I chew.

Lucas's laugh is deep, longer this time. I try to focus on the delicious, deep-fried part as I suppress my reflexes with every bite.

"How does it taste?" he asks as I open my clenched eyes.

I strain my neck to swallow. "Sensational," I say. I push the plate up to him.

He looks down. "I'll take your word for it," he says.

I press a hand against my collarbone. My T-shirt hides my welt. "Your host will be offended," and I give him my best puppy dog eyes.

His smile lingers as he snatches a frog leg from the plate. He stuffs the entire leg in without flinching. He chews fast. "Interesting," he says.

I sit up straight and watch him chew.

"There," he says.

I close my mouth, stifling my laugh. He has a frog leg stuck on his front tooth. I can't keep my laugh covered; it bubbles and bounces across the table.

"What is it?" he asks.

My laugh reaches my toes, and I can't breathe—I slap my legs a couple of times and snort.

"Amelia," he starts laughing with me, "what's so funny?"

I point to my teeth, mimicking where it is stuck. He focuses and digs at the frog piece with his pointer finger—he plucks it out.

I bend over, laughing again, and he joins in. It has been a long week, and this is the release I had no idea I needed.

Sydney passes, and I ask for mustard. She whips a bottle out of her apron, and I pull the poor ketchup elephant toward me and let the mustard work its magic.

"There," I say.

He studies the plate. "That does look like a lion...and your dog."

I smile wide. "Yes, Neme does look like a lion."

"Is that why he's named after a lion?" he asks.

"You found me out," I say, like I'm drunk on carbs. "You must be familiar with Hercules' labors and his curse." My smile is wry.

"I know a thing or two. I've read a book," he says.

"Wow, I'm proud." I wave my fry around in the air. "You could remember what page it was on and show it to me sometime?" I raise my eyes.

He hides his smirk well. "I bet you like reading."

"What gave me away?" My stomach feels like it opens a little.

He asks me the one question you never ask a true book lover. "What book is your favorite?"

I can't even get to the question because I have to explain to him why it is impossible for book lovers to answer. He laughs during my entire explanation, and I can't pretend that I don't see the twinkle in his eye when he is enjoying himself.

Time slips. We talk and laugh the night away. He orders us both milkshakes, and I behave, mostly. He laughs as I use eight more napkins on the cool whip that somehow gets all over my cheeks and nose.

Sydney turns off the open sign, and we stand up. We drive in silence back to his Snob Acres development.

"Thank you," I say, breaking the silence. He nods and pulls off to where my car is parked.

He straightens his face as my hand rests on the door handle, but he reaches for my arm and holds it.

He clears his throat. "I will be fighting for the apartments."

"I can't let you win," I say.

He nods his head.

I tug my hair free, step out of the car, and strangely, I'm relieved. He will never be nice to me again—dinner meant nothing; it was all about him winning.

"Amelia?" He rolls down his car window.

I turn back and look over my shoulder.

"I don't lose."

I am glad he is honest with me. "I'll fight with everything I've got," I say and spin around, letting my hair spray out underneath my hat, and I jump into my car.

The only words I can find myself saying on the way home are: *Bring it on, henchman.*

But my mind is frozen on repeat, replaying his strong jaw chewing frog legs with a straight face—he paid for me and forced me to have a wonderful time—I shake my head.

He is a henchman who knows precisely what he is doing.

Chapter Eight

Lucas

I will avoid Amelia today. I need a day to consider the best way to collect unbiased data.

I'll see her soon enough, I tell myself. The ketchup on her chin makes me smile—she hides nothing—and my soul drinks that up. Even when she tries to lie, I can see right through her.

Fried frog legs were exactly what I needed, with the inheritance box and rezoning weight on each shoulder—I feel like I can actually breathe a little right now.

I called Apollo late last night and told him everything about Amelia breaking in and Neme chewing on the envelope. Amelia loosens me up so I can face this: my brothers and the inheritance box situation. The more I catch myself smiling about Amelia, a small drip of guilt pools up in the back corner of my mind—I am the villain in her story, and she's made my life irrevocably difficult.

Data will tell the truth, and she'll have to accept apartments instead of a library—data will be the bad guy, not me.

My phone buzzes before I reach the soda shop's door. Apollo wants to meet in person and update me about the passcode, so I pull my phone out before I step inside.

Mitchell Ricks-The Big Boss: *How'd the engineering assessment go?*

Next, a picture of the newspaper headline "Chernov partners with Noil Construction for future apartments: City postpones rezoning" comes through. The photo is a stunning rendition of apartments with a bold new roofline and extra beams.

It's beautiful.

Me: *Rescheduled for next week; I'll keep you posted.*

Mitchell Ricks-The Big Boss: *Thumbs up emoji.*

Mitchell Ricks-The Big Boss: *Good work. The article points out that you knew your stuff; you made Noil look good. What would I do without you?*

Me: *You should promote me.*

Mitchell Ricks hearts my message.

I open the door to Creamy Meets Crusty, a small mom-and-pop soda and pastry shop. I see two teens huddled in the back corner with my brother—a girl spinning on the orange chair, and a boy on his phone. Apollo hops up to greet me.

I tighten my jaw. This place is crawling with tweens and teens that are loud and smelly.

"Thanks for meeting us somewhere public," Apollo says.

I grunt.

The neon lights are draped from wall to wall, making anything white, including teeth, stick out. I can't hear what type of music plays from the speakers; too much lunchroom chatter.

I catch a wrapper in midair and toss it right back to the boys laughing in the corner. They stop laughing as it hits the boy right in the face.

Apollo leads me to the back corner by his two friends—BO smell isn't as strong in the corner. The girl looks too cute for a small town, and the boy has a flat face with tall hair. They both stand up when I get to their table—I tower over them and watch their pupils dilate. I don't do a thing to settle their nerves.

"I-I've studied your state game, and I must say—" the boy fiddles with his hands— "you are a legend, and I-I finally get to meet you."

I clench my jaw and shake their hands, not easing up on my grip.

"My fumble?" I ask.

I see the boy's Adam's apple move; he nods like a timid dog.

Apollo rolls his eyes. "These are the best two people I know; go easy on them."

My lips curve down. "Are you so sure about that? I checked their credit scores." My head shakes in disapproval. The girl's eyes widen, and the boy seems to sink more into his seat.

"Stop," Apollo says. "I know you don't want to be here, but they don't deserve your cold side." The boy seems to shake it off, but the girl studies me like I am a crime.

"Fine, I'll stop being a jerk."

"Speaking of money...I'm helping you because I'm a good person. You should think of a way to compensate them both. They are exceptional...investigators." The boy is chewing at a piece of dead skin on his hand, and the girl doesn't break eye contact as she sips her soda.

"I'll be the judge of that." I try to breathe and take it down a notch. I can't help it—I can't get Amelia's face out of my mind, and it makes me irritable that she holds some of my brain space.

Apollo pulls the letter out of an envelope and out of a clear plastic covering. "I thought about what you recently shared, and you might be onto something." He scratches his head.

I'd mentioned how the hole was too clean of a cut. It seemed too slick of a view to Atticus's face yesterday, the one over the passcode.

"The likelihood that a dog's tooth made this hole..." He holds the letter up in the dim neon light. "I don't know what to think."

The girl cuts in. "AP says that the seal was unbroken, correct?"

My eyebrows go up. "You going by AP now?"

He blushes. "Just by some close friends." He clears his throat. "Let me start with what we discovered today." Apollo reports that the bank won't accept more than three passcodes a day. "Sort of like if you forgot your online banking password before they locked you out and made you call to unlock it, only three tries. Or they make you wait 24 hours for security purposes."

I nod. That makes sense.

"We've analyzed the paper all day. Our best guess is six or seven letters long." He takes the letter and carefully puts it back away in his backpack.

"I think we should start with the six letters; then we will move up." I do like his logic. "I don't mean to seem sus, but..." He leans in close. "If the dog didn't punch out the hole, then who did? I don't think we should tell many others about this." He sits back down, and his friend sips a soda like an eight-year-old, loud, full of air bubbles.

My stone face glares at him—he stops drinking.

"You think a brother could have done this?" the boy asks.

Could others know about Dad's plan from a year ago? An enemy would be more like it; Dad had many.

"All I'm saying is that if Dad created clues, got all of these 'projects' to lay dormant for who knows how long, legal documents, and a passcode of some kind to retrieve the 'inheritance box' from who knows where for each son, who's to say he didn't have help?"

He takes a silent drink and taps his fingertips on the table. I look at his friend as if to say, *That's how normal people drink.*

Apollo puts his drink down. "Okay, let's be real." His eyes get so intense when he is puzzling things together. "There is no way Dad could have done this on his own. He had accomplices." He shakes his head. "But if there are people who know about assets that we don't know about...it's sort of a big motive to keep us out."

I nod and look at his friends. "You trust them?"

My stone-cold eyes bore through them. The girl hugs her stomach and taps her foot and the boy coughs.

Apollo looks at them. "Cams and Dev? I trust them with my life."

"Fine, get digging. I have to stay focused."

"On the librarian?"

I wipe the boyish smile off Dev with one glance. I re-adjust my blazer. "It's work-related, so yes."

"For what it's worth, sir," the girl's voice is soft and smooth, "Amelia is among the best people I know. I think you should get to know her. She could be a useful ally."

I do a *you have no idea what's going on* nod and look at Apollo.

"We've created a spreadsheet with all the possible options according to several online dictionaries."

"How long could it take?"

He wipes his face like I do when I am stressed. "Almost three and a half months."

I nod.

"That is if you go to the bank every business day. Every day you miss bumps it back a day."

"You'll have fun going to the bank for me," I say.

Apollo holds up his hand. "You must show your driver's license each time you go in. They might even scan your face; I don't know. They made it clear that no one except you could have access to the box."

I press my lips together and close my eyes.

"Okay, thank you for your help...can you send me the passcodes?"

He whips out his phone. "Already shared it digitally with you. Just check off the ones you use."

"Oh, one more thing," His girlfriend says while looking at Apollo.

He rubs the back of his neck. "Lucas, we need you to get Amelia's dog to bite a piece of paper."

I shake my head. "Not going to happen."

"Fine, then get her to our mansion with her dog. We'll do the rest."

"Fine," I say. "Thank you for your help, Apollo." I fish some cash from my wallet and toss it on the table. "Drinks on me."

Dev picks up a bill. "Bruhh, right on. It's two hundred dollar bills!"

I walk through the wall of BO and out into the cool air. Fall is coming—and so are apartments.

I try to convince my mood that managing rezoning, Amelia, and the passcode is doable.

Chapter Nine

Amelia

I am excited for work today. Grandpoppy is still sleeping, and I habitually check if the blankets are moving up and down before I leave.

Neme follows on my heel. "Stay here, boy. It's not your day to come."

I really don't know how he'd take the bats. I have been looking forward to this day all summer—bat day at the library has finally come. I started planning this event six months earlier; I secured a day with the Bat Association Ties (BAT) of Virginia. They are a nonprofit that helps protect endangered bats. I sent flyers to every school in the district when school started and had every local church announce the event at their children's and youth services. Hopefully, that will blow our average of five people in attendance out of the water. In a way, it would be perfect if it could get a lot of people in the door for my plot chart to show the library board.

I waited for Lucas to show up all day yesterday. He never did. My data and I don't need him—I can collect data on my clipboard just fine without him.

Brenton Hill is representing the B.A.T., and I have to let him in early. I pull in and search my work bag for my keys as I walk to the front and give Bart and Gert a kiss. I need all the help I can get with Lucas on the prowl. My pace is fast as I rush to the door, fumbling through my bag—and of course, I have to run square into the chest of a man waiting outside the front door.

A hard chest—fresh soap with a hint of mint today.

"Lucas?" I ask. "What do you want?" Butterflies start to form in my stomach, and I have a hard time looking at his brown eyes. Our frog leg dinner hasn't left my mind, and the cold truth that the enemy had already breached the lines before business hours unnerves me.

"Do you need to get inside the building...for your library card?" The morning fog still hangs close to the ground, covering everything.

"Ah...ya," he says. "I wasn't sure when you got in."

"I'm usually here at nine but came early today." He watches me unlock the door, and I click my tongue. "Don't tell me you want to check out a book about...frogs?"

He shakes his head. His face looks tighter today, more calculated. "I came to collect data," he says.

My lips open a little. "Data...you mean help me set up a survey? I'm pretty sure we both have some strong bias. My clipboard survey covers the basics."

His face lets a smile peek through. "That's why I came. The library board told me there are no extra funds for data gathering or surveys. Neither of the companies I represent feel great about...funding research that could potentially stop their plan for this land."

I smile. So there *are* some uncertainties. "The only way to collect data is for you to..."

I wasn't born yesterday. "You didn't want me collecting the data." I put the keys back inside my bag, "Afraid I'll skew things?"

He nods. I pretend to look offended—I sort of am.

"Well, in that case, the library is closed today." I blink.

"Excuse me?"

My clipboard system is perfect. Plus, I need to focus on the bats and the kids today, not this battle.

He walks over and points to the door. "Bats in the Air, Friday THIS WEEK at 10 a.m." He points to the flier on the door. "That's today."

I pull it off, slip into the door, and lock it behind me.

"Amelia, this is violating a written rule!" he says through the glass.

I lift my hand and squint. *I can't hear you*, I mouth.

"Amelia, this isn't going to help your cause. I am your best bet here."

I nod and place my hands on my head, pulling my hands out. I mouth, *Big head*,' and point at him.

"Ha, ha. Very funny. You need me, Amelia. Let me in; it will work better if we have a plan."

I smile slightly and shake my head. He really has no idea how much I love this library and how I will chain myself to the front door before I let anything happen to it. I hope it doesn't come to that, but a librarian will do what a librarian has to do.

Mom would agree.

I shrug and wave goodbye as I walk through the second set of doors.

It feels so good to hear him bang on the door—I hum to his hitting on the glass. I even dance a little to his beat. If he can't get in, I will stay one step ahead. Every bang he makes is a reminder of my first win of the day.

I turn on all the lights and set up the chairs. The pounding stops after fifteen minutes. I am impressed; he is diligent.

I print off more bat coloring pages and fact sheets in case it is a smashing hit. I adjust all the bat books on display and smile at how awesome I am. Seriously, a BAT demonstration in the early fall is such a good idea. Some of the bat cutouts I have hung up fall off the wall as I circle each room, taking shards of paint with them. "Shoot!" I can see the baby blue paint underneath the dusty white color. I print off bigger bat cutouts and use duct tape to hang over the peeling paint.

Perfect.

I hear voices talking outside. The high-pitched voice of my boss, director of the library, Mr. Marcus Mettle, zips up my spine.

"Dewey, Dewey, Dewey!" I say, running to the door. I scrunch my nose—I have to work on not using the Dewey decimal system as a curse word.

He pulls back the door. "Amelia May Anderson!" He says it like I am a child. His high-pitched voice matches his high-rise pants—I am confident they pass his belly button every day. His glossy bald head beams shame right to my toes. "This is *no* way to treat patrons!" He stomps his foot, and I jump.

I glare at Lucas, "It-it's not opening time."

He stomps again and looks up at me—his denture breath is metallic and eggy. "*You*, young lady—" a little of his spit lands on me— "made our guest speaker wait out here. I'm so glad Mr. Chernov was here to keep him company." He shakes his head like he doesn't know how to discipline his naughty cat. "He was so kind to call me and tell me what *you* were neglecting to do!" His eye twitches, and my stomach drops.

I look to Brenton, realizing Lucas knocked on the window to let someone else in.

"Oh, sir, I'm so, so sorry." I can't stop my red face from pulsing. "I should have been paying more attention."

Lucas smiles like a schoolboy who just won the top of the hill—I shoot my laser eyes at him. He winks.

"Come, come in!" I ignore the fluttering my skin feels when he gives me attention like that.

Brenton bends down and picks up the clear Tupperware tote with two small bags inside. Laminated signs are taped on all sides of the tote: "LIVE ANIMALS," "DO NOT TURN OVER," "BEWARE, LIVE BATS," and "RABIES HAZARD."

Brenton bristles. "At least some people in this town respect other people's time," he says, hunching his shoulders more. "I'm glad it wasn't too hot or cold out for Char Char or Benzie." He is tall and thin, with a pasty white face. I had wondered if he only goes outside during the night, like the bats, when I first met him months ago, visiting their building a few towns over.

He carries the box through both doors and follows Mr. Mettle into the building.

I feel my hair stand up as Lucas Chernov walks toward me and stops. He is the width of an epic fantasy book away.

"You need me," he says in a quiet voice, trying to hide his gleeful tone. He watched me every minute of my boss's public scorn. His dark complexion is softer and more addicting today—I can't look away.

I cross my arms. A slight breeze must have picked up and pushed us closer together. I don't breathe through my nose, no more smelling him today.

He chuckles a little. "Simmer down, Milly, your face is the shade of a ripe raspberry."

I lift my hands to my cheeks, and my jaw pops open.

He bores his gaze deeper. "We will go farther if we work together," he says. This is part of his tactic, tricking me into working together.

"The board wants us to work together. I think letting the data make the decision will be the most helpful."

"Maybe—maybe not." My chin is held high, and I keep my hands on my cheeks, hiding my actual color. I won't let him see what he is doing to me.

He pauses. A piece of my hair flies up to his face. He pushes it down, smoothing out my hair. He brings a little of my hair between two of his fingers and lightly rolls his fingers over the strands. Our eyes connect for three heartbeats, and then I turn and leap away. Another second, and I would have drunk him in and agreed to anything he asked.

"Fine," I say over my shoulder.

Chapter Ten

Amelia

I round the library several times, making sure the vanilla scent is on, bats are still hanging up, and Brenton is settling in okay, but really—I'm avoiding Lucas. Mr. Mettle helps him with a card, and he checks out a book. I am not allowed to pry and see what book he is reading, at least without him knowing about it.

Mr. Mettle stays with Mr. Benton, and I watch the rest of the library. I tap my fingers on the desk—patrons will come. I stare at the clock. Patrons have thirty more minutes; *have faith, Amelia.*

I walk toward the corner Lucas has staked out and straighten some books. I bend down and find an angle where he can't see my eyes. I bet he's reading another middle-grade book—I smirk. I don't judge what book anyone checks out except for Lucas Chernov. I can feel humiliation from my earlier scorn morph into agitation, and my nettle leaves start to perk up. I'd give him the horror novel, *Hauntings of the Librarian Who Didn't Get Her Way*, not like that is an actual book, but I'd read it, write a personal note in it, and give it to Lucas. I don't like him in the library at all. He doesn't belong here.

Bat day, I tell myself. *It is going to be perfect.* He pulls out an iPad and makes some notes. Good, he doesn't dog-ear the book—maybe he isn't a lost cause after all.

The door opens, and I see an older gentleman walk in. His zen music gives him away every time.

"If it isn't Joe Gunner. I've missed you." I smile wide. He is a library board member who stops by to say hi.

"Your hat has some new feathers," I point to a few smaller ones I don't recognize.

"You noticed, Milly? I found those on the trail last night."

"What were you doing on the trail last night?" I ask as he smiles wide. I can see his gold tooth twinkle back at me. I cross my arms and tap my foot. "Don't tell me you were cannonball hunting?"

He doesn't even flinch. "Pumpkin Spice, come now. I thought we agreed to disagree."

I grimace. There is a slim chance Lucas didn't hear what Joe just called me. I peek at him. I can't tell if he can hear us; my gaze pulls back to Joe.

He loves the legends and lore of our small town. He believes General Lee shot a cannonball into the river over 150 years ago. General Lee had been the president of a nearby university before his death.

I shake my head. "Not if it means you're out late all alone looking for a cannonball in the Marrow River by yourself."

He holds up his hand. "I brought Mev."

I roll my eyes. That makes it worse. Mev isn't any younger than he is, and he's lost most of his sense of danger. "Promise me you'll only look for your treasures in the daytime?"

He keeps on a soft smile. The low tones of his music summon smiles everywhere he goes.

"Tell you what, I think the other two myths you always tell me about, the gold mine and the lost jail cell, are much more promising leads." He twists his head, and even his feathers perk up.

"We can find references to both in our history section." Now I have a stupid wide smile on my face.

"I know you think all treasures come from the library, but I think no one wrote about these to keep them safe. I've never had any luck searching."

I pat his back. "I know just what to do."

I show him the history section and pull one of our nicer leather chairs in front of the bookshelf. "There. You don't even have to move." Next, I push over the return cart. "When you're done looking, place the book here, and I'll take care of it for you."

"I'm glad you're not married." His eyes look through the books.

"Why's that?" I ask.

"So you can save me a dance at the retreat." His feathers hold still, and I see his broad smile again.

I smile and push my hair behind my ear. I catch Lucas's eye as I walk back to the circulation desk. He needs to leave—librarians are the only ones allowed to eavesdrop.

I stare at the clock again and make sure all the coloring pencils inside the boxes are in rainbow order.

Ten minutes later, he enunciates my name, "Amelia."

I look at him like I am bored. He is wearing black today, and it brings out unshaven facial hair—I wonder if his chin is rough and prickly. It would match him.

"This iPad is for data collecting. Can we place it on that shelf?" He points to a display shelf right by the main entrance and exit sign.

I pull the iPad from him like a teacher confiscating a game console.

I tap the screen, and it flashes questions like, *What do I use the library for?, What things does the library offer that I use most?, What needs do I have that the library could meet but doesn't?,* and *What's your opinion on the library's current location?* with twelve options for me to tap or a spot where I can fill in answers. I keep tapping, and it asks about my current housing needs, a few demographic check marks to push, and then it pops up a book. *One free book will be donated to your library for your input today. Thank you!*

One minute and twelve seconds of survey time—I am impressed and force myself to look annoyed.

"Who's donating the books?" I ask.

He doesn't smile. "An anonymous donor. I think it's a good idea."

His hand brushes my bare arm as he reaches for the iPad. It blossoms up my torso.

I can't haunt him if he touches me. It distracts me. I take a step toward the display by the door.

"Do you think this will work?" he asks.

I nod, my voice not working.

"Can you make a flier about the survey?" He points around to the walls and shelves.

I nod my head again.

"Fewer fliers," he whispers, "will go a long way." He turns and goes back to his chair.

Ten minutes later, I have them printed and am taking down some of my 'Get a library Card' flyers for 'Take our Survey and enter to WIN.' I highlight a book being donated for every survey completed.

Lucas stands up and nods at the flier. I'll use the raffle at Halloween for both initiatives—I smile at my own genius.

"I like it. Was the clip art necessary?" He frowns at the cute clipart lion reading books.

It is the cutest thing I have ever seen, and I cross my arms and bristle until I hear both doors pop open, and a small Batman runs up to me.

"Mikey!" I put the extra fliers on a shelf. "You made it!"

"Miss Milly! Of course, I did."

Mikey Edgewood is the smartest second grader I know. Today, his lips and tongue are stained red—I can imagine he enjoyed his red slurpy too much.

"You know me." His eyes go wide. "I won't miss this for the entire earth." He lifts his arms, showing off his wings.

I bend down. "Mikey, your outfit...is batastic!"

He giggles and covers his mouth.

I giggle a little, too, and catch Lucas staring at me with a soft smile.

My stomach tightens, and I hope I'm not drooling. I look back at Mikey. "Is your grandma coming today?" He nods and points to Sandy, who is already searching in the western section.

"She's over there..." He waves me down to his mouth. "What happens if I scare the bats away?"

My heart melts a little. I kneel, "Mikey, I'm sure the bats are nervous about today," I wink at him, "but I think your costume will help them feel less nervous."

He smiles big. His two buck teeth started coming in two years ago, and they look bigger than his eyes. I can't believe how much he has grown since he started attending craft time.

"Oh, I almost forgot!" He pulls my arm. "I have something for you."

He reaches into a small black pocket in his costume and pulls out a paper.

"What's this?" I ask.

Lucas moves behind me and looks over my shoulder.

"A plan, Miss Milly. You told me about that handsome henchman who is trying to crush the library." He lifts his wings up and down again. "I wanted to help you."

Red face—check. Red neck—check. Are the whites of my eyes turning red? I am sure that is a check, too.

I finger the paper and stand up. Lucas is breathing down my neck and is towering over me like a wrecking ball. I know he is reading the paper. I can't hide sweet Mikey from him now.

I hold my breath and read the note:

TO MISS MILLY – my favorite librarian

Step one: don't let him see how much it's falling apart. He drew the separating carpet and foundation.

Step two: beg. He drew Neme drooling over a dog bone.

Step three: wear lipstick and make him love you. He kissed the paper with red paint. Aw, it wasn't a slurpy. I bet Sandy, his grandmother, had to scrub his face for an hour.

Step four: compromise. He put a band-aid on the paper.

Step five: cry...a lot. He drew a face with tears.

Step six: make a new plan and try again. He drew hands shaking.

"Mikey..." I say, "you are the best library patron any library has ever seen." He wraps his arms around me. My eyes are big, and I can't hide my red anymore.

"I-I..."

He pulls the list out of my hands and snaps a picture. I snap it back.

He studies my face.

"Handsome henchman?"

I want the Mariana Trench to open and swallow me whole. I can live off the nectar of stories for the rest of my life and never face Lucas Chernov again.

He laughs. "Wear lipstick?"

"Kids these days." I let out a nervous laugh. "They say the cutest things. I don't believe most of what they say."

"Miss Milly!?" Sandy calls for me.

I am by her side in a blink and peek back through my peeping spot. I can see Mikey talking to Lucas. "Oh, Frankenstein," I say through my clenched teeth.

Mikey is ratting me out, and there is nothing I can do about it.

"I wanted to congratulate you and Mr. Chernov," she winks at me, "for being the newest board members. Young, fresh blood is just what we need." I walk her western large print book to the computer and check it out for her.

"Don't look at me that way," I say.

"I know you have eyes, Amelia; you were peeking at him again."

I use the book to wave in front of my face to help simmer down my blush.

Sandy continues, "The retreat is in a couple of weeks. You better make sure you get work off."

I nod. "Can you get me the exact details about the retreat so I can be prepared?"

She taps her nose and nods.

"No meddling, Sandy."

She attempts to look innocent. "Me? I would never meddle?"

"How many examples do you need, Sandy?"

Her eyes get big. "Amelia May Anderson," she lifts her hand to her heart, "cross my heart, I won't."

"You won't what?"

"I won't—" A friend of Sandy's walks into the door. She smiles as if she queued for the interruption herself. She pushes her walker toward the new group of people walking in. I shake my head at her. She shrugs her shoulders like an innocent church girl would.

She doesn't understand I am small potatoes—just a librarian, with her books, her dog, and Grandpoppy. Lucas can choose any girl on the continent, and all of Russia, for that matter. He is so far out of my league; I know that now. I will stick to my corner of Herasburg and protect it.

My head is still shaking at her as I walk back to the corner where Lucas and Mikey are. He has somehow climbed onto Lucas's lap and is looking at photos on his phone with him.

"See!? That's what an earth dragon looks like. I can't believe it! Miss Milly!" he says, pulling Lucas's phone out of his hand and pointing it toward me. "His Chinese zodiac is an earth dragon!"

I nod my head as I hear the library door open more. Several other families walk in, some of whom I have never seen in the library before, and I lead them toward the children's room, where Mr. Mettle and Brenton set up a camera and a portable screen. I try to wave Mikey in, but he is demonstrating something with his wings to Lucas. Several other families come, and I make sure Brenton has a drink of water. There are no extra chairs. I see Lucas holding Mikey's hand and walking him into the presentation, and my heart is not allowed to squeeze at the sight of a small hand wrapped up in his ginormous man's hands. Mikey pats the seat next to him on the ground in the front kids' section, and Lucas sits down.

He fills up two colored dot spots, and I pull my lips in to hide a smile. Lucas won't ask more about Mikey's note if he knows what is good for him.

I hug my middle—my sigh is soft. I love my job. Mikey deserves a library medal, and I know it is entirely my fault. I shouldn't have opened up to a second grader. Maybe I do need more adult friends to talk to?

Mr. Mettle motions for me to dim the lights and get the children settled in. "Excuse me, children." He motions for me to come up to the front. His face twists, and his excessive blinks make his words choppy. "Miss Amelia will introduce our very special guest today."

I walk up to the front. He walks out and into his office and closes the door, noise always triggers him.

"Welcome!" I say with a big smile. I can feel Lucas's eyes on me. "Don't forget to check out our books about bats on the way out. And!" I point to Lucas. "Please stop by the iPad on your way out and complete a survey for the library. Your input is invaluable, and for every survey completed, the library will receive a free book."

The kids cheer.

He nods.

I extend my showcase arm and give an elaborate introduction for Mr. Brenton. The families cheer, and I settle in the back, eyeing Lucas. He seems squirmy. The presentation is going better than I would have expected.

"Repeat after me, Crepuscular."

"Cruppussccullarr," the audience sings back.

"Bats are crepuscular animals, which means they hunt in twilight. They use echolocation to find their food," Brenton says. He continues, and the room goes silent when he pulls out a bat and holds it up to the camera. It projects on the big screen. "Now, don't go thinking you can get a pet bat. I must always carry around my permits. I've had my extra shots to keep myself safe." I can see Lucas cross his arms and squirm more.

"Char Char is a Red Bat," he says. "He is very skittish." He bends down, pulls the bat out, and handles him with a gloved hand. Lucas hops up and walks to the back of the room, next to me.

He is sweating.

"Lucas Chernov," I lean into him, letting our arms and shoulders touch, "are you afraid of bats?"

He doesn't meet my eyes, and I let out a small laugh—Brenton scowls at me.

"It's a long story," he whispers.

I cover my mouth. He leans into my shoulder, and my skin hums.

"Be quiet, librarian," his lips graze my ear, and his breath tingles down my neck.

My ears burn.

Brenton pulls out the next bat, Benzie. "This fellow is a Big Brown Bat." He continues to talk about white-nose syndrome, light pollution, and how we can help bats repopulate.

The only thing that really sticks is how close Lucas is to me.

The lights go back on, and all the children go to the craft tables I've set up out by the circulation desk.

"Brenton, can I do anything else to help you?" I ask, finally moving away from Lucas.

"Oh yes," he says. "Benzie is wiggly right now. Can you help hold the flap open? I don't want to drop him."

"I actually have to help out the other children, but Mr. Chernov, the kind and helpful gentleman who helped you get into the building," I wink at Lucas, "will gladly help."

I leap to the door; I have to help check out any of the library books and make sure Joe is still comfortable by the history shelf.

I can see Lucas's mouth drop open as he shakes his head at me. I bite my lip and swear I see a vein in his neck pop out like topography on the town map.

If I am not mistaken, Lucas Chernov is flustered, and I like it very much.

Chapter Eleven

Lucas

I wake up too early, my mind restless. I try to drown out the noise by lifting weights, each rep burning in a satisfying way. "Re___e" words echo through my dreams. And Amelia. The way she smiles when she leaves me alone with Mr. Brenton is worth an award. And Mikey's letter? I rub my face, feeling unfamiliar strings pull at my cold heart. Her hair, smelling of vanilla and mildewy paper, lingers in my thoughts. She made me stand inches from a bat yesterday. She's the most aggravating woman on this side of the Appalachian Trail, with the most striking green eyes to match.

I plan to go to the library every day to check in on the data until the retreat. A small voice in my head is telling me: *It's her rage wrapped up in her smile again that's unpredictable, not the data.*

My max weight rips micro muscles through my shoulders and chest as I push hard on my final bench reps. I reason I'm not the bad guy here. It's unfortunate—maybe I can find a way to help her cope with the loss. Olympus always helped a younger version of me; is she too old to enjoy Olympus?

I dab my face with a towel and step outside for some cardio to clear my mind.

My inheritance box and passcode fog my brain, and Amelia is a beacon of light in the distance. "Maybe the inheritance box will turn out to be a good thing," Andrei had said. My chest relaxes as I walk to the edge of our driveway. The crisp air clouds up my breath, and the leaves change into vibrant colors, reminding me of Amelia's hair.

I've been to the bank and checked off the spreadsheet's first three words this week: rebate, rebase, and reshoe. It's not like I think those are the actual passcodes, but I want it over sooner rather than later. I pull out my phone.

Me: *Are the passcodes in a specific order?*

Maybe Apollo has a strategy I don't know about.

I shove in my EarPods, and sweat slowly peels back the real problem. I'll be stuck here for months because of Dad. I'm not sure how much longer I can deflect her smile—it's so wide.

My mind volleys back to Andrei; he uses his words like a bucket of oats. Shaking the temptation of being second in command at Noil Construction. He knows how hard I've worked, and the last thing I need is to have my brothers pull out and move the location of the apartments—I was certain if they did, Noil would not get the bid to build the apartments.

Pumpkin? Is that what the townies call her? It fits.

Sweat forms and falls into the crevices of my feelings. Rezoning shouldn't be this hard.

Baba is right—I'm cursed, not with not finding a girlfriend but with fulfilling my job. Kim's face flashes in my mind. I'm sure I'll summon her to town if I don't get the rezoning data soon. Mitchell is too nervous not to have his spy, his daughter, and my ex-fiancé on the ground with real-time feedback.

Mitchell will send in his reinforcements, and I want Kim to stay far away from Amelia.

Maybe I'm cursed at both.

Why do I keep thinking about the woman who has made my life so difficult?

My track skips to my rage music section as I make it to the flood wall along the Marrow River, and the woman running up the second entrance with her large dog doesn't notice me.

I mute my rage music and slow my jog to match her pace. She finally sees me and jumps back.

"Hades, Lucas!" she says, touching her EarPods. Her leash has steadied her fall. "You're in my morning...again," her tone sounds like it's her required spinach dosage for the day.

"This is only the second morning," I point out. "But I'll easily change that." Maybe she likes spinach.

"Unbelievable. Your arrogance is fired up at the crack of dawn. A true sign of a Chernov."

My face straightens. "After my family tree now?" I tap my EarPods back on and try to speed up.

She taps them back off, her finger skimming my wet ear. "I'm just saying that you appear right as I push you out of my—" she stops herself.

My arrogant lips twist sideways. "You were thinking about me, Pumpkin? Is it my charm or my smile that's on your mind?"

She tries to push me off the trail; it feels like a koala's love tap.

"Neither." She sounds equally annoyed and a little guilty.

"I bet you were thinking, how did my thoughts magically make him appear?"

"No, I wasn't." A small smile touches her lips.

I take her in—she smiles, genuinely enjoying my sentiment; her shirt is green, her pants are blue, Neme's leash is wrapped with multi-colored duct tape, and her hair is pulled back tight. "My mind has reserved a permanent spot for you, labeled—don't touch my books."

Nothing about her matches, and it staples her to my brain.

"How far do you run?" I ask.

"Neme likes three miles. On weekends, I get in five sometimes." He seems to know the trail.

"How about you?" Amelia asks.

"I usually jog for an hour most days." I see her eyes run up my workout suit. "I lift, too."

Her eyes jolt away to the gravel trail in front of us.

I laugh a little. "It's okay if you think I'm ripped, Amelia."

She shakes her head. "That's not the most arrogant thing you could say right now."

I chuckle. We fall into a natural pace together; it's too easy. She's taller than most women I've dated, and her legs can keep up with my stride.

"Do you already have plans to throw me out Monday when I come to the library?"

She suppresses a smile.

I won't tell her the engineer will meet me there next week to get a formal examination of the building's structure.

"Well, if I did, telling you would ruin them, wouldn't it?" Her puff cloud of breath wheezes a little, and my stride pulls back, but she powers through—Neme now falling behind her.

My legs pound down faster.

"You want a race, do you?" I speed past her, looking back to smile, but she's on my heel. But for how long? I push until my lungs feel like they're going to burst, and she seems to have been waiting for me to get tired.

My pace slows back, and she sails past me.

I bend down to catch my breath and put my hands on my head. She starts to slow down and walks back to where I'm dying.

A drop of sweat drips from her nose.

I hold up my hand. "You run fast."

She nods, "Can I beat you though?" The twinkle in her eye gives away her double meaning.

No, Amelia Anderson, you can't. I'm touched that she tries so hard.

The end of the trail is in sight, and we walk to the large barrier that stops the trail.

A large bench faces the river, and I sit on one end—she sits on the other. I feel the pull to her side and give in, moving to sit close enough to feel her warmth, legs touching.

"You run here often?" The sun is now peeking over the Blue Ridge Mountain range, and a few rays dance through her ponytail.

She nods. "Years…" She looks around, taking in the morning. "It never gets old."

She drops Neme's leash, and he walks over to me and drops his slobbery mug over my legs. Tiny bubbles and slick slime pour onto my jogging pants.

I shudder. Amelia's laugh is contagious, and I stand up and whip the dog juice off, but it spreads like sticky liquid glue. She laughs more; all I can do is wipe my hands off in the grass and keep Neme away from me.

She reaches into her fanny pack clipped around her waist and gives me a large cloth.

"Thanks." I wipe my hands off.

"He likes you," she says, petting him.

"I guess he has a sixth sense," I say, sitting back down. She sits next to me this time, and I brush my legs against hers again.

"I think he really does." She doesn't pull away.

We watch him make his way down to the river while I wipe the sweat off my brow. I'm tempted to grab her hand and watch her cheeks turn mercury red. I have sweat and dog slime on my hands now; she'd recoil.

Her soft smile flees, and she scowls out of nowhere.

"You're thinking about the library again?" I ask.

She nods and furrows her eyes at me. I want to laugh at the visible trigger it is for us and point it out, but I also want to walk home in one piece. "Amelia, who do you think owns the building?"

She tips her head back. "It's the library board. Or the greater regional library. But it's in the same system."

I shake my head. "Amelia." I pause—she really has no idea, does she? "Chernov and Sons own the building and land. We've been letting the library live rent-free for years."

A small dimple forms on her cheek as she presses her lips together. If this is what humble pie looks like on her, I want a bite.

She fiddles with her ponytail slowly. "I had no idea...Wow."

"The deed, the document you tried to destroy?" I say, watching her wide eyes start to get a little wet. "That was proof that the Chernov trust owned the land and the building." She watches Neme take a drink. "You must have missed that part of my presentation at the public hearing."

She lets out a belly sigh. "I wasn't entirely having my best day. I could have missed that."

A soft smile pushes up my temples as I revel in her newfound meekness.

Her eyes follow Neme, and I look up as he lunges into the river.

"Neme, No! Come back, boy!" she yells. The dog takes several paddles out, then turns back around and swims back to the stony beach. I can hear the dripping of the river water across all the rocks as he jogs back up to us. She hops up and grabs the slick, muddy leash.

The pull I've felt toward her since my hand was trapped in her hair is noticeably growing; I wonder if she feels it, too.

"He listens well," I say.

She looks down at him with kind eyes. "When he wants to. But I guess I'm kind of the same way."

Neme turns his head and does a small bark through the trees; I can see feathers bobbing up and down through the bright foliage. Two men emerge holding metal detectors. Neme barks again, louder this time.

"We come in peace," the man with a feathered hat yells across the meadow.

I hear faint zen music approach, the same music I heard yesterday in the library. But the sound spooks Neme. He runs forward and around my legs, then around Amelia, clamping us together. He does it again for good measure, putting us in his protective fence.

Our knees and hips seal together. My sweaty clothes wiping into hers. Amelia's wrist is trapped between our chests as he pulls tighter.

"Neme!" she says as we wobble to stay balanced. "I'm, I'm—"

I place my finger over her mouth—she grows still. I want a sliver of a moment to see her as a woman, not as my competition.

The morning rays light up her eyes. I tug a piece of her hair and rub it with my fingers, and I wonder for the briefest of moments if she would let me kiss her.

"Lucas Chernov," she whispers.

"Hmm?" I hear the zen sounds get louder. Her lips are full, her cheeks warm, and her skin glistens with sweat—warmth flows through me.

She doesn't break eye contact as she whispers, "You're stepping on my toe."

I blink.

My shoulders and hip wiggle back, trying to force some slack, and the leash tightens around her trapped wrist; at least I can move my foot off hers.

"No need to stop on our account!" The men appear on top of the trail.

I cough and run my hand through my hair.

The man in the baseball hat says, "We ain't born yesterday!" He winks at me.

I don't know what to say.

"Joe," Amelia says. "What on earth are you doing with those metal detectors?" I see two speakers clipped to his leather belt. Joe has a hat on with long feathers sticking out.

"Cannonball hunting, Pumpkin Spice!"

She laughs. "Here?"

"Where else, Pumpkin Spice?" Joe says. The man in the baseball hat pulls out a map, and Amelia's cheeks blush.

"You forced me to read those books yesterday, so it's all your fault—I got a new idea." The man she called Joe says.

She covers her mouth, her eyes twinkling.

"I was looking in the wrong spot all along. Your books helped me." He nods. "We'll strike it rich if we can find General Lee's lost cannon."

I don't even want to know.

Neme weighs over 100 pounds, and hc lays down at her feet. I try again to pull at the leash to loosen it. He moves enough for me to step out of the leash trap—but I decide I like Neme now—touching Amelia makes my sweaty skin hum, and I swallow.

Amelia faces both the men and talks with her hands. "Did you learn anything about the jailhouse or the gold mine?"

He frowns.

"It did mention it, but I got so excited about trying out the new spot I didn't pay attention. I'll have to go back in when I'm ready to read more of your books."

She beams, and I can't help but smile. I wish it weren't connected to the library—her happiness.

He slaps my shoulder. "Can't wait to get to know you better, son. You're coming to the retreat with us; we're on the library board."

The men pull out a map and show Amelia where they have looked for the lost cannon. Neme is lying down again by Amelia's feet, covering his ears.

"Think you can turn down your music?" I ask.

"Nope! It's our good luck charm. Getting the universe on our side. We're hopin' the fish hear it and lead us to the cannon."

I mouth, *Wow*, to Amelia, and she smiles and nods like this is a typical flavor of tea she sips every day.

The men walk farther downstream, and we jog back, talking about the river, Neme, all the flavors of people living in Herasburg, and our running routes. Our bodies' connection still warms my skin more than any jog could, and her easy smile cools my face.

I forget entirely about Dad for three miles. She ducks off, and I jog the rest of the way home.

Next week is just around the corner. Getting kicked out of the library is a new highlight I'm looking forward to. And the retreat.

I'll let the data be the one to break her heart, not me.

Chapter Twelve

Amelia

Step one: don't let him see how much it's falling apart

I tell myself that the storm clouds are dark—that's why no one came to craft time today. I haven't seen Lucas since our weekend run.

I look at my hair, replaying when he touched it. Instead of nervously pacing the rows of books because no one is coming to the library, I sit down and make the craft all by myself—not sulking.

I color in the words "I HEART THE LIBRARY" with markers and add yarn and popsicle sticks. If anyone comes, I'll bust out the buttons, too. Heck, even the forbidden glitter just to reward them.

Neme leans up from his sleeping cushion in the corner and moans.

"Don't look at me that way," I say as I sit on a child's chair, with an entirely empty library. "The storm clouds scared them away."

Mr. Mettle left for bingo two hours ago, which is fine with me. Sulking alone is my favorite—I slump my face into my hands. I can see the bank from the picture window, and I see Lucas walk up and walk out in a matter of minutes.

Is he dropping off a love note to one of the tellers?

I bristle—Katie Dale is not his type, so I put little baby bat stickers on the sign. Library plus bats? This sign is Lucas's worst nightmare.

Anger, skin tingles, comfort, irritation, gut-ripping laughs, and, let's be honest, a little swoony are all the things I've felt since he came into town. I clench my teeth—I am not falling for Lucas Chernov.

He needs to give up and leave town so I can use the retreat time to win over the board; I will do whatever it takes to push him out.

How can I swarm these signs around Lucas? And his brothers, for that matter? Maybe I can heart attack his lawn with bats and I-heart-my-library signs?

I imagine sticking hundreds of small popsicle signs into his mansion yard, and I'd run rows along his driveway—not only adorable, but I'm confident they would get the picture.

"Listen to the small signs in your life right now." I can have a ghostly voice recording on a loop. With that, I'll get his entire family's attention; I know Apollo and Dimitry would listen to me.

A stroke of insight washes over me, and I stand up, the chair falling over—*I'll offer to help pick out a different spot for the apartments*. Why hadn't I thought of that before?

I will even donate my blood—no, my plasma—to help fund some of the needed updates to the current library. Pushing over the library isn't an option.

Just then, I hear a loud muffler stop and turn off.

I walk to the door and see a short, stout man with a pencil behind a well-fitted tool belt walking along the side of the library. Lucas meets him halfway; he's carrying a ladder.

I run outside as they turn the corner. "Hey," I run after them, "Hey!"

Lucas turns and looks at me. I eye him up—looking that good in a plaid shirt is a sin.

The short man sticks out his hand.

Lucas plasters on a fake smile. "Milly, just who I needed to see," he says. "This is Steve."

I look at his hand. "I don't want to meet Steve."

He clucks his tongue. "Manners, Milly."

I cross my arms.

"Steve, this is Milly. She loves the library and doesn't like us." Lucas rests the ladder on the rooftop and the ground as a clank vibrates my soul.

I don't think the roof can hold both, as I shift my weight in a catty way—maybe that's the best thing for me, both men break an ankle falling through the roof.

"That adds up. Is this the lady you said would give us a h—"

"In the flesh," Lucas cuts in. "Now, Milly, I'm going to make this as simple as possible."

I hate his cuteness and how he tries so hard to undo me.

He takes several steps closer to me, and I step back. If he isn't so close to me, I can keep my resolve up and think logically. Well, at least my level of logic.

"This kind and benevolent man, Steve," he holds his hand back toward him, "is doing his job. Both of my companies are paying him to inspect the building. We need to start with the roof." He points up to the clouds. "We want to beat the storm, Milly." He readjusts the clipboard in his hands. "Milly," he taps a pencil, "let him do his work."

I watch Steve take a few steps up the ladder. "What if I don't?"

He walks toward me and bends down to my ear. "I told Steve the librarian had claws, but they're sanitary, mostly." he pulls back and winks at me.

My stomach does a back handspring.

"You are playing that role perfectly. Now, if you're extra good, I'll..." he taps his chin. "I'll bring you to the bookstore."

This is a trick.

Steve starts to climb up the ladder.

"Hey!" I yell out.

"Milly, we are doing an entire building inspection today." He presses his hands together like he's saying a prayer. "Maybe, just maybe, you could kindly cooperate and help point out all the repairs you know need to happen."

The man whose name I won't name has made it halfway up the ladder.

"Over my dead body."

He laughs and leans close to me again, "Would you like me to restrain you, Amelia?"

I swallow. Touching him will make me useless. "No," I say.

"Tone it down then, Mills." He flashes a deeper smile. "Or should I say Pumpkin Spice?"

I drop my jaw and push him away—my skin prickles.

"In all seriousness, this is a legal part of the process that is required. Who knows, maybe it could help your side of the argument." He shoots me a half-smile that probably makes gaggles of women swoon.

"No one needs to get hurt." He starts climbing, "Pumpkin. I like you alive, so much more alive. Who'd be the spice in my life?"

"Don't use my nicknames," I growl through clenched jaw and tightened fists.

He laughs and squints. "Oh, I wouldn't dare, Pumpkin."

I flare my nostrils so he can't see my heart squeeze a little.

The men disappear on top of the roof. It's a mansard roof with a flare of second empire angles, tight shingles near the outside, and a flat top. I know exactly where the seven major leaks are. That's why we closed off the top floor of the library. My kind heart will let them get a full day's work in. Finding every. Single. One.

I know the terrible truth in my heart, whispering, *there are too many repairs*. I brush the thought off my shoulder and walk back inside to see a patron plugged into her headphones. She's a mother working online, and I watch her son, Gregory, play.

"I love this!" He holds up a piece of paper he has colored all green. "The bats sort of look like pterodactyls."

"Yes, they do." I wave at his mom. She waves back and focuses again on her laptop. When he finishes, he slips over to the play corner and grabs the dinosaur tote, dumping everything in front of Neme.

"No chewing." He points at Neme's nose. He sets up the entire set of 45 dinosaurs and intermingles people and cars. I love watching him reenact Dinosaur Park in the middle of Herasburg. "Wait, Neme, it's not your part yet," Gregory says.

The men stomping on the roof echoes through the top two floors.

"Miss Milly, what's that noise?" He pushes his blonde hair out of his eyes.

"Oh, sweetie." His forehead is pressed together, and his eyes are glued to the ceiling. "Maybe raptors or some pterodactyls?" I make my eyes big and walk back to where he's playing. "They are looking for a new place to make a nest."

He covers his mouth and laughs. "Miss Milly! Dinosaurs are exskunked!" he says.

"You're right." I tousle his hair. "Will you help build a nest for..." I tap my chin, wincing like I'm in pain, grasping for a dinosaur name.

"An Oviraptor," he says.

"Oviraptor," I say. Gregory knows more about dinosaurs than most adults. We read dinosaur books together when his mommy is in her college Zoom classes or working through her tasks. It reminds me of the countless hours I played or read while Mom sat at the same desk completing her degree. He bends down and pulls more toy bins out, going back to creating a masterpiece.

After Gregory and his mother leave, I wring my hands and pace back and forth. The footsteps still ring through the floors and itch my ears.

Finally, Steve walks in.

"Nature calls," he says.

I tense—he'll get a front-row view of the cracked floor, broken faucet, and cracked ceiling.

"You're not just playing cards up there?"

Steve shakes his head. "No, ma'am. We're finding all the parts of the roof that are exposed, rusted, or missing fasteners. Cost repair analyses are thorough reports. It's not easy up there." He leans in closer. "Especially with Mr. Chernov leaning over my shoulder."

I nod in an *I know exactly what you are suffering from* type of way. Seriously, that man needs to be taught a lesson on letting people do their jobs—let librarians be librarians.

I hear him flush and pick up a call. He runs to me. "Ma'am, I am so sorry to do this. My wife's water just broke. It's real this time!"

He shoves his phone in his pocket. "Can you tell Mr. Chernov for me?"

I nod. He probably doesn't want his head chewed off for backing out right in the middle of the inspection.

"Of course!" I help him out and practically open his car door for him, watching him drive away.

I run back to the other side of the building and grab the ladder.

"*Hey!*" Lucas yells as I try to pull the ladder down.

It's heavier than I imagined. I stumble backward a few steps and force it to tip to the left, doing my best to prevent it from crashing into the building next to us. It hits the ground with a vibrating crash.

"*Amelia Anderson!*" His head peeks over the edge. His hair is hanging down, his shirt sleeves are rolled up, and lots of facial lines are forming—he does not look happy.

"Steve had to step away," I shoot up. He stands up and walks to the west side to check out the parking lot.

He shouts, "Where did he go?"

"His wife—" I smile wide— "is going into labor."

He comes back to where I tossed the ladder down and runs his hands through his hair. "Great. Just great." He puts his hands on his hips. "And you thought this was a perfect chance to catch me?"

I twist my hair with my finger. "Correction, I thought I could trap you into submission."

He laughs a little. "Amelia." Then, like a grumpy professor, all the laughs and smiles disappear. "Put back the ladder."

I back up a little.

"Amelia," his voice flatlines.

I shake my head back and forth and inch closer to the corner of the building. "Don't go!" he says as I almost turn the corner. "I'll shout your nickname to the world if you leave."

I force a smile—Mikey would call me Pumpkin Spice forever. "I could take that hit for the library," I yell up.

He nods. "I could...buy you a better leash for Neme."

"What's wrong with my leash?" I've taken care of the fraying parts with lots of colored duct tape left over from craft time. "It's original," I defend.

"Okay," he stammers out. "I can't ask what you want—"

"I'll say the library?"

He nods his head. "I can't do that..."

"What if you help me get an audience with your brothers? I can thank them for letting the library live here for free and petition why the repairs are a better route than apartments..."

"No," he says, chopping his hand in a downward motion.

"*Fine!*" I yell up.

I'll let him sit on it, like an adult time-out.

The wind picks up as I walk to the front of the building and tuck myself underneath its small awning.

"Hey, hey, hey!" he yells out. "Amelia! This isn't playing fair!"

I cover my snort; he sounds like an upset fourth-grader who lost his kickball.

I tuck inside and turn off the vanilla freshener, keeping myself busy for a solid twenty minutes straight reshelving books. I also stare out the window, listening to him walk back and forth, imagining his face's tight lines and clenched fists.

The sky is getting darker, and he has his phone, right? He can call someone. I haven't heard him for a while, and a loud drop hits the window. Not a tiny drop, but a Virginia raindrop, large and juicy.

I walk outside. The clouds are all dark, but I don't see lightning yet.

My arm muscles strain, and my back shakes as I hoist the ladder up. It hits the roofline with a scrape of metal, and I start climbing up. If he agrees to let me talk to his family, I'll let him down. It's a solid next step to give the library a fighting chance.

I take the final step off the ladder, bracing myself to fall through the roof. It holds my weight, and I put my feet down softly. My eyes search across the roof—no Lucas. Maybe he jumped? I walk back to the edge and look down. Yeah, that would've broken something for sure. My feet take several steps away from the edge, and the rain starts to fall.

Large arms wrap around me, and I yelp.

I try to wiggle out of his embrace, but he doesn't budge. He whispers in my ear, "Amelia." His tone is way too soft, and I stop moving. He breathes in my hair, and I swear he kisses the back of my head. Rain begins to fall, filling the air and clinging to our embrace as my heart feels exposed. "I'm going to turn you around. I'll let you go if you don't move."

He loosens his grip and turns me to face him, keeping his arms at my waist. I look into his dark brown eyes and let the rain splatter across my face.

My breathing hitches; I can't slow my heart.

"My brothers..." He shakes his head. "We all own this building, and we..." His eyes dance across every feature of my face.

I've already had to swallow the news that they own the building and don't charge us rent. That's terrible news. That wasn't fake nice; that was real-authentic kindness. My stomach feels like he's trying to stir up oil and water with a whisk ever since our leash entanglement. I can't hate someone nice. I look into his dark eyes through his dripping eyelashes.

I blink and lose my voice again.

"You need to know that they only see the library as a leech, a massive drain on our resources, myself included," he whispers the last part. "Some of my brothers are far worse than me." He looks down. The sound of the rain pings off like a ping pong ball tournament. It bounces up and drenches our pants and shoes. "Some of my brothers will resonate with your plea, but you must know there's a chance you will regret this. Are you sure that's what you want?" His voice is loud now.

A small roll of thunder speaks out and slaps across the sky; rain drips steadily from his hair, and my eyes become glossy.

"I really want to give the library a fighting chance," I yell. I'm stripped of all my walls.

He bores his eyes into me, staring down at my lips. The electricity in the air charges my body, and it hums everywhere he touches me. A raindrop drips off his nose, and I can almost taste the rain mixed with his salt.

I feel a tear drop from my eye.

He reaches up and wipes it away, and I'm perplexed as to how he found it. "The only way I think it can work is if you are..." His thumb wipes away a few more drops of rain off my cheeks. He swallows. "My date."

I know I can never un-know how it feels to be in Lucas Chernov's arms, and I quiver. His hand goes to my chin, brushing away more large water droplets. I nod, my voice so small through all the rain, "Okay," I mouth.

His hair is plastered to his head, and I feel my shirt cling tight to my skin. He leans into me, and the urge to taste the rainy salt on him again is too strong.

He comes so close to my lips as a crack in the sky flashes bright.

We bend low and dash to the ladder. He goes down first, shouting, "Be careful, it's slick!"

Rain drips down my nose, and wet dreadlocks stick to my face. My feet move quickly following him, but the rungs are wet, and my hands cling tight to the sides. A roll of thunder booms overhead, and I lose my grip.

I slip several rungs down before I feel his strong hands around my waist. He slowly lowers me to the ground. I turn around to face him. My hands conveniently sprawl out across his chest, his hands still on my hips.

The thunder rolls away, and his stare pierces me, soaking me through more than any storm.

Another crack of lightning lights up the sky, and I pull both hands away, but he catches one hand in the air.

Our wet skin seems to conduct the static in the air, and he turns my hand over and places a paper-light kiss on my wrist

His lips zap my resolve, unraveling every strand. My world tilts and cracks a little. My heart stops now, and I have no voice again.

He turns and picks up the ladder, yelling, "I'll see you tomorrow."

He loads it inside his truck parked along the road. I hadn't noticed it earlier. I stand stone still, like Bart and Gert, watching him pull away.

Several moments pass before the next crack of lightning snaps me back. I wipe the rain from my face and run to the library entrance, leaning against the door. I stare at the skin he kissed. My chest heaves as drops fall—it tingles with unspoken warning.

Falling in love with Lucas Chernov will ruin everything.

Chapter Thirteen

Amelia

Step two: beg

I watch him leave the bank every day for two weeks; then he comes to me—I mean the library. He comes in every day, even on Saturdays, and checks on the iPad throughout the day.

We've barely spoken a word since our kiss incident. He lurks in the shadows like a good book, hidden but there. I try convincing myself that he's a boring book, but he catches me stealing glances and holds my stare.

I walk through the aisles of books, and he follows, always an aisle away. We don't talk like it's a rule—because if we do, I'll remember who he is, and I'll hate him again.

Instead, I stare and flip through books. He looks away when I try to catch him staring. When he's reading, I study him in very hidden ways. His brow, the way his hair touches his forehead, the way he taps his lips when he thinks—it makes the place where he kissed my wrist pulse.

I'm tempted to pick his book up and flip through the pages.

When he sits there in the corner reading the history book he checked out, he always stops and makes sure anyone who walks in the door takes the survey. He's civil and even lets several genuine smiles peek out. During my weaker moments, I feel like a tiny kiss has turned us into a budding romance, and I have no sense of what's real and what I want to be real.

Other times, I remember who he is: the head contractor of Noil Construction, the library killer—my library killer.

The fog clears occasionally, and I remember he's the type of book where everyone dies in the end—he will break my heart in more ways than a simple lover could.

The library is my world.

But he agrees to give me an audience with his family. And finally, on Friday, I blurt out, "Stop lurking."

I bite my lower lip but then stomp my foot lightly. "I know you're not reading. And I'm not going to tamper with 'the data.'"

"You have no idea what I'm doing," he says with his eyes still on the page.

I scrunch up my forehead with my hands. "I'm a librarian. I absolutely know when someone is real reading and not just reading the same thing over and over again."

"Fine." He closes it. "You got me. But it's not what you think."

Right.

"You're thinking about world peace and the source of dark matter?"

He presses down his lips. "Close."

I shake my head—arrogant Chernov.

"I'm thinking about my family."

I leave him to sulk.

"Amelia," he says. "Family dinner is tomorrow at six."

I bite my lip again without looking back. He's following through, actually letting me have an audience with his family. Is he giving the library a chance...or is he giving me a chance?

Family dinner tomorrow, then the retreat the day after that.

I get a weekend of Lucas, finally.

I don't want to know if he's regretting letting me bully him into a date, but it doesn't matter now. Tomorrow, I'll get to defend the library to the Chernov brothers.

It's "fake date" day, and I'm angry with myself—no, I'm magma. My "I love my library" baseball hat will hide my blunder of the year. I'm late for work again, and I hope Mr. Mettle isn't there. I go to pull open the door, and it's unlocked.

Inferno.

I open it and look around; Lucas is lurking already. "Why are you here so early?" I ask. "Did you pass your love note off to one of the tellers already?"

He tilts his head, and his slow smile is telling. I wouldn't be as tempted to touch his face again if I knew he was pining for someone else, well, maybe just his lips.

"Why are you so late?" he asks.

He brushes my question off, so I brush off his.

I rub my forehead; I'm glad his silence means he's pining for someone in the bank. Knowing where we stand with each other before our forced date begins is a gift.

This is a forced date—I bullied him into it, that's it—nothing more, is on repeat in my brain.

He stares at my hat and puts the book down on my desk. "You looked like you had an entire conversation in your head without me."

"No, I didn't." I force a blank stare.

He puts his hands in his pockets. "You are the worst liar I've ever met." He points to my shirt. "Is that what you are wearing to dinner tonight?" He winces as he reads my t-shirt out loud. "I'm a Librarian: I know everything." He wrinkles his forehead and chuckles. "Milly, no." He says it like he gets to pick what I wear to dinner. "I'm sorry, just no. My brothers will eat you alive. That t-shirt is for an intimate family gathering, not a family dinner."

I lift both hands. "I thought that was the definition of a family dinner, 'intimate family gathering.'" I use my hands for air quotes.

He shakes his head. "Not with the Chernovs. Baba takes family dinners seriously. We dress up." He points to my shirt. "Don't you have a nice day dress or a Sunday dress you could wear to dinner?"

I bark out a laugh. "Lucas, the nicest thing I own are sweaters that say, 'I LOVE CATS AND READING.' It has nice sequin—"

Someone shoves the door open wide, and we both swing our eyes to the woman who barges through the door.

"Oh dear," I say with a sigh. "Rosabell."

Lucas looks at me and back at the woman. "Don't think you're getting out of this, Amelia. You must own something..." he says under his breath, then crosses his arms, leaving a runway for Rosabell, a loyal patron with some of the biggest feelings in town.

"Amelia! I need your help, honey; this is an emergency!" Rosabell's heels are as high as three romance novels stacked up. Her toe tips are pointed, like a witch's nails and her yellow blazer matches the bandana on her Shih Tzu dog, which follows her heels.

I walk around the circulation desk and bend down. "How's my Patty today?" My fingers scratch the top of her head, and she kicks her leg in the air. She smells like shampoo with a twinge of tree bark oil.

Rosabell looks down at me. "What in the devil's gate are you wearing, Milly Bean?" I wince at another nickname Lucas will have in his arsenal against me.

She lifts off my hat, and I count to three before opening my eyes.

Both jaws drop open wide.

I pull back the hat, put it back on, and then stand up.

"Oh, pothole on Ninth Street, swallow me up. What in the church's name have you done to your hair?"

I gulp. "It's nothing. I just..."

The truth is I can't tell them the truth. I wanted to look nice for dinner tonight. I wanted to look beautiful; at least, that's what I told myself in the mirror last night at one in the morning because I couldn't sleep. A few snips to help tame my mane: I thought it was a good idea...until it wasn't.

Lucas stifles a laugh—my jaw juts out.

"You look like Billy's weed-eating job. Who in the world did you pay to cause that type of damage?"

I look down and mumble, "Me."

She stares at me. "Honey, you are a woman of many talents, don't get me wrong." She shakes her head. "Don't you ever try cutting your own hair again."

I nod and feel moisture pinch the back of my eyes. I won't cry. The YouTube tutorials made it look so easy last night.

Lucas tilts his head. "If you tilt your head and close your eyes halfway, you can't see the step-down shelves as much." I would've slapped him back into his lurking corner if Rosabell wasn't there.

His eyes soften as I push a finger to the side of my eye, forcing tears to stay in. "Mom used to cut it," I blurt out.

Both stare at me.

"Are you tellin' me," she pauses and shakes her head, "Milly Bean, your hair hasn't been cut in over ten years?"

I play with a corner of my shirt with a small stain. "I haven't gotten around to it since she passed."

My emotions peek out of my eyes, and my gut drops as I watch Lucas count every single one of my thoughts. So much for being strong, full of vengeance, and not letting him see my vulnerabilities. I focus my eyes on the computer screen at the circulation desk. "What about your emergency, Rosabell?" I ask.

"Oh, it will have to wait. This is much worse."

Lucas turns and steps outside. I watch him on the phone through the window.

He thinks I'm a hot mess that looks like a weed patch, that apparently Billy doesn't even know how to cut.

"What came over you, Milly Bean?" She searches my eyes as I watch Lucas through the window. He paces back and forth on his phone.

"Oh, Rosabell." I sit back down at the circulation desk. "I really wanted a chance to talk to all of his brothers because I know I can convince them how important the library is here and that the remodeling is worth it. But then I made him get stuck on the roof, and then it rained, and then he didn't want me to talk to his brothers. He thinks I can't handle it. But then he said it could work only if it's a date, and I hate that I want it to be a real date, not a date that I got because I trapped the man on a roof in a lightning storm." I hiccup and use my shirt to wipe my cheeks.

"Come up for air, Milly Bean." Rosabell bends down and places her elbows on the circulation desk. "Milly Bean, you've got it bad." She can't hide the small smile on her face.

I hate that she can see me—really see me.

I put my face in my hands and try to take a deep breath. Hearing how Lucas thinks about my hair makes me want to curl up.

"Is Susan in today?" She holds her phone up to her ear. I didn't even see her pull out her phone.

"Oh, dear me, lemon pie," she says. "How long has she been out for?" Rosabell nods. She helps every shop in town to keep in the loop about what the other shops are saying about each other. A professional small-town gossiper with an eye for sentence structure—she edited my speech for the last public hearing, and she'll help with the next one, too.

Lucas walks back in as she ends her call.

I hope only to lurk.

He comes straight to us, but Rosabell speaks first. "My girl is out watching her grandchildren who have pink eye." Rosabell cringes. "That will spread like wildfire through here, honey. Just watch out."

I wipe my eyes again.

Great, pink eye, too. Will the roof fall in next? I shove that thought away. I don't want to challenge the universe to make it so.

Lucas's eyes are gentle. "My barber can take you anytime today. He'll work you in." His tone is smooth, and he doesn't take his eyes off me.

"Oh, I couldn't, I can't—" I don't know how to say I can barely afford to pay for dog food and our cardboard frozen meals, let alone a professional haircut. Plus, that means I owe him—like, really owe him.

"Amelia, it's on me. What's your number?"

I must've stood there in shock for too long because Rosabell snaps her fingers in my face.

"Oh." I take his phone out of his hands and type it in. He turns and walks out of the library, and my eyes follow him every step.

"Oh, Milly Bean, you're a goner."

I swallow and try to focus on helping Rosabell with her emergency.

She needs a new book for her upcoming book club. New books are only checked out for two weeks at a time, and we find one she feels she can read in two weeks and "enough in it to keep those prattling women talking for months."

Her knowing half-smile spreads as she says, "Have a great time, Milly Bean. You deserve it. Your mama wants you happy." She makes my eyes water again as she leaves the library.

Chapter Fourteen

Amelia

Step three: wear lipstick and make him love you

Mr. Mettle lets me have an earful. "Not only are you late," his high voice always sounds louder than it is because it's high-pitched, "but you're requesting to leave two hours early so you can fix your hair?" I might have fake-cried a little, too. I figure it will help my odds.

"I hate female tears," he gruffs, stands up from his office desk, and walks to the circulation desk. I take that as a yes and dash out the door.

Lucas has texted me the address of his barber.

Lucas Chernov has texted me. I save his number—Henchman Lucas Chernov. Just as a fresh reminder, I stare at the name. Their family is technically letting us stay in the library for free...I delete "henchman" and put "Lucas Sinful Hair Chernov." I push on the link he sent, and Google Maps takes over; it takes thirty minutes to get there. I'm glad I left early.

Parking is a near-death experience, but I finally walk in.

The middle-aged man has tall hair combed back slick with a little around his ears and neck.

He points to my hat. "Lucas's friend?"

I nod. My heart takes a little courage; Lucas has called me a friend.

He smiles. "Your hat looks like you're hiding something."

I shrug.

He laughs. "No judgment here. Let's see what type of creative haircut you have." He points to a seat. He takes off the hat and runs his fingers through my hair. "Wow, your coloring is so—"

"Unusual, I know."

He shakes his head. "I was going to say original. Women pay an arm and a leg to get this type of hair color. I also haven't seen thick hair like this for years."

He grabs a brush.

"Oh, I don't know if you want to do that," I try to hide my face.

He laughs a little. "It's what I do. Promise you can't scare me away. I'm Brian, by the way."

"Amelia," I say. "Thank you so much for working me in."

He nods. "Today was my day off."

I cover my mouth, and my eyes go wide. "Oh no! I'm so sorry!"

"Oh, don't even think about it. I'd do anything for Lucas." He pushes down my shoulders and smiles. "Serious, I'd do anything for Lucas."

I relax a little as I roll those words around in my brain for a few moments—anything for Lucas. I watch in the mirror as my hair instantly springs up, big and static as he brushes out my hat hair.

"Wow!" he says.

I frown—it's terrible. I am not only a mess, but I am a failed mess. I drop my eyes to my hands.

"Amelia. Take heart," he says. "Your hair will love my curling regime."

I scrunch my nose. "Regime is not a word that sounds normal for hair." I have so far failed; I wipe my cheek.

He softens his voice. "You have amazing volume and natural curls hidden under this fluff." He takes my hair and crunches it up in his hands. "You, Amelia, have a gold mine of natural beauty; it just needs a little taming."

I laugh a little, but he can see the water in my eyes. I try to blink quickly; I don't want to turn into a blubbering mess in the chair. I have nowhere to hide.

"I want to help you love what you have." He looks at me through the mirror. "Your true self." He winks.

I take a big breath.

"I'll blend in some of these creative layers." He smiles. "Then I'll walk you through every step so you can do it in your sleep." He places the comb into his apron. "Amelia, have hope."

I take heart in his focused face and his hands' quick movement. He takes complete control over my hair, squirting it, snipping it, pulling it high up, and snipping along every strand.

He takes off a little of the length, and I'm surprised he leaves it longer than I expected. The tips reach the middle of my back like a soft hand bracing me up. He takes out a tooth-like set of scissors. "You've never had your hair thinned, have you?" I shake my head no and don't want to admit I've never had a professional haircut, ever. The cost is never something I feel I can spend—I had Mom back then. She gave me the perfect haircuts.

But Brian gives every strand attention.

I let myself sink into the chair.

We both turn our heads as the doorbell jingles open. "Sorry, it's by appointment only. We're closed today."

The young woman holds a package that's in a long white box. "Oh, just a delivery, sir."

He drops my hair and walks to her.

"Thanks." He brings the package over to me. "Pumpkin Spice?" He looks at me in the mirror.

My cheeks flush. "Oh, um..." I squirm in the chair.

"Is that you?" he asks.

"I think so." My eyes scan the large, flat, white box. I take the card taped to the box.

Brian returns to cutting my hair. "Almost time for a wash."

I nod as I pry open the letter.

Dear Amelia,

I know we haven't made life easier for each other, and you won't listen to me if I ask you to do something for me. In that case, will you wear this for Baba? She will appreciate the sentiment. I would be lying if I didn't say I would enjoy seeing you in this dress, too.

Yours,

Lucas.

I bite my lower lip. My heart squeezes tight again, and even my throat feels butterfly tickles. I read the words several times again until Brian says I can get up, and start opening the box.

"From Lucas?" Brian asks.

I nod, not trusting my voice.

"He's a good man. I've always been in awe as he's helped his mother and brothers. He's navigated strong personalities better than most."

I swallow as I run my fingers along the box, lifting it to feel the weight. I'm too nervous to open it.

"You can open the box after we wash your hair."

I nod, and he sits me down and massages my head, lathering in the liquid. "The real work begins."

I let him crunch, scrunch, apply, and twist.

He shows me his regime: curling shampoo, cream, gel, hairspray, hair oil, and, lastly, a curling rod. I only listen with one ear as I keep eyeing the box. A warm sensation fills my chest and abdomen with every curl he perfects.

He brushes through my hair with a wide-tooth comb, softening all the curls.

Lucas wants me to look nice because he'll enjoy it too.

No one will recognize me, I think, as I study the image blinking back at me through the mirror. I look put together and smooth.

"Oh, Brian, thank you so much." I run my hands down my hair. It doesn't feel like me at all; it looks like a hairstyle right off the magazine shelf.

He turns me to the box.

I open it like a timid kitten—the navy blue chiffon falls out as I hold up a flattering dress. It has a fitted bodice with three-quarter sleeves. The neckline comes up past my collarbone. I smile; my welt is gone, but I like high neck protection now.

Brian lets out a long, soft whistle. "You are going to sparkle tonight."

Lucas is transforming my life, and I haven't decided if it's for better or worse.

Chapter Fifteen

Amelia

Step four: compromise

I stop my car and put it in park, glancing back at Neme panting in the back seat. I'm surprised Lucas wanted me to bring him. Neme wags his tail as we both spot Apollo in the front yard.

I splashed some makeup on, and I'm glad Grandpoppy is out for the evening at the retirement center. The driveway is lined with cars, and I pat Neme and then my hair. My dress fits well, and I can't help but take a small spin as I step out of the car—this is not a Goodwill dress.

Apollo, in his well-fitted suit, looks like he belongs here. "Amelia! I'm so glad you came!" he says, reaching out to give me knuckles.

"Can we play with Neme for a bit? I want you to get settled in," Apollo says.

"Okay, that's thoughtful of you," I say, feeling a bit relieved.

His shoulders relax. "Just so you know, it's going to be an interesting night," he says with a smile and two thumbs up.

"Oh no, should I be nervous?"

He nods. "You kind of should be." Then he takes Neme out to the yard and picks up a frisbee.

Neme will be in heaven; and I am glad one of us will be because Apollo just set a beehive loose in my nervous system.

I walk through the door and large entryway, past the kitchen, and then several steps down into their massive family room with an entire wall of vaulted floor to ceiling windows. With every step, it smells like lemon-fresh, warm pie. Every surface sparkles back at me—I better not touch anything.

Everyone is out on the massive deck or in the yard, wearing blazers or sweaters, and the handful of women I see are in dresses. My T-shirt would have crumbled.

I frown. My dress might be a little much, but it's just enough to stand out in a *save the library* type of way. Lucas knew.

The soft music pulls me in—excessive bulb lights strung above, and the sun is about to set—and I see him. Lucas, leaning over the deck's side, looks out over the evening light. He's slipped on a blazer and has his hair slicked up.

"So," I say and lean against the porch railing, "a girl just has to trap you on a roof to be treated like a queen?"

He turns and drinks me in, his breath hitching.

"Amelia," his voice is low. He blinks. "I'm sorry about your hair." He reaches for my hand without thinking, then pulls away.

My fingers act fast, wrapping around his.

"You wore the dress," he whispers.

I nod, and we hear several footsteps approach. He leans into me and wraps his arm around me. "You're exquisite." His warm breath makes me go weak in the knees. "I'm glad you're here. Truce? For tonight?"

I nod, thoroughly melted.

"Lucasss," a tight voice says behind us.

Lucas presses his face against my ear. "Amelia...forgive me." His breath lingers on my ear. "I didn't know she'd be here."

He turns slowly, and I savor his soap and scent for a moment.

"Who is this new sunflower you picked up?" The woman's voice drips with disdain. I turn to stand next to Lucas.

Her skintight black dress makes her look like a black panther—the gorgeous, mean kind. She has dark, auburn hair and long, dangly earrings that the kids at the library would love to play with and probably rip out. I stare at her hands to see how long her nails are, just to be ready.

I feel like a small farm kitten hiding behind the farmer.

Her eyes run up the length of my body, and she glances away like I'm a one-star hotel. She raises her eyebrows, waiting for a response.

"Kim, this is my beautiful—" he looks at me for approval—"date," he says as if he's going to kiss my forehead, "Amelia Anderson."

If he keeps this up, I should hoist up my white surrender flag for eternity.

I have no power over blazer-wearing, quasi-fake friendly Lucas, one-night truce—and a pang hits me as Kim seems she's ignoring me on purpose.

Lucas is right; this kitten can't play this game.

"Some may say otherwise," she says, staring at Lucas.

I look away and see Apollo lingering—Neme must still be out front. Apollo had warned me; bless him. He gives me the smallest nod.

I channel my inner courage from all my favorite stories and jut out my hand, "Hi! It's nice to meet you, too! Your name is Kim?" I hold my breath to see how well my duck feathers will hold up.

She looks annoyed while reaching out her hand; her handshake is light as a germ. She rolls her eyes, and I think fast and ask, "How are you connected to the Chernovs?"

The music stops, and every eye looks at me.

"Lots of different ways, actually," Lucas says, cutting in and pulling on his neck collar.

A small smile ticks up on Kim's face. "And how are you connected to the Chernovs?"

"Well..." How can I say I'm the passionate librarian who was infatuated with Lucas all through high school and recently vowed to hate him, and I'd infiltrated their house illegally and made it my life mission to stop one of the bigger projects they're currently working on? Oh, and I think I'm falling in love with Lucas for real this time.

"Work," I say, looking stern.

She tilts her head. "Interesting. Me, too."

"It's time to eat," a brother yells out. Dimitry walks up and wraps his arm around Kim.

"I'm Dimitry." He sticks out his hand.

I take it. "Dim, it's me."

He tilts his head, and his brown eyes go wide. "Amelia Anderson?" He gives me a hug. "Wow, I didn't even recognize you. You look amazing!"

I'm beet red; Kim is sharpening a claw.

"Let's get caught up some time," he says, reaching for Kim's hand. She tugs on his jacket, and he leans in for a kiss.

Lucas looks away, his jaw tightening. They turn and walk in; Kim laughs at something Dimitry says.

Two-faced cat—I want to hiss a little at her. I flex my fingers to make sure I don't have claws myself.

Lucas leans into me again, lingering. I try not to close my eyes and savor it more than I would the world's best cheesecake.

"Well done. That was just the kiddie pool, though," he says, pulling my hand through the crook of his arm. "You sure you want to follow through with this? It might get ugly."

I've come this far, so I nod.

He pulls away and looks out in the yard. "I'll have to stay close to you to keep my brothers—" a Nerf football flies past us— "in line," he says.

Several college-aged men run toward us, down to the back deck past a guest house.

Two are in sweats, and one is certainly not.

"Is he wearing a—"

"A speedo, yes." Lucas frowns. I try not to stare while Lucas rubs his eyebrows. "He swims a lot. But his mom," he points to three women sitting at a side table, "is glad Atticus is wearing anything at all."

I cover my mouth.

All three women look over and wave at us.

"Are those..."

Lucas nods. "My Dad's exes? Yeah, they are. Family is family if you're a Chernov. They're like aunts to me." He adjusts his blazer. "That doesn't mean we play nice."

My eyes become teacup plates—*hold up duck feathers.*

"Change, boys!" Lucas hollers as they get closer.

"Lucas, man. Come on. You know we want to be more casual when people come over." The brother, wearing slim joggers and a gray shirt with a ketchup stain, looks like he stepped out of a magazine cover. He's a little shorter with lighter golden hair and a half-smile.

Who am I kidding? Each one of them looks ridiculously handsome. I feel like I'm the dull color in a special edition pack of vibrant, washable markers.

I lift my hand to cover up my view of the speedo.

"Not the right time to try that, Vincent."

He scratches his chin. "Just don't think we are going to act all fancy for your new girlfriend."

Lucas shakes his head and ignores him. He points to the man I'm keeping covered up from my view. "His mother let him run naked in the forest as a child. That's what we blame it on."

I bark out a laugh but stop when I see Kim mean-eyeing me through the window.

"Go on, then, get ready." Lucas raises his arm to the left wing of the house. All the brothers walk in and disappear down the hallway.

He drops my arm and grabs my hand. I'm on a Lucas high and don't know how to get out of the clouds.

The sun dips behind a ridge, leaving orange-kissed clouds. It softens all of Lucas's features. I take a deep breath as everyone starts to file around the large table at the back of the family room by the windows.

Elaborate greenery and autumn colors scatter in the middle of the table. Name tags are placed on each plate. Meats, potatoes, vegetables—steam fills the air, rich with the flavors of more sides than I could get at a buffet.

"Is this a wedding reception?" I ask Lucas.

He shakes his head and points to his grandmother. "Welcome to the over-the-top women in my life."

I swallow.

Lucas lightly touches my curls and twirls a strand, heat traveling up my back.

He leads me to my seat, and my stomach twists with nerves. Self-consciousness bubbles up: I don't belong here. I don't have a family like this. I don't have resources. I don't have fancy dinners in ginormous houses with a bazillion siblings—I can't do this. I start to push back my seat.

"Hey," he says in my ear, stopping me in my tracks.

He reaches out and squeezes my hand. "I still don't think it's a good idea for you to talk about the library." His eyes don't tease at all. "But just be you. Your story is powerful."

I squeeze back, and he releases my hand as an older woman approaches. We both stand up to greet her.

"We welcome you to our family home," her Russian accent is refreshing. I watch her red lips and expressive hands bounce her double chin when she speaks.

"You're pretty as a flower,. she pats Lucas's cheek. "Remember your lion." She shakes her finger in front of Lucas's face. "Simargl will help you."

He side-hugs her, not even blinking at her words.

"Simargl?" I ask.

She just winks at me, taking in my dress and hair. She looks pleased.

"Baba, this is—" he pauses before he says, "Pumpkin."

I scrunch up my nose.

"Pummmpkinnn." She lets the letters dance on her tongue.

"She loves to read, Baba."

"Pumpkin is perfect for Chernovs," she says, patting both of our cheeks.

The woman pulls me into an embrace and says, "Lucas loves the flavor of pumpkin! He asked me to make—"

Lucas clears his throat. "Baba," his voice is stern.

She brushes him off. "He's trying to surprise you. I'll behave." She looks up into my eyes again. "Do you really like to read?"

A smile reaches every part of my face, and I nod.

"You are my favorite then. He never has brought home a reader. I know deep in my bones: If you are a reader, you are a nice person." Her hug lathers me up with a welcoming courage I didn't have a minute ago. "A nice reader can help Lucas break our family curse."

I smile and look at Lucas. "A curse?" He'd mentioned something about it before.

She reaches out and squeezes my hand. "I will tell you."

Lucas adjusts his sleeves and collar again.

"Zolton's boys are cursed." Her eyes go wide. "I have family dinner to help the Chernov brothers..." she lets out a loud sigh, "...work through their troubles. There are many," she points at Lucas. "And to help boys find good women to help make good strong grandbabies."

I pull back my hand.

"You see, Lucas is a big, tough guy. But really," she points to his heart. "He cares about us all. His heart is so good, Pumpkin."

"That's enough, Baba. She's already terrified of us. I don't think—"

Baba slaps his cheek again. I stifle a giggle. "Stop thinking! Break curse, boy." She points around to all the other visiting girls, a good handful of them, "Then the others might actually work."

She winks at me again and moves off to the next couple to interrogate.

I cross my arms. "Fess up," I say, turning to stare into his dark brown eyes.

He shakes his head. "The curse?"

I nod.

"Over my dead body," he says.

I look over my shoulder. "I think we can arrange that. Kim's claws look like they are set to kill," I say.

"I don't disagree," he says. "Only one family secret per full moon."

I nod my head. "Tell me about the curse, *or* who Kim is to you," I say.

"Fine. Kim." He sucks in a mouthful of air. He rotates his jaw and turns toward the moon. "She's my ex-fiancé."

My eyes almost pop out. "Your brother is dating your ex-fiancé?"

He bobs his head in a slow trance, and I feel a claw poke out of my own skin. "What type of brother does that?"

He shakes his head. "It's a long story."

I stare at her and Dimitry. Her laugh seems forced, and I see Lucas cringe.

"The worst part is—" he shakes his head— "she is my boss's daughter."

I cover my mouth again. "Noil Construction?"

"That might be the only part you care about. Her dad wants the apartments, not a library. If I do a good job, I get the promotion I deserve."

I suck in a breath. I've never stopped to think about Lucas's situation with the library.

Vincent and Atticus enter the room, looking fresh and dressed to match Lucas.

"Let's get started!" Baba's voice is loud.

My stare bores into my dinner plate, and I realize his *why* for the first time. In the same stroke of insight, my overpowering brain shows up and pushes any ounce of compassion for him to the side.

The library is more important.

We all take our seats, and Baba blesses the food and each of her grandsons to send to her grandbabies. Everyone jumps up so quickly after the prayer that the awkward feeling in the room leaves within moments. All the food is on a massive serving table across the room.

"Try Baba's grape juice," Apollo says. "She grows her own grapes." It looks deep and full of flavor through the glass pitcher. "It makes everything purple." he flashes his purple teeth.

I cover my smile and am glad there is vinyl flooring here, not their white carpet in the front of the house.

I meet Andrei and the local lawyer, Magnolia Grace. She is impressive, and I can't believe I've never met the local lawyer before.

We steer clear of Dimitry and Kim.

Nikola has a date, and we wave to both of them.

When we sit down, he points out all the brothers to me.

Apollo walks by and whispers, "Neme is safe out front." I nod. "Lucas, I got the paper I needed; thank you. Do you know where you put the hole-punch?"

Lucas looks confused, then his eyes focus. "I don't know where it is. Are you sure?"

"I'm sure," Apollo swings his gaze to me, "that a hole punch is what I need. Don't worry; I'll be looking for a hole punch until it's found."

My lips pull to one side. "You know there are five in my desk, right? Just come by the library, Apollo, and I can help."

Both look at me with a strange strain in their eyes.

"Amelia," Cams and Devon, Apollo's friends, wave at me from across the table. I smile and wave back, and Lucas gives them a nod like a boss would a minion.

"Such good kids," I say.

"I know," Lucas says. "I think some of my brothers are good despite how rough I've been on them."

He points to each brother. "Let's see how well you can keep us apart." He points around the room, "Andrei, Nikola,

Dimitry, Atticus, Anton, Maximillian, Vincent, Apollo, and Remington."

Wow, just wow. The testosterone in the room is thick now that he's pointed each one out, and they each look ready for an impromptu photo shoot. My eyes go around the room several times, and I repeat their names under my breath. "Where's your mother?"

"She's stuck finishing up a job in Russia."

"She's a very capable woman." I say. But really, I'm saying that she's stunning. I've seen her around town, even in the library, and I always watched her from afar. She raised boys who turned into strong men, dealt with a difficult husband, and thrived despite rumors about her family.

"Mom is a tough bird; she's been through a lot. I hope she gets back soon." He pops a grape into his mouth. "Let's have you share your speech when everyone is eating before everyone breaks off for games."

"Games?" I gag a little.

He nods. "My brothers love games."

My hand rests on the table. "Games don't bring out my best side." my shoulders tighten.

He puts his hand near mine. "Don't worry, I'm on your team. I'll curb your impulses."

Warmth inches up my arm as his pinky caresses mine. I square my shoulders. "I'll just get it over with and go now." I want to use some of the euphoria Lucas is spoon-feeding into me.

We both stand again. "Everyone, I'd like to get your attention," he announces.

I push my chair in, pat my hair, and run the napkin over my face for good measure.

"As some of you know, Amelia is the librarian for Lionstone Library."

The room quiets. My hand starts to shake, and I stick them behind me. Kim picks up her butter knife, probably to sharpen her claws.

"She kindly asked to share a few words with us about the library." Lucas's smile is steady as he sits down.

"Who's Amelia?" Baba shouts from the head of the table. "I thought your name was Pumpkin?"

Everyone laughs. "It's Amelia," my voice squeaks out over the side conversations that erupt after the reveal of my nickname.

"Let her speak," Andrei shouts out.

I look at Lucas.

"Go on," he whispers. "Share your story." And he gives me another soft smile.

Several brothers poke their food, and others put down all their utensils and stare me up and down like I'm a pimple in the room. I'm going to die—the autopsy will say death by swarming sharks and a wild panther.

"Thank you, everyone, for letting me share a few of my feelings." My fingers find my napkin, and I twist it. Lucas reaches over, tugs out the napkin, and slips my hand into his. His large steadiness is contagious, and I take a deep breath, "I recently learned that Chernov Trust has never charged rent for the library these past twenty years."

Everyone's eyes are on me now. "My mother started her long path to getting a college degree that same year, twenty years ago when the library opened here in town. We had no resources for technology, and the library offered free help with college applications, the internet, and computer space."

Tears spread over both eyes. "The library is more than just books to me; it is interwoven into a better life for me and Mom. The library was able to fund other resources because they didn't have to pay rent or a mortgage, and I know that now. I had more books to read as a child and more toys to play with as my mom studied and obtained her degree, all in the Lionstone Library, so first and foremost, *thank you*."

I look into as many faces as possible before my pause becomes too long. "My mom was able to live her final years in a much more comfortable financial situation because of the free resources the library offered. It eased single parenthood for her and gave me," I wipe my cheek, "a home away from home." I take another deep breath, "How we run the library now is more than just a book exchange; it's a place to help direct and connect citizens with so many things. It's a ho—."

One of Lucas's younger brothers shouts out. "We don't want the library gone, Pumpkin." It's Vincent. He wipes his mouth with his napkin, "Just move it somewhere else."

Some voices agree.

"I don't think that is as viable an option as it may seem. In this region, six small-town libraries have been closed down due to building safety, funding, or not enough patrons. We will be next if we move locations. My regional director has let me know if we move, they will cut our branch out of our town. They won't have the funding for the move or logistics for the new location. We stay, or we leave town forever. I get this in better context now, knowing that regionally, they pay little to keep our branch open because of the Chernov generosity." I toss my hair over my shoulder. "Risking the library isn't an option. It's in the heart of town. It's so accessible to so many citizens, thanks to the Chernov building." I feel my defenses rising.

Lucas drops my hand, and I hide both behind my back.

"Fixing up the library would be a way to help rebuild our town." I shake my head. "It's one of the best resources we have, and for a town that is trying to rebuild. It's vital to support it and not destroy it or move it." My face feels flushed, and my voice cracks. I pick up my water, but my hands are too shaky, and the glass slips.

It tumbles down to the ground and shatters. Water splashes all over my dress. Kim and Lucas jump up to help.

Lucas has his napkin, and Kim walks around the table with a napkin in one hand and her drink in the other. She takes a misstep and her grape juice spreads across my face and chest, and down the front of my dress.

The room is as silent as a lion's den before the kill. Or maybe after the kill.

Lucas looks up and pales.

"Oh my," Kim says. "I'm so clumsy. I am so sorry." Andrei and Magnolia Grace jump up and pick up the glass pieces off the ground. I wipe the juice off my face.

My hands shake more, and hot tears form and spill out. "She's a leaking pumpkin now!" Kim says. "Pumpkin, I hope you don't cry when we squash your library," she says with a forced southern accent and looks at me with a veiled concern.

I feel her clean claw slice down my front.

Several of the brothers laugh. I slowly back up as she cracks another joke about me. The room erupts this time.

My duck feathers all blow away. I hold my sob in and flee. I run across the room, not looking back.

Baba shouts, "*Boys*! Enough!"

When I reach the front door, a hand catches my arm. "Amelia, stop. I—"

Tears are coming, and I can't meet his eyes. "You warned me." A silent sob shakes my shoulders.

He comes up close. "This is my fault, not yours." He lifts my chin to meet his eyes, and I look away, wiping my cheeks.

"It's my fault for forcing you to date me. Goodbye, Lucas," I say, tugging out of his grasp.

Neme jumps off the porch swing, across the cement, and into my car.

I don't look at him standing in the driveway, focusing with all my might to see the road through my blurred vision.

I've been such a naïve fool.

Chapter Sixteen

Lucas

Fire crackles in my belly, and smoke comes out of my nose. My heart twists up tight—that was a disaster, and I need to hit someone. I run back into the family room and over to the table. Most of the party moves outside; everyone can see us through the glass.

A front seat to the next Chernov drama episode. I don't care one drop of juice what anyone here thinks; the only opinion I care about tonight is Amelia crying her eyes out and driving home.

Dimitry and Apollo are yelling. "What type of brother brings his ex-fiancé to a family dinner?" Apollo's voice echoes off the glass.

"What type of brother destroys the passcode to get our inheritance? He left us, Apollo! He just up and left before Dad died! That is not what a brother does." Spit flies out his mouth and lands on Apollo's face. "He wasn't here when we needed him when I needed him!"

I push Apollo back. "Don't take your fight out on Apollo." I point for Apollo to go outside, but he shakes his head. "You are mad at me, not him," I say to Dimitry.

Dimitry shakes his head, "Dad screwed us all when he thought starting with you was a good idea."

"I didn't ask for this. I didn't ask for him to leave breadcrumbs." I feel my neck vein swell, "I don't even want to know what he wants to give me!"

He pushes my chest.

"Hit me," I say. "You'll feel better." My hands clench.

"You know what," he takes off his suit jacket, "I think I will." He rolls up his sleeves, "But first, let me warn you." I don't blink. "I know there was footage deleted from our security cameras, and guess who authorized it?" He nods his head. "You." His finger hits hard on my chest, and I stumble back. "You know what else? I just so happen to know that your *Pumpkin's* car was reported to have been parked in the area at that same time." He smiles. "I know she is part of the missing passcode—I don't know how, but she is."

My nostrils flare, and I feel a crackle of fire in my ears.

"Don't you get it, Lucas?" He shakes his head. "She is playing you. She is destroying our family all because of the stupid library. She stole the document, saw the passcode, then punched a hole in it—who's to say she isn't swimming in your inheritance right now?"

"She has nothing to do with me not being here when you needed me, Dimitry."

He lets out a bark of a laugh. "Oh, you think that I need you now?" He shakes his head. "I don't need you anymore; I don't need anybody," he says, getting close to my face. "I will squash her just to watch you squirm." His breath is warm and sour. "I will turn Amelia in; spoliation of legal evidence is a hefty crime, along with breaking and entering. How would your librarian like some jail time, Lucas?"

"Leave her out of this," I say through my teeth.

"It's way too late for that." He raises his voice. "We need this deal, Lucas. I have other investors watching how we manage this deal; it could be the start of so many more for us."

I push his chest to get his breath off me.

He stiffens and gets close to me again. "If you don't get the rezoning passed and the board's approval, I'll turn her in. I could make her shrivel up in jail for—"

I take a step back and swing hard. The contact on my fist shoots up my arm, and it knocks him back. He lands on the dining room table, crashing into the plates. A woman screams, and I hear the patio door swing open.

Dimitry swings back, and I don't block it. His hit sends my head spinning. I feel a trail of blood on my face as Andrei pulls me back, and Vincent, Anton, and Nikolai pull Dimitry down the hallway.

"I am going to the bank every day," I shout to him down the hallway. "I will get Andrei his letter—not because of you,

Dimitry. Because that's what a good brother would do—not blackmail him."

Dad would blackmail.

Baba looks through the window, and I see her shoulders sagging. I hear her yell, "Party's over; we're cursed!" as she points everyone to the side of the house. Kim meets my eyes and has a soft smile on her lips. She holds up her phone right as I feel my pocket buzz.

I pull it out.

Kim: *Do you want me to tell my dad that you're too emotionally compromised for this project?* Embarrassed emoji.

Kim: *Oh, and just a friendly observation: Your new girlfriend is too soft for this family…I'm glad I could meet her.*

Me: ***I will text him. Leave Amelia alone.***

She believes I'm on Amelia's side.

How can my heart not be involved now?

I practically fed her to the wolves—I cover my face with both my hands.

She is everything Kim could never be.

Amelia is kind—the realization sinks deep. Kind in a way that would feed my soul forever.

I drop my hands, stand up, and go to work cleaning up the dinner and broken plates Dimitry's fall caused.

It does feel like a curse. Everything I've done to push Dad out of my life seems to prove one thing.

I'm more like him than I ever thought possible.

Chapter Seventeen

Amelia

Step five: cry...a lot

Teardrops mix with my wet dress. Neme sticks his face up by mine while I drive—he licks my cheek.

"Oh boy," I say quietly. "I've failed badly." I let out a quivering sigh.

I don't wipe tears or dog juice off my face as I put my car in park and walk inside. The keys drop on the formica countertop with a thud. Grandpoppy is hopefully sleeping. I don't want to talk to anyone.

Neme's paws trot behind me, and I kneel and give him a hug.

"Let's go to bed." He looks at the leash hanging up. "I don't have anything left in me."

Grandpoppy is sleeping in his TV chair. I put a blanket over him and turn on the shower.

It doesn't matter how hard I scrub; the grape juice is under my skin. It'll leave a mark I need to remember—I will never talk to Lucas again. Logically, I know it wasn't him; it was Kim and his brothers. But he's a part of the Chernov reign that causes pain.

I pull my hair out of a shower cap, letting Brian's magic set in as long as possible. Too bad it can't take away the sting in my chest.

I'll have to talk to Lucas tomorrow on the retreat, and we'll have to create a plan for the library together. After that, I'll not talk to him again. I slip into my mourning pj's, the same ones I wore for years after Mom passed. I wrap myself up in my burrito blanket and collapse onto my messy bed.

My hands are stuck at my sides in the blanket; I pull them up and run my hands through my hair.

I will have to face him again. At least twice. He didn't refute anything Vincent or Kim had said. The library is as good as gone, and I've made things worse.

Do I even go to the retreat?

I call Neme and pat him up on my bed. He jumps up, and the entire bed wobbles. He settles in right next to me, taking up more space than I do.

My shoulders relax, my jaw fully loosens, and my hand instinctively reaches out for the closest book on my nightstand. The book starts to drop down as I doze, and I turn off the light.

Right as I feel my breathing deepen, a knock at the door rings through the dark house.

My eyes blink open.

Nope. I do not care if a fire is coming; I'm done peopling.

The knock comes again. And again.

Neme jumps off the bed and trots to the door. Then he starts to whine from the other room.

"Argh," My body unrolls out of my warm burrito, and I sulk to the front door. I see Grandpoppy's hearing aids on the counter and know he won't be making an appearance anytime soon.

"Who is it?" I pinch the bridge of my nose.

"Amelia, let me in." His voice is muffled, but I know the voice of the man I plan to avoid for the rest of my life, except for two approved times.

I don't answer, but he keeps knocking. Neme whines again. "Stop!" I say. "I'm not letting you in." I walk up to the window, pull back the blinds, and push my forehead against the glass, cupping around my eyes to see him.

He holds up a bag, and he has flowers, too.

I shake my head. "I'm not talking to you." The lighting on the porch is too dim, and it makes him look way too genuine with his lips pulled down.

"Amelia," His voice too soft. "I don't expect you to forgive me. I just wanted to make sure that you're okay."

I close the blinds. "I'm still not talking."

I go to the door, and I let my fingers linger over the handle.

"Baba sent pumpkin bars."

I slip the door open and look at the bag he is setting down on the ground. "Squirrels will eat it." I whisper as I pick up the bag.

He jumps in front of the door, closing it, blocking me and him outside. He smiles. His face is soft and darkened.

Before I protest, my eyes snag on his glowing red cheek. "What happened?" I take a step closer to see his red circle and a small cut under his eye.

He fingers his cheek. "Problem-solving."

"Oh, Lucas." I forget myself. "I hope that didn't happen because of me?"

He takes a small step forward and meets me in the middle. "No. It was about me and how I've lacked sorely as a brother." He lifts the flowers up, "This is for you."

Our fingers graze. "Thank you for the dress," I say as I breathe in the flowers. "I loved it."

He puts one hand inside his pocket.

"I'll return it after I get it—"

"Amelia, it's a gift." He smiles. "It's not a library book."

I hold the flowers in my hand. "I guess I learned a life lesson: Never trap someone into going on a date," my voice hitches.

He grimaces, his swollen cheek stopping me from meeting his eyes. "I guess that's the other thing I need to clear up." He pulls a single red rose out of thin air; he must have been hiding it behind his back. "You didn't trap me." He shakes his head, touching the rose with his nose and lips. "I wanted to go on a date with you, Amelia."

He hands the rose to me and then lifts my left hand up to his lips. He closes his eyes and kisses my hand—like cool strawberries against the top of my hand. I revel in his touch.

In my defense, I was emotionally compromised the entire day, starting off with my hair-cutting debacle. Any other day, I'd chase him off my porch in a blink, and I open my mouth to try, but a high-pitched hiccup leaks out instead of words.

Lucas's wide grin breaks, and I cover my mouth. "Thank you for coming. And I'm sorry I ruined your family d—" A louder hiccup escapes my lips.

"How dare you say you ruined my family dinner?" He shakes his head. "You were the best part for me."

He turns and takes a slow step, swaying back and forth away. "I'll see you at the retreat tomorrow?" he asks.

I nod with a hiccup, lifting my chest and watching him drive away. I have flowers in one hand, a bag of pumpkin bars around my arm, and a rose to my lips.

I sleep with the rose in my hand the entire night and tell myself it doesn't count toward my last two times talking to the henchman.

My library killer.

Chapter Eighteen

Amelia

Step six: make a new plan and try again

I love it when the weather matches my mood.

Grandpoppy leaves me a card on the table.

Good luck on the retreat! Clyde told me all about it. Show them what a librarian is made of. I believe in you.

I slip it into my bag.

The wind and rain splash against my bedroom window, and Neme whines as I shove the only clean clothes I have inside a bag and brush through my new hairstyle with my fingers.

"Don't worry, boy." He looks at the leash again. "Carrie is coming. You love Carrie. She'll walk you the next few days. Grandpoppy will, too. It's going to be okay."

He tilts his head, and I know what he's asking.

"I'll manage." I bend down and give him a hug. I push my head up against his. I know there is no chance I will enjoy myself this weekend.

I guess one would say I woke up with a small change of heart—an updated perspective.

A thorn from the rose I slept with pulls me down from the clouds and back to Magnus Avenue. It helps jolt me awake, and I use tweezers to pull the thorn out and tape a band-aid around my finger. My realization makes me cringe more than lemon drops—my Lucas will choose the apartments over me.

I tossed and turned all night after that.

I douse my fiery feelings and smother my butterflies as long as possible. He has an admirer over at the bank anyway. I know there is no way I can compete with the girls over at the bank; they are cute, wrinkle-free clothes and know how to make pies with lattice tops.

Last night's dinner made me realize how much work I really have to do. I can't convince the Chernovs; that's clear—they don't want the library; they want apartments.

So, I'll put all my lifeblood into convincing the board. Then they'll help convince city officials to keep the library safe. A lot of board members come to the library, and they know all about the peeling paint I hide. They know how few patrons we have, and worst of all—they know me.

The rain is heavy, and the mountains hide behind the mist that expands upward. I love misty days; it makes me feel like I am drinking more oxygen, and I need the resolve of an ox to make it through any version of Lucas.

Even with his tender apology last night, I can't trust him; he only wants apartments, which means he'll take my world away from me.

He doesn't want me.

I park my car in the bus lot, in the shared parking space with the post office. My feet step out of the car, and I cover my head with my hoodie.

I have no idea what to expect at the retreat—why didn't I hunt Sandy down for a packet?

My shoulders knots are getting tighter, and I finger my thorn prick band-aid. *Good attitude*—I remind myself, *having vengeful feelings toward Lucas would be a swell of a time.*

And I'll use it to save the library—I smile; I'm back.

I pop the trunk, grab my duffle bag, and look at the small bus. The raindrops smear across the front windshield, and I walk fast to the accordion door. It opens, and I take the two short steps up into the bus.

Blaire—board member and the bus driver. He's a loyal library supporter. *Yes, he's a secured yes vote for the library.* I smile and wave at him.

Mrs. Licket walks up the aisle. Her neon blue pants make her tummy look bigger than it is. She was my piano teacher during my glorious three-month concert pianist phase before I quit. She said I lacked commitment—she'll need attention. I will have to listen to her talk about her recitals. Maybe I will have to restart lessons again?

She passes a blanket to Sandy, who is standing up between two seats. Where is her walker? I scan the ground and can see several walkers stacked up in the back.

Lucas is in the front row with an empty seat right next to him, like he is inviting me to his lap, to his side, to his *apartments.*

Never.

He looks at his phone, and I imagine him sending dollar bills and kiss emojis to the bank teller ladies.

His black and red plaid shirt is sin again; I just won't look. It is the same flannel as the pocket on his pajamas. I've seen the light and know Lucas will always choose the apartments—shielding my eyes to him will be as easy as cataloging.

My white fitted skirt with a blue half-buttoned-up shirt looks classy, convincing, and not flirty.

I have purpose and resolve.

My eyes scan the rest of the bus—only one seat left. It's on the very back left. I hold my duffle bag close and set out to part the Red Sea. I feel Lucas's eyes crawl up my back like a spider.

The tiny seat over the tire promises claustrophobia and safety from Lucas.

"Excuse me," I say to the woman with a tight white bun. Her face is tanned with sun splotches.

"Yes?"

My eyes gesture to the empty seat next to her.

"You want the wheel seat?" She touches my hand.

I nod, and a kind smile comes across her face. "I'm Gemma." I push toward the window. "You must be Amelia."

"Yes, ma'am."

Clyde, the library board director, clears his throat. "Welcome everyone!" Clyde is a loyal jogger, like a slug to a wet rock. He stops by the library to use the restroom on his jogs, and he never complains about the leaky faucet, how you have to flush the toilet twice, or the cracked floor that runs across the entire bathroom floor and stops at the toilet. He even showed me how to pop the floaty black thing in the back of the toilet to make it flush—it gets jammed regularly. I like him.

"We are excited to get away, have some fun, and hash out our strategic plan! Now, two of you are new. Can you stand and introduce yourself for a quick minute?"

I hate getting put on the spot, but I always have a few backup lines to use in most situations, so I don't have to think about it.

I stand. "Hi, I'm Amelia Anderson. I'm a librarian, and I love spending time in the library. My favorite flavor of ice cream is pistachio. I love getting caught in the rain, and I never have enough books."

Everyone usually oohs or aahs at that or even a, "She's so cute." Others would then report back to me in a month or so that they tried and now love pistachio ice cream, too. I love sharing that flavor with the world; I could be the flavor ambassador. Maybe the royalties could help fund library bathroom repairs?

Instead, there are crickets, and everyone stares at me.

Lucas tries to hide a smile—I glare at him and sit back down.

"Hold on just a minute, Amelia," Clyde says.

I sink a little deeper into the seat.

"Do you even know what we will be doing over the retreat?"

I have no idea; I should have followed through with Sandy to get the itinerary. I nod my head and say, "Yes."

"Good, you're in for a re-'treat!'" His fingers do the quotation marks right on the last syllable. Everyone laughs at his bad joke. He turns towards where the henchman is standing,

"You were put on the board in a rather unconventional way. We've been searching for board members who are under the age of 35 for some time now, so I can't tell you enough how much this means to us. Lucas?"

Lucas stands up. "Hi," he says in such a way that the entire bus says, 'Hi,' back at him. "I'm Lucas."

And everyone says, "Hi, Lucas!"

I cross my arms.

"I love exercising and building things."

"Like those muscles?" Sandy points with her crooked finger. "You were practicing those muscles recently, weren't you?" She points to the cut and red mark on his cheek. Someone sends out a cat call, and several shout a yee-haa.

I rub my forehead.

I will have to get Sandy into a new genre that has no muscles. Hobby gardening books are a safe option, or canning. I will have to dress it up in a western for her to even turn her head.

He smiles in a modest way, like he's a little embarrassed. "I like building beautiful things." He puts his hands in his pockets. "Buildings that are beautiful gathering places bring me joy. They always have; creating them is a dream." Everyone nods except me. "I think being on this board is an opportunity that I wasn't expecting but will help me in so many ways." He looks at me; I look out the window. "I'm excited to help offer ideas for the strategic plan over the weekend."

"Hear, hear," Joe cheers at that. He holds his feather hat on his head and lifts an arm up.

The bus roars on, and we start to drive away. Gemma closes her eyes and lifts her hands like she is meditating.

I pop in my EarPods.

The curves of the Blue Ridge Parkway lead me through my own roads of thought. The rain makes my window blur, so I focus on my own internal view—the only road I let myself explore is the thorn I have for my henchman.

The tight turns back and forth spark nausea and a headache. I look for motion sickness medicine in my bag and don't find any; it isn't bad enough yet. I'll tough it out.

My eyes close, and I let my forehead lean against the cool window; it helps. I doze in and out of consciousness and decide feeling sick the entire weekend isn't a great option.

After thirty minutes of my playlist, I hear a loud thud and a pop outside my window. My neck doesn't have longer than a breath to respond, and my head slams into the window hard enough that I look at the window to check for cracks.

There aren't any.

The bus starts to merge off the side of the road onto a very small pullout. I take out my EarPods and hear the tight commotion.

"What in heaven above?" Sandy hollers out over the chatter.

"Everyone stay seated," Blair's accent is strong and assertive. "I'll call roadside assistance, and we will be on our way again in no time."

"Blair, did you hit something?" Joe yells out again over the bus like he is a conversation or two behind. He looks out the back of the bus.

"I didn't hit nothing, Joe. Now sit back down until we get it fixed." Joe turns around and winks at me. He holds up his hand like he is going to tell me a secret.

"Blair always hits the potholes in the road." he leans over the seat more. "Raccoons too." Then, as if he is noticing my forehead for the first time, he says, "You got yourself a big sleep mark there, Pumpkin Spice."

I feel my forehead. The throbbing hasn't settled in after the initial shock of the flat tire. Sure enough, I feel a lump start to form like it is a wart on a pumpkin.

Blair, Clyde, and Lucas stand up; all three men walk down the two steps and out to the back of the bus to investigate. Lucas points to the tire right outside my window and leans over, starting to look underneath the bus. He points to the back area of the bus, and both men walk back around. They pop the back and start taking out luggage, and I peek back. Underneath the back panel are a jack, tire wrench, bolts, and other tools I don't know.

My headache presses down, and I need some fresh air, so I step over Gemma and walk up the aisle and out the doors. Cool and damp air hits my face, and I attempt to breathe out the wave of nausea. The storm has let up a little, and soft, tiny drops catch in my lashes and cool my forehead.

"We've got everything under control," Blair says as I walk toward the flat. He points to the bus. "Go back on in there, Milly. We've got this; you'll get soaked."

I don't object; I just don't move. "I need the fresh air," I say.

Lucas's legs are sticking out of the side of the bus. "I can see the spare. It looks a little old."

I bend down and can see up Lucas's nose. He taps something, and dust fills the air. He coughs.

"Do you even know what you're doing?" I ask.

He lifts his head. "Milly."

I ignore his tender tone.

"Yeah, I know what I'm doing."

I stand up, crossing my arms. "I think we should call roadside assistance." There is no way I trust a library killer.

Lucas stands up, brushes off his clothes, and stands way too close to my face. His man soap is faint today. Good, he'll be less poisonous.

"There is no service here; Blair tried." He looks into my eyes, and I wonder what part of last night he is thinking about—when I dropped my drinking glass? When his brothers laughed at me? His kiss on my hand?

"You'll get dirty." I'm not thinking as clearly as I want to. He is already a mess and getting wet with every passing minute.

"Do you doubt me?" Lucas asks.

I don't answer. He reaches up and touches my forehead, and I feel the warmth pool into my stomach. I pull back.

Lucas lets his eyes wrinkle. "Don't worry, Milly. I've got it."

"Which is entirely why I am worried."

"Your forehead doesn't look good. It would be best if you sat down." His tone is confident.

Blair walks up, and Lucas points to my forehead. "Milly, your forehead looks like a baseball bat got you on its follow-through. Don't worry about this, honey."

"It looks worse than it is." At least, that's what I imagine.

Lucas squints at me. "Fine. I'm glad you don't have a headache or anything." He takes a small step back. "I need an assistant." He plops the jack down and crouches over. He starts to twist the jack. "I believe you are a perfect person to help. Amelia, do you think you can get everyone off the bus?"

My nostrils flare as I take a deep breath.

"I need everyone off the bus, and I know you know how to manage all types of personalities."

"You mean I'm bossy."

He smiles.

I turn, and the rain begins to come down in sheets as I climb back on the bus and channel my inner Lucas, faking nice through my head throb. I do a decent job getting everyone off the bus and helping them keep high spirits. Joe smiles the entire time I hold his hand and guide him down the small trail to benches and a pavilion that seems to be the start of a nearby trailhead.

When everyone is settled and every spare umbrella except one is being used, I take it and go back to Lucas. He is wiggling the old tire, his shirt stuck to his body, and his face twists as he lifts the tire off the long bolts.

I run up to him and hold the umbrella above his head. He rolls the tire to the back, and I follow him, keeping him covered. He has the spare tire out, and he rolls back, dripping, and I am mesmerized watching his defined arm muscles flex as he lifts the tire up to the bolts. He wiggles the tire on, and I look away.

Thorn, Amelia—I rub my band-aid again.

"I will have to apologize, Amelia Anderson."

Finally.

"That my looks are off the charts right now."

His arrogance is out of control. I cluck my tongue, "Lucas, I still don't want to talk to you. Rose or not." The umbrella pulls as the wind picks up a little, and his tender eyes drink me up. It is cruel. "Don't look at me that way." I look at the road. "You're the only one that can get this bus going again."

I force my gaze into his eyes—I can't take it and bend down to the tire. He moves away and continues spinning the bar around, tightening up the bolts.

We are silent as I keep the umbrella over him, and the rain begins to lighten up.

"We're almost done," he says as he tightens the last bolt. He twists the wheel and makes sure it is sturdy. "It will do," he says as he twists the handle on the jack, and the spare tire lowers back to the ground.

He pulls the jack out right as I see the car.

It comes fast around the curve, and I am surprised at how much the water spreads like a large wing. I feel arms wrap around me and pull me tight against a wet, muscular body.

Lucas.

He cocoons me up and slams his body into the bus as the car barrels past us. The sheet of water splashes over us like a wave. The car brake lights light up as they realize they almost hit me.

I don't move. His warm body presses against mine, and I feel his heart beating through his chest.

His chin brushes near my ear. "Amelia," his voice is rougher. I feel warmth surge from my toes up to my arms, where he is holding me. "Are you okay?" he asks.

In the smallest moment of weakness, I close my eyes and swim in his warmth and the swirling awareness of his skin. "Thank you," I say, letting his softness pull me in.

A voice interrupts, "Sorry to ruin a moment," Blair says.

I pull away.

"It looks like you are the flat tire hero, Lucas. Can we load back up?" he asks.

Lucas nods.

He can't know the power of his touch, so I force my cheeks to behave. "What cut you?" I ask. Blood runs down his hand, and I'm surprised it didn't get on me.

"Not sure." He wipes it on his pants.

Blair walks a little down the muddy path and cups his hands, "Let's load up, troopers!" The others cheer as I check my watch. Less than thirty minutes.

I find the first-aid kit underneath Blair's seat and pull out an alcohol pad and a band-aid.

He cleans up the tools and pushes the flat tire up toward the entrance of the bus. He bends over the tire. "It doesn't look like he hit anything; I think it was just too tread bare."

I frost my heart and snatch his hand, ripping open the alcohol pad. "How did you know how to change a tire so fast, on a bus no less?"

I scrub at the blood. He grimaces; I smile.

He watches me. "Practice," he finally says.

"I don't believe that's the only variable." I'm not blushing, and I keep my tone even.

I twist the band-aid around his finger. It isn't that deep, but it needs more than one band-aid. I have Blair pass down the kit, and I find another band-aid.

He points to my band-aid. "Paper cut from your books?" he asks.

I lower my voice. "Your rose."

He stares at me, and I hope he catches all my meaning. I turn to climb back to my corner.

Lucas waits for everyone to get on the bus before he loads up the flat tire.

Sandy shouts, "Mr. Muscles, are you up to date on your tetanus shot? Heaven only knows how rusty this bus is."

"Lucas is fine," I blurt out.

"It does sting," he states, "but I think it's a small price to pay to make this trip a win."

Sandy starts clapping. "You deserve a round of applause, baby." Everyone claps, and Lucas smiles at me. I look out the window again, this time not so close.

It is my heart I am disappointed in.

Chapter Nineteen

Lucas

My face needs to relax; I'm being a baby about my finger. It was in the way as I hoisted the new tire onto the rusty bolts. I didn't shout; I didn't want to scare away Amelia. Not any more than I already have.

Mr. Blair pulls into the parking stall. My heart feels raw for what I put her through last night. Her talk about the library and her management of it are inspirational and good.

It's clear how much I've hurt her, and I can't think about anything else until I make it right.

I scroll back over my text with Mitchell.

> Me: *I've run into some unexpected complications. Let's consider modifying our original location. There might be an al-*

ternative that works better for the town and can yield the same profits.

Mitchell hasn't responded yet, and I figure my cell service won't work once we reach the cabins. I hunted down Mr. Clyde for a packet last week and had time to think about how to use this time to make plans to my advantage.

I frown. I don't know what advantage looks like anymore.

A message pops up.

Apollo: *Is the spreadsheet up to date?*

Me: *thumbs up emoji. I shared it with all the brothers, too. I want to make things right, Apollo. I bumped up the word* re-prove *last week.*

Apollo: *salute emoji.*

Me: *Put the best options up next. You didn't answer my last text. Can I go out of order?*

I don't like the last three: rename, repave, resile. I thought it was reprove, so I used that earlier, and nope, I was wrong.

Apollo: *Stick to the list. I'm okay if you change the order; just record it. And just in case you didn't get my hint at dinner last night, it's a confirmed hole punch marinated in dog drool. Repeat, a dog DID NOT eat your inheritance passcode. We'll start digging in to figure it out.*

I shove my hands in my hair; someone is trying to sabotage our inheritance.

Me: *Fine. Thanks. I'll add the ones I like. I think I'll be out of service.*

Apollo: *thumbs up emoji.*

Apollo: *kiss emoji, makeup with the librarian. I like her.*

The feeling is mutual—and I've got service. Mitchell just isn't responding.

Apollo is such a good kid. I equally hate and love all my brothers. It's worse than being on a long see-saw all day. Is that normal? Am I normal?

I look back at Amelia; she is listening to her seat partner. The way her eyes open wide and her ears perk when she listens is intoxicating. The rawness in my chest feels like it will make me pop or go mad.

I wipe my face; I am glad I came. Changing a tire in the rain is something I'd never tried. Amelia will be safe from my brothers' reach here; Kim's venom can't reach here either. I want every free moment with Amelia to make it right, to prove to her that I am trustworthy.

I let re___e words dance through my mind. The sooner I get the passcode, the sooner I can mend things with my brothers—reshine, release, reawake. I smile, reptile.

Why can't Dad be normal and give us normal inheritances?

Amelia's hair has dried halfway from all the rain and lays comfortably along her face. Brian brought a masterpiece to life.

Everyone gathers up their things as we funnel out of the bus. A shaky hand lands on my shoulder. "I know the best thing for a hurt hand."

My eyes meet the woman who commented on my muscles. "Sandy?"

She nods as she searches through her purse. Her glossy eyes read each tube she pulls out of her bag. "Here!" She hands me pink lotion with red kiss logos all over it.

I take the bottle. "Sweetheart's Touch?" I raise my brow high.

She pushes it toward me as I try to give it back. "You should read the instructions; it says to have someone else do the application." She winks, and I bite my cheek. She points behind her to Amelia, who has magically appeared behind her.

"Sandy...no meddling," Amelia cuts in.

Sandy leans closer. "Just try it; you'll see the magic."

"Promise," I say.

She smiles wide as Blair helps her to the group gathering outside.

Amelia studies the bottle, then jerks it out of my hands. Her cheeks match the kiss color as she reads the back of the bottle.

I like it.

She starts to walk out with the lotion, and I lean over her back and tug it up from her hands.

"Lucas, look!" She does the old trick: look at what I'm looking at out the window. I fall for it, and she jerks the lotion out of my hands and runs off the bus. I can see her practically skip away.

I grab both my bags and step off the bus.

The camp director is a tall, willowy man. His cargo pants have all the extra pockets bulging full, and the brim of his hat is extra wide with an attached bug net rolled up in the back.

Clyde counts the group once I arrive.

The camp director clears his throat. "Welcome! We are hosting the southern cities and organizational training all this week. We share the facilities with all campers, and new friends rotate in at their reserved time." He points to the nearest large cabin. "The main cabin is open until eleven each evening. Your customized rotations of our camp offerings start tomorrow. Your schedule is posted inside your rooms. Oh," he points to Clyde, "speaking of which, can I have a word?" Clyde nods his head and steps off near the edge of the group.

I take a step closer to the talking men.

"I didn't know you'd have this many," Clyde says.

Amelia steps in, too, but then I'm so focused on her nearness that I can't hear the rest of what they are discussing.

The camp director steps back over to the group. "If you go inside, you'll see your assigned cabin." The board is unusually even, five men and five women, and Amelia and I push the numbers up to twelve.

Clyde walks over to Amelia and me, rubbing his hands together. "Sooo." He blinks more than he usually does. "I thought Sandy had requested two extra beds for you both. The message didn't make it in time."

I know where this is going. "We don't have beds," I say.

"They're booked up. There isn't any room in our cabins either; we had to get the ADA ones, and we've maxed the number of campers for them both per their policy."

I nod and watch Amelia's wide eyes.

"Are there any tents we can use?" Amelia asks.

Clyde opens his mouth but stops before he makes eye contact. "Yes, but there was a bear sighting last week. Your options are to sleep on the bus, sleep in an older cabi—"

I cut him off. "What cabin?" I ask.

"Well, they are all full except one," Clyde grimaces.

He puts his arm on my shoulder. "I'll give you my spot—"

"No," I cut him off.

He looks at Amelia. "I'll see who wants to trade spots with you then, Amelia, so I don't..." *make you both sleep in the same cabin.*

Alone.

Amelia shakes her head. "Clyde, don't do that. I know our coming wasn't part of your original plan." She looks at me and blinks twice as if she is saying words without thinking, "We'll make it work."

Impulsive creature—she squirms like an overactive kitten, looking everywhere except at me.

Clyde takes a deep breath. "I'm so relieved. We know you two aren't—well, I was at the meeting." He shows his teeth. "You two gave quite the show." He looks down at the ground. "I think I just asked a cat and dog to room together."

"You did," I cut in. But from the sounds of it, there are four beds in a cabin. We can have a canyon of space between us.

I look at Amelia. "You promise you won't cut my hair, glue my mouth shut, or poison my toothpaste?" I want Clyde as a second witness just in case Amelia jumps on an idea that she'll later regret, and I'll have to deal with the consequences. Again.

She lets a small smile out. "Don't tempt me."

I nod. "She will promise not to succumb to any temptation." I look at Clyde. "Promise I'll be a gentleman. I'll stay in my own room."

He nods. "It's settled. They'll show you the last open cabin," he says. "It's down by the lake."

I wink at her and watch her face blossom spring pink.

Clyde lets out a sigh and leans into me. "I was more worried about what she'd do to you. I'd sleep with one eye open."

My very life could be in danger, but the promise of spending more time with Amelia is worth the risk.

The camp director has one of his staff members drive us down to the lake in a golf cart. I sit in the back and hold tight to the side—the path is gravel and has a steady decline as it drops down to the lake. The clouds are starting to push out to the edges of the sky, and the sun is warming up the air. I turn my head to get a full view of the bowl-shaped lake—the rainwater tops it off, and the vibrant orange, yellow, and red trees reflect off the lake. I'm glad the rain hasn't taken down all the leaves yet.

Other cabins pepper the hillside close by the main cabin. Adults I don't recognize are splashing and screaming out in canoes on the cool lake.

He drops us off and tells us it is the unlocked cabin.

Amelia runs up to the nicest cabin and shakes her head. "It's locked."

I walk to the smaller cabin next to it. It has a broken window, the rain gutter has been ripped off, and the door is cracked open.

"Hello?" I say as I walk in. I flip on the light. No power.

I go to the small sink—It works. I wash the grease and dust off my hands and arms. I open my bag and take out a towel. My damp clothes will take forever to dry.

The wind blew in leaves and rain and must have opened the door.

Amelia walks in and goes straight to the room just off the main room. There are not four beds to choose from—one bed in the room and one couch in the main room. Maybe it is an old staff cabin? Or just for couples?

"Interesting," she says, and she turns on her phone light. The curtains are closed, making that room dark and cozy.

She screams, drops her phone, and runs behind me.

"What?"

She points as a small raccoon runs out of the room and clamors out the open door. She holds my arm tight.

"You okay?"

She unclamps her hand. "Oh my." her hand flies to her forehead where her lump is.

"You don't like raccoons?" I ask.

She sneaks back into the room, grabs her bag and phone, and jumps back out. "Not where I was hoping to sleep," she says.

I laugh as she rubs her arms, her clothes still damp from the storm.

"I can't sleep in there," she says.

"You want to share the couch?" I ask, making my tone hopeful. She swats the same arm she just held.

She sits on the couch. "I'm not going back into that room."

I nod and turn the corner into the room. I pull out my phone and turn on the light. The bed blankets look messy, and I see rodent feces along the floor.

"I don't blame you," I say. "I'll sleep in here." I push back the curtains, letting the light in. I don't want Amelia to sleep somewhere she doesn't feel safe.

My bag drops by the bedroom door, and I watch her shiver again.

"Thank you," she says.

I open the cabin door and step out to give her privacy.

I follow the path up the inclined hill, rubbing my hurt hand with every step, thinking about 'Sweetheart's Touch.'

Ten minutes later, I make it to the main cabin—the retreat is already more exciting than I can bargain for.

Chapter Twenty

Lucas

The schedule is full—I hold the paper in my bandaged hand. The flat tire doesn't put us behind schedule at all. I haven't seen Amelia for forty-five minutes, and I'm too prideful to admit that I probably need stitches—and a shower, too.

I breathe through my nose—I can do this: icebreakers, dinner around the fire, workshops, and service activities today and tomorrow cleaning cabins, and then heading back on Sunday.

And kiss Amelia to complicate everything.

I shake my head and take in the main cabin. It's full of all the board members except Amelia. Sandy catches my eye and winks at me. I look away and chart a path around the room to avoid her.

The main cabin has wooden floors, old couches along the edges, and plush polyester curtains pulled back on every window: cedar, earth, and old furniture dust linger in the air. Yellowish doilies and nature pictures are on every windowsill, and two large fireplaces are on the outside walls, with cross-stitched Bible scriptures framed above both mantels.

My eyes snag on Sandy again, who's still watching me, biting her lower lip. I might have to add eighty-year-olds to my "beware" list.

I check my phone, and there are no bars, just SOS in the top right corner.

Refute, rescue, revive. Rescue or revive, maybe? I like both of those words a lot. Rejoice, rewrite, receive. "Re, re, re," I mutter under my breath.

I put my phone down, scan the room, and scratch my head. I need to socialize—that's the backbone of my game plan this weekend—and win Amelia's over.

In the first circle I pass, a woman with noticeable buck teeth is talking loudly. I pass.

"Oh, that chicken was the best they've served yet. I believed it when they told me it converted the entire congregation. Could you imagine heavenly chicken with a side of coleslaw?"

I move toward the front.

"Do you see why I think taxes really aren't as high as all the townies think?" A man wearing jean overalls say., "The housing market is cheaper by a hundred k.. If people started to think about the entire financial ecosystem of money flow within our city, they would begin to see that the flow of money is critical to get things done." His voice rings through the group. Neither of the women blinks, frozen like the man in overalls doesn't know how to have a two-sided conversation.

The chill of the rainwater lingers on everyone, and both fireplaces are overcrowded. I glance out the window and see Amelia walking slowly up the dirt path. She bends down to collect something—pinecones. Each time she bends down to get one, another slips out. She tucks in her shirt and seems to scold herself. Her damp hair lies against her chest and back, smooth with soft curls. She's changed into a dark blue hoodie and jeans, making her look like someone I could laugh half the night away with.

I need a drink of water and start to search for it when Clyde walks up and pats me on the shoulder. "You really saved us today. Thank you." He shakes my bandaged hand. "My back freezes up now and again," he says, bending his back. "Thank you, Lucas." He pulls me a little closer, tugging at my cut through the wrap, and says in a quiet tone, "I know why you're here. Your presentation at the city meeting was impressive. Go soft on Amelia. She hasn't had it easy."

He nods and steps away as two older women stumble in front of me. The younger one says, "Sandy told us...you're single." Her hair has enough hairspray to be an ideal bug trap.

I am no bug.

The older woman has white hair that is cut tight to her head. "Boy, oh boy, do we have the best thing for you!" Her smile is flat, and one of her eyes droops.

Both women look related, and I force myself to crack a smile.

I want allies. What I need are real friends who can help Amelia through this transition.

"My granddaughter is the sweetest thing on this side of the Mississippi." The white-haired woman holds out her phone with a photo on it. Her shaky hand makes it hard to focus on her photo.

A blonde. I always seem to get matched with blondes. Maybe she'd be Amelia's perfect friend. I don't know of anyone Amelia talks to who isn't a library patron, her grandfather, or her dog.

I can deflect earnest mothers in my sleep. But I see Amelia by the fire out of the corner of my eye.

"Wow!" I say. "She looks great." I really do despise mothers who thrust their daughters in my path.

"Mom, show him the family photos we took last year." The bug-trap-haired woman takes the phone and starts swiping.

"You know she's the assistant at the Holy Sheep Shop," the grandmother says.

I glance at Amelia, who's rubbing her arms as she leans into the fire.

"The sheep cheese factory outside of town?" I ask, staring at Amelia's bulging pockets.

Bug trap lady nods a stiff bob. I imagine a bug getting scooped up in her side-winged hairstyle. "You get all the free samples you'd like if you know the right someone..." she says.

Both women frame a smile, and I am disenchanted with faking interest anymore. My smile drops for a moment as I collect my thoughts, and I feel a soft touch on my elbow.

"I need Lucas for a moment, Mary and Maryanne. Do you mind?"

Her hand is cold, but it warms my blood.

Both women smile with an eye squint that is polite but loaded with flavor.

"Anything for you, Milly," the bug trap lady says.

Milly shoots the same smile back. She pulls me over to the fire. "Have you not been warned about the mother-daughter duo?" she asks.

I like that she's still holding onto my elbow. "You rescued me, Pumpkin," I say.

She pulls her hands away and rubs them against the fire. "Don't get used to it." she glances over her shoulder. Both women are talking in a hushed tone, staring back at us. "You are giving me the couch," she murmurs.

I nod. "You know, normal people wouldn't see that as a positive?"

She nods. "Good thing I'm not normal."

Her self-awareness does the worst thing to my body; it warms my skin from the inside. I take a step closer to her.

She stares up at me, and I can see the green mingled with the golden specks again. "I think I'm beginning to prefer not normal."

Clyde's voice cuts our trance. "Board members," he continues without everyone listening "get ready for team-building activities!"

My flinch and moan are loud. Amelia covers her soft laugh with her hand—her smile is one of the most genuine on the planet, and it makes her face sparkle.

"For me, normal means that you're not true to yourself, that you have to be someone that you're not, or that you have to live up to someone's expectation of what normal is. So, Amelia, your 'not normal' interactions are becoming the most refreshing ones I've had in a long time."

I watch her swallow, realizing those were some of the most honest words I'd shared in a while.

I rub the throb in my chest—if I pick the path of demolishing the library, I will be the one to break it—her smile and her not-normal self.

Get-to-know-you games have got to go on my list of worst things to endure. At each icebreaker game, they reward you with first-grader treats like Skittles, M&M's, or Suckers. The attempt to bribe falls flat. But not for Amelia. Her loud cheers have everyone turning, wishing they could be her partner. In a matter of two hours, I've become irritable. It's because of the get-to-know-you games. Or maybe it's because I'm not in Amelia's group.

We have lunch in breakout sessions and assemble humanitarian kits and school supplies for a local school district. I'm not in Amelia's group again, and I focus on the bags, helping assemble hundreds of kits with hygiene products, writing materials, and books.

We're finally wrapping up our long day, and I stretch my arms and hands out. I need rest and have looked forward to spending time with Amelia all day.

I'll show her the data tomorrow, see how she responds, and go from there.

"It's hot dogs and s'mores tonight!" Clyde says as he goes to the back corner where the kitchen is.

My stomach clenches and growls, and I hop up to get the fire started.

The cool air weaves into my nostrils; pine mixed with tree bark and wet leaves mingle in the air. I take lots of deep breaths and search for dry wood. I find some neatly stacked and covered near a shed and start the fire.

Everyone pours outside with jackets on, pointing up at the sunset. Purple and blue clouds splash the sky as the sun dips behind the mountain range, and I want to find a way to walk with Amelia around the lake.

I see a blue hoodie slip out and join the food line. She walks up to the fire but keeps her focus on her plate.

"Do you know everyone's names?" I ask her as I poke the fire.

She nods and pushes some of her hair behind her ear. She keeps a Dumdum sucker in her mouth. Amelia's lips perk up. "I wanted to warn you." She studies her blue sucker. "I am going to win everyone over here, so you should just give up now." She purses her lips. "I don't want to talk about what happened with your family, but—" she puts the sucker back into her mouth—"I will win the board. You just wait, Lucas Chernov. You just wait." Her eyes twinkle, and her voice is strong. She leans into the fire, warming the backs of her hands.

My heart pricks, and I drink in Amelia Pumpkin Spice Anderson. My eyes trace the outline of her long hair poking out of her hoodie. The curl and color match everything about her; it just had to be uncovered for me to see it. My eyes follow her lips, smacking and puckering at her sucker.

"You think?" I ask, rubbing my hands and placing them over the fire, moving closer to her. The air chills my damp socks and shoes. I curl my toes tight. I can't look at her lips again. "Amelia, I don't—"

She holds up her sucker. "I'm only talking to you because you gave me the couch and because you sorta saved my life today." She tries to lift one eyebrow, closing the other eye.

I lift one of my eyebrows and keep both eyes open.

"Not fair." She points to my brow. "Will you teach me sometime?"

"To arch an eyebrow?" I let out a small chuckle.

She nods.

"For you, yes." I watch the fire reflected in her green eyes.

She stands up. "Last free tip before I go back and win votes."

I lift one eyebrow again. "Go on."

"I overheard Sandy has plans to dance with you tomorrow night." Her cheeks blush as she pushes the sucker into her mouth.

I cross my arms. "I will only if you dance with me, too."

She freezes. I take her smile as a yes. "If she asks about the lotion, say you lost it, got it."

I lift my eyebrow one more time and nod my head. She smiles wide, pushing the sucker stick to the side of her mouth.

Joe walks over with Sandy to the fire, holding his arm. He lowers Sandy down, right by me.

I let out a nervous cough and poke the fire. Small embers fly up. Amelia disappears into the mingling crowd.

"It's ghost story time, kid!" Joe's eyes look a little bloodshot, matching the wild feathers in his hat, but no one else seems worried. I let him take over the entire conversation while I watch Amelia weave in and out of different circles.

Her laugh fills my soul.

Joe rants on about legends, hidden or lost things in Herasburg, and his war stories. He catches my attention when he talks about his current goals: to find a lost cannonball in the Marrow River, a hidden jail cell, and a hidden gold mine on Dinky Hill. His feathered hat bobs up and down as he shares the things

Amelia helped him find in history books in the library. If anyone sat close to him, he would have poked them in the eye.

Amelia seems to bring out the not-normal, real, authentic, genuine side of everyone around her. I leave Sandy's side a few times to add more wood and return each time. She pats my leg in approval—she can see through the fire what I'm focusing on.

Amelia.

Chapter Twenty-One

Lucas

The water swallows up the last burning embers of the fire. Joe could talk for hours, but I don't want him to prove it. When I see Amelia bringing the leftovers back into the kitchen, I tell Joe he should go to bed. I make sure everyone gets safely back to their cabins, and I linger by the main cabin for three more minutes, hoping I can walk down with her.

She turns off the lights and steps out.

"Hi," I say. "Can I walk with you?"

She puts her hands in her pockets. "I was hoping you would. I don't know how I feel about meeting a bear alone."

"Not on your agenda?"

She shakes her head. "It doesn't help save the library, so sadly, no."

We walk in silence for a few moments. "If the library's fate were not endangered by a 'library killer,'" I point to myself, "I have been wondering what you would be focusing on right now."

Her pace slows, and she takes a deep breath. "You just had to ask, didn't you?"

I know what I would be doing, and it certainly wouldn't be having a moonlit stroll with a firecracker of a librarian. I frown at the thought.

"To be honest, I'd probably be looking for someone," she clears her throat, "to fall in love with, or at minimum, a date. I need a date for a friend's dinner at the beginning of the year."

My smile presses against the cut on my cheek. "You need that much time to find a date?"

She lets out a nervous laugh and plays with her hoodie strings. "I know, it's kind of pathetic. I wanted to convince my friend that Neme would pass as a date. I come off kind of intense, so yeah, it takes me a long time to find someone willing to give me a try."

I swallow. Every one of her intensities, I want all to myself.

"Amelia Anderson would want to love something other than her library?" She pushes my arm. I wish I were quick enough to grab her hand, but I'm not.

"You're going to think I'm crazy..." Her words are light, and I wish I could see her smile in the dark.

"Too late, so there's nowhere but up from here."

She laughs again, and it echoes against the dark wall of trees that surround us. A few crickets rub their feet, and the wind flows through our hair.

"In all fairness, you've survived a night with my family. You've seen what Chernovs are like. If you don't think we're all crazy, I don't know what is."

She pauses, and I can tell she's debating how much to say. "Promise you won't laugh?"

I hold up my pinky. She shakes it, and I don't let it go. Our hands drop to our legs—she doesn't pull away.

The hum between us has always been there, and I'm ready to admit that. I want to lean into it as much as she'll let us. I want to stop lying to myself; this is a woman I want to be close to.

She swallows. "I've always wanted to fall in love with a bookworm."

My laugh sneaks out, and she pulls her hand away.

I cough and straighten up. "I'm sorry. I wasn't expecting that."

She puts her hands on her cheeks. "I know it sounds silly."

I put my hand out in front of me, making my intentions clear. For three steps, she hesitates, then slowly touches the palm of my hand, then spreads her hand wide and slips her fingers between mine. She's cold, and I love how my large hands cover hers like a blanket.

"What's your definition of a bookworm?"

The low sounds of the forest wrap around, growing louder as we walk farther down the trail.

"I guess there are two qualifiers I need to explain."

I squeeze her hand as an invitation to keep talking. It's like teasing a kitten out from a stack of hay—and I'm holding warm milk.

I can't blame her after my family, and Kim running her out.

"Mom and I spent a lot of time in the library like I shared with your family, and I know it's silly, but I guess somewhere along the way, the library felt like it was...mine. Naturally, my future bookmate would fall in love with me in 'my library,' Lionstone Library. He'd love reading as much as I do, and we'd play hide and seek in the library, sit in the sun, and hold hands while we read, or I'd stare at him while he was reading...we'd eat a ring pop sucker together, and then we'd go play in the river when we needed to stretch our legs."

"Amelia, how old were you when you decided on this?"

She lets out another soft laugh. "No going to answer that." Our pace continues to slow. "I really haven't been into too many guys in my life, so I never revised what I really wanted in a relationship; that was my next life step—before I heard about the rezoning of the library land, that is." She lets out a long, deep breath. "After mom died, I took care of my grandparents. I worked two jobs. I didn't really socialize much, and I wanted to make sure I took care of the family that I had left. So when my grandmother passed, Grandpoppy really encouraged me to go to college and graduate school. He said, 'Life is too short. And getting a graduate degree changed the course of your mother's life.'" She kicks a rock on the path. "I focused on my studies and went home on the weekends to be with Grandpoppy and Nemean. I never really dated."

"Why didn't you start dating after you graduated?"

She smiled. "I tried. Like I said, I'm intense."

I smile and pull her close. Her genuine self seeps into the cold crevasse of my stone heart and makes it pump—I breathe in her campfire and floral lotion scent.

"I imagine you never wished for things that were childish. I bet you were an eight-year-old businessman who finalized building projects every year." She says, then with a lowered voice, she adds, "Hi there, city. I can knock you all off your socks with my charm, bar graphs, and, might I say, my perfectly styled hair."

I touch my hair like it's fresh-baked bread. "You're right. It is perfect." She shoves my arm again while she laughs.

I lean into her shoulder. "When I was ten, I wanted to build a tower to the moon. It was the best idea I'd had up to date." I lift my hand to the visible part of the moon.

She lets out a little laugh. "Why a tower to the moon?"

I look up to the sky. "I wanted a big enough house for all my family to come live in, where we could all have our own...slides."

She laughs.

"Did you tell your dad or your mom about this brilliant proposition?"

I nod. "I did. I guess that's why Dad built me Olympus."

"Olympus?" She leans forward and looks into my face. The reflection of the moon dances along her cheeks.

"It's a treehouse."

Her eyes glow. "I have never seen Olympus, and I've been to your house tons. I have to..." her voice trails off.

One of my eyebrows pops up, and I tug one of her fingers to my brow and let her trace it. I swear I hear her voice hitch.

My voice is more gravelly now. "Our rule was to never share it with our friends." The cabin is in view. "How else do you think Mom survived when all my half-brothers came to visit? If we kept it a secret, then it stayed special to us. I haven't been there for years. I'll show you sometime...if it's a date?" I hold my breath, worried I've pushed her away again.

"I think I'd like that."

We arrive at the cabin, and I tug her arm to the lake. "Walk with me."

We walk in silence and our pace matches. "Tell me about your mom." My thumb swirls in a slow circle around her hand. I want to walk all night long with her hand in mine.

"Mom was determined and kindhearted." She shakes her head. "Her world changed when she was a teen pregnancy statistic, though." The soft pulse of the lake against the rocks relaxes my shoulder. "She got pregnant when she was eighteen, and my father supposedly disappeared. Mom never talked about him. Mom and my grandparents raised me. She worked at the factory outside of town but then one day decided to go back to college to make a better life for us."

"Did she finish her degree?"

She nods. "In English. Go figure. She was a teacher at the high school."

"I don't remember a Miss Anderson."

She tugs on my arm. "She started teaching freshman English when you were a senior. But...she knew who you were."

My hair rubs along my forehead as I shake my head. "I was a tough nut to crack back then."

She smiles. "I know. Not much has changed."

"Were you ever in her class?"

Our pant legs brush as she starts to walk slower. "Yeah, I was in her first class right after she graduated—her first real full-time class." She looks down and kicks a few of the rocks again.

I squeeze her hand again as a whisper to keep sharing.

"I wasted the final year I had with her." Her voice is soft.

"What do you mean?"

She lets out a long sigh and takes in the lake, letting the thrum of nature surround us more. "When Mom was diagnosed with ALS, it was the kind that attacks your mouth first—speech and breathing. Bulbar ALS. I didn't take the news well at all..." She wipes her cheek. "You know why Joe calls me Pumpkin Spice?"

I have wondered.

"Losing Mom meant losing everything. So, I took it out on her while she was still alive." I can see the tear stains on her cheeks now. "I skipped school. I never went to her class, and I never went back to the library. Reading was something we shared. My friends and I even toilet papered the library once or twice; I even painted a scene of burning books in all black and red on the underpass leaving town..."

I stop walking and lift my thumb to her chin. I wipe both of her cheeks. Everything about *her* makes all the sense in the world now.

The moon touches her lips, and I can't stop staring. My feet take a small step toward her, and I hover over her lips. She doesn't move. I move as close as my self-control allows, and then I stop.

I let her decide which way to go.

I feel her breath flutter, and her finger rubs over the band-aid on her hand, still resting in mine.

I hold my position. One heartbeat, two heartbeats, three heartbeats, four heartbeats—my skin is burning.

I don't want to force her into anything she'll regret, but I know kissing Amelia is the first thing I'll do in years that I won't regret.

My chest swirls as I feel her lean.

I can feel her skin on the corner of my mouth, a sliver of a touch. Her lips open as she speaks. "Unwritten rule—" she pauses— "No kissing library killers."

She pulls away, and the cool of the night nips at me as I watch her run back to the cabin.

I want to burn her rules.

Chapter Twenty-Two

Amelia

I run, and my chest heaves.

With some sleep, my resolve will be stronger. That was too close—way too close. All my indicators of *real* nice blaze inside my head. Was Lucas kind, thoughtful, and wonderful, and had I been blinded because of the library? What villain wants a treehouse and slide for each of his brothers? I lean against the outside of the cabin to slow my heart, watching him walk slowly along the lake in the moonlight.

I can usually talk about Mom now without crying, and I practically lay bare my entire heart. If I wasn't mistaken, he fully accepted every single piece.

I push open the cabin door, turning on my phone flashlight to scan the entire cabin to make sure I'm alone.

A kiss would have sealed my fate, and I've never wanted it more—like waiting years to get the final book in a series or wanting to know the end of a story more than anything, but you don't peek ahead.

It's all those combined, plus a cherry on top and extra cool whip.

But can I love a library killer?

I open my bag and take out another painkiller for my head; I imagine sleep will be the best thing for me now. Not kissing.

The window lets moonlight fill the room, and a flashlight bobs out by the lake.

My goosebumps activate, and I decide to add extra layers of clothes as PJs. I pull out every shirt I brought and slip them on. My sweats fit over my pants. Good. A little better—the popping gooseflesh comes down a notch.

The cold, stiff leather of the couch seeps through my sweats. Oh...so not cozy. Just in case I can't control myself, I slip my shoes on, too, for good measure; if I need to run away from Lucas again when I can't control myself, I'll be ready.

The door creaks open.

"Lucas?"

He steps in, his light staying on the ground as he closes the door, sealing my fate. "It barely stays closed. A small wind could open it," his steps are stiff as he picks up his bag and drops it by the door. "There, that's the best security system I can get you."

I hug my knees.

Lucas takes a few things out of his bag and goes to the bathroom.

The night is projected to get down to the thirties, and I can't admit how ill-prepared I am. The small blanket I brought will only cover my legs. If Neme were here, he'd chase away the critters and keep me warm.

I'm not going to survive the night.

Lucas comes out, and I flash my light toward him. "Are those your favorite PJs?"

He pinches the plaid pocket. "Yep, you found out about my secret. Flannel PJs with bad jokes on them are my favorite," he says.

"Too bad you don't have a reason to run through the meeting cabin. I think Sandy would give you a double wink."

He tosses me a crooked smile and shakes his head.

"Whoever bought you those, I like the way they think." Our near kiss makes the empty air between us feel like there isn't enough oxygen. The faster sleep comes, the better. I clear my throat. "I'm tired. I'm going to try to get some sleep. Night."

He nods and disappears into the other room. I hear him shuffle around, and he steps back out and opens the cabin door, tossing out the blankets that had been on the bed.

"That should help the smell." He says, and he disappears back into the room. I feel the floor bend and creak.

"Are you sleeping on the ground?" I yell through the paper-thin wall.

A grunt of a moan sounds through the wall. I laugh. "Good night, Amelia," he yells out.

I rub my band-aid. "Thanks for helping again with the tire." He pushes himself along the ground to where his door is and peeks his head out.

"You mean saving your life?" His voice is soft.

"Yes. Thank you, Lucas." I rub my eyes. "Good night, for reals."

"Good night for reals, Pumpkin Spice," he says. I curl up to the arm of the chair and let out a silent shiver.

It takes my mind an eon to get off the almost kiss and his strong arms saving me. That should not have been the last thing I brought to our attention before bed. But it was.

Lucas is still in the doorway; his eyes are closed. I hear his deep breathing, and my shivering slows. I think I doze off until I hear it—soft enough to stay hidden but loud enough for my sensitive eyes to pop open like a confetti can.

It doesn't come from the door or even Lucas's room. It comes from across the room where the cabinet is.

It's a nibbling sound. Then a crunch. Then, a small shriek.

"Oh, my holy book stack," I whimper.

Crunch, crunch, crunch.

I'm sure it's coming from the cabinet, so I put the blanket over my head. A small squeak follows. A mouse? But then it does a low-pitched grunt that is not a mouse squeak.

My fingers push my ears tight, and I decide staying camouflaged on the couch is the best option.

Then I hear a small hiss.

There's more than one. I pull the blanket back. "Lucas," I whisper. He remains a frozen masterpiece of Michelangelo.

"Lucas Chernov."

Crunch, crunch, crunch.

Do I even dare make it to him? I shove through several layers of my shirts and find the uneaten Skittles.

In the library, I'd wad papers up from the trash that needed to go in the recycling bin. On the slow days in the library, I practiced my shots into the bin.

It's all in preparation for this critical moment of my survival—I pull one of the Skittles I'd won from the getting-to-know-you games earlier—and let it soar.

It bounces and rolls off to the right.

Again.

It hits the wall, right by his chin.

Again.

I kiss this one for good luck and let it fly. Bullseye, right in his forehead.

He flinches and rubs his forehead.

Another squeal and a not-so-soft hiss ring through the cabin. How is he sleeping through this?

Another kiss to a Skittle and a flick of the wrist. This one hits his lip. He cringes and opens his eyes.

"Lucas," I hiss. He focuses his gaze on me and sits up like he doesn't remember where he is.

"Amelia," his voice is groggy, "are you okay?"

"Do you hear that?" I stare at his face and point my phone light at the cabinet across the room.

A small scamper followed by a gnawing sound fills the cabin. He nods.

He stands up and walks to the small cupboard. I follow him with my light. I stay right behind Lucas and tilt my shoulder into his back. It pulses with warmth.

We listen. Nothing. He tosses one of the doors open.

Four beady eyes look back—a wet black nose, striped tail, and black arms and legs.

I scream.

Both animals bolt out and run into the bedroom.

"Lovely," Lucas scratches his chin. "They planned a sleepover."

I grip his arm like it's a baseball bat and direct him like he's my shield. "Will they bite?" My shiver chatters my teeth. "Or should I go wa-wake up the camp director, or should I wake up Clyde, or should—" I stumble a little as I follow him to the room.

He twists and catches me.

"Just breathe." His warm breath reaches my frozen nose. My teeth, I swear, start chattering to the pulse of my heartbeat. Why does he have to be so warm and calm?

"I can't." My voice is small. "It's kind of impossible when there is a critter planning to scratch out my eyeballs."

"I think they'd only go for one," he says, snatching my hand as he walks toward the bedroom. "You're freezing." His touch is warm. "Your scream scared them," he whispers. "You breathe, and I'll keep your eyeballs safe. Plan?"

I nod. He opens the bathroom on the way and snatches out the broom attached to the wall. Good weapon of choice.

They've jumped up onto the bed, and the light of my phone flashes their hissing teeth at us. I squeeze Lucas tighter. "Don't make a sound," he whispers.

He slowly steps on his sleeping bag and inches along the wall. I'm the koala on his back and mirror his every step.

Lucas lifts the broom up. "Easy, buddies. We're friends," his soothing and steady voice says. "Let's get you outside so you can find your family."

He uses the bristles of the broom to slowly push toward the raccoon on the bed. One of them turns and sniffs the broom. Its little black finger-paws grab some of the bristles and snarl again. I keep my squeal in my mouth.

Is that foam I see coming out of its mouth?

"Lucas," I whisper.

"In your nose, out your mouth, Amelia."

We have to get them out without anyone getting hurt. My arm shoves back into my hoodie pocket, and I pull out a Skittle and toss it onto the bed. The farther raccoon moves toward it and starts eating. I toss another piece to the other raccoon. Both raccoons gnaw on the Skittles. Lucas turns, and I feel his breath on my cheek.

"Skittles?" he whispers.

"They solve a lot of problems. Didn't you know that?"

He slowly pulls the broom back as I toss two more onto the bed. They grab and eat them faster this time, pushing the entire candy in at once. Lucas tiptoes out toward the cabin door. I toss two more out of the room. They jump off the bed, and I bite my tongue; they are so close to me. Lucas opens the outside door. I toss two more—one by the door and the other bouncing outside.

I smile as both critters run after each other outside. Lucas slams the door and puts his bag back.

Our breathing is heavy, swirling with warm puffs between us. A small laugh escapes his mouth. It grows into a bigger one. I blink and can't help but follow. He bends over, laughing so deeply, and it fills the entire cabin.

"Do you mind if we push the couch against the door? I don't know if that's how they got in or if they were in here before we came."

"Good idea," he says.

We push the couch against the door, and it faces toward the window, the moonlit lake.

"My phone is dead. How much battery does yours have?"

"Five percent," I say.

He nods. "Let's save it, just in case..." And like that, I'm in a dark moonlit cabin with Lucas Chernov, alone.

"Do you think that is all of them?" I crinkle my nose.

"Yes."

"You have no idea." My smile is wide. "You just want to sleep without waking up to flying Skittles."

"A man can have hopes, can't he?" He scratches his head. "Very resourceful, Milly Bean." That is the first time he's called me that. "I want you to get some sleep."

I curl back up on the couch. Lucas is only three steps away now. He slips into his sleeping bag and looks at the ceiling.

I close my eyes. The coldness of the couch has reset, and I twist back and forth. A bird starts hooting. I sit up. One of Lucas's eyes opens.

"Just an owl," he says.

Ten minutes go by, and I think I hear Lucas breathe hard again. The wind picks up, and tree branches scrape the roof. I sit up again.

"Amelia, you're safe. Can you sleep?" His voice is groggy.

"Just anxious, I guess," I say. "Don't mind me; go back to sleep."

He slowly hoists himself up, grabs his sleeping bag, snatches the broom, and props it up by the couch. He unzips his sleeping bag and sits right next to me, draping the sleeping bag on us.

He's far enough away that we're not touching. My fingers itch toward him like he's a new book, so I sit on my hands.

"Sleep," he says. "I'll keep watch."

His eyes look puffy.

"No, no," my voice cracks.

He looks at my face. "You need your energy to convince the board, remember?"

He's right. I dig around in my hoodie pocket and hold out my hand. "Just in case," I say.

I drop candies into his hand. He doesn't grab my hand, and I sneak it right back underneath me so they don't betray me. A soft smile rests on my lips. My breathing instantly starts to slow and deepen. His warm sleeping bag surrounds me.

Lucas will keep me safe.

Chapter Twenty-Three

Lucas

I wake up feeling warm. I crashed when Amelia turned and snuggled into me like I was her pillow sometime after five a. m. I guess she thought I was her Neme, not Lucas. I swirl my thumb across some of her loose hair. My eyes are scratchy, and I don't want her to wake up yet.

If the puddle on my shirt is any indication, she's in a deep sleep. Far away, I hear bagpipes. Sun rays dance along the top of the water; it's time to ruin this slice of heaven.

Her hair smells sweet, like candy. I close my eyes, taking my last moment to soak up the kindest creature I've ever met, and decide I'll listen to her today—really listen to her reasoning. No matter what.

I stop rubbing her hair as she props herself up. She looks back at me, horror written in her eyes.

"Good morning, Pumpkin," I say as she covers her mouth.

She wipes her mouth and points to a huge wet stain on my PJs.

I nod—I feel the puddle through my shirt.

Her shoes hit the floor. "I'm so sorry, I didn't mean—"

"You kept me warm. Thank you," I say. The cool cabin air fills the empty space between us.

"Time?" she asks as she starts to shuffle through her pockets.

I pull up my watch. "Seven-fifteen."

She takes a deep breath and closes her eyes. "Good; I promised Gemma I'd make it to her yoga session at seven forty-five."

I nod. "You'll make it. You don't have to get ready." I point to her clothes. "Except some of them are inside out."

Her cheeks flush bright as she grabs her bag and runs to the bathroom.

She comes out wearing a red sweater. "Thank you for sharing your sleeping bag." She's pulled her hair back into a ponytail.

I nod. "Anytime," I smile. "It will be a night to remember."

"You know, I didn't say anything about the condition of the cabin to Clyde or the camp director, just so I could...make you suffer." She frowns, tossing her bag next to the couch. Her smile is so readable. "But you keep surprising me," she says.

All I do is nod as she leaves, and I have a chance to change, hoping a raccoon isn't watching me fumble through my buttons. I flip a small bag over my shoulder with the iPad. All our things are next to the couch, so I drape the sleeping bag over it. If the friends come back, I want our things to be safe.

Breakfast is at nine, and I feel the lake calling to me, so I walk down by the water. Leaves fall and pile up at the rim of the shore. Soft ripples topple over each other, and I find a rock to sit on.

My lungs expand as I suck in a forest breath and hold it for a moment. I need this. The space to clear my mind. I don't feel angry, and it's noticeable.

I bend down and pick up a small rock. Its slick sides are trouble-free—I toss it in.

I'm a nice person, right? Was I always angry? My first thought is to blame it on Dad. But as the soft ripples expand out across the lake, I'm not so sure. If I want to be the opposite of Dad, I need to stop being angry and running away.

"Beautiful, isn't it?" Clyde's yellow puff coat stands out as he walks closer to the shore. Every button is done up, and small wisps of breath hang right in front of him.

"This lake always gives me peace. It's taken me a long time to learn how to capture it." He closes his eyes like he's letting each slap of water cover him up.

"It's breathtaking." I fold my arms. We stand there long enough to watch a good handful of leaves join the lake.

"Did you rest okay?" he asks.

"Well enough." He doesn't need to know.

We both watch the soft pulse of the water. "You know, I knew both of your parents—Amelia's and yours—and I must say—" he smiles at me— "you both remind me so much of them. Your Dad had a way with an audience." He shakes his head. "I don't think people realize how much good he did behind the scenes. Most only saw his coldness."

I don't know what he's talking about.

"And Linda Anderson, Amelia's mother? She was one of the most stubborn women I'd ever met. I thought she'd beat the statistics out of sheer determination when I heard about her diagnosis." He smacks his lips. "It didn't work out like that for her." He takes a step closer to the water and points out over it. "Amelia is someone who's let her mother's legacy live on." My eyes follow where he's pointing—some deer bend low to drink along one of the bends. "I think that's why she is against any alternative. She is so loyal. She doesn't know how much her mother lives on through her and her overwhelming goodness. She doesn't need a library to share goodness."

I rub my shoulder.

I ran from Dad. I turned and pushed away his ghost. Dad caused so much pain; I didn't want to see what good he had done. Focusing on the pain is what I was good at.

He turns to go. The calm slosh of the water makes me think twice before I clench my jaw. "Amelia Anderson is one of the best-kept secrets the library has been hiding." He looks out over the lake. "And you are a leader, just like your dad." He shares a soft smile. "Maybe we all can learn something from Amelia, no matter what our family dynamics are."

I watch as he turns and walks up the hillside.

Being a leader is the last thing I asked for. All I want is to make a name for myself.

Everything I've done since I left the family business looks like it has Dad's handiwork all over it.

I lift my hands up behind my head. Amelia has done just that. She's defending her mother's shadow with all her heart. And all I've done is the complete opposite.

I let the waves splash my thoughts around; *we all can learn from Amelia.*

There's enough time for me to walk around the lake twice, but my eye still twitches, and my mouth won't stop yawning. The group gathers inside the cabin, and I see Amelia sitting by Sandy.

Amelia sees me, and I give her a soft smile. We don't break our stare until I hear, "Yoo-hoo! Mr. Dreamy Mountaineer, how is my Sweetheart's Touch working?" Sandy lets out a whistle and moves close to my side.

I glance back at Amelia, who is covering her smile up with her hand. "Will you help me dish up my breakfast? I'd always wanted a hunk of man to eat in a cabin with me," Sandy asks.

I nod, and she traps me all morning right by her side. I don't mind, not today.

Clyde stands up after breakfast. "It's time. We have sandwiches prepared in the kitchen whenever you're ready for lunch." He points back into the kitchen. "Pick up a bag when you're hungry. Amelia and Lucas, that room right over there is for you." He points to a big office with a whiteboard hanging up and a large window looking out into the main room. "That's where you can work together." He points to the group. "We think it's best for you both to hash out what plan you think is best and then present it to us."

Everyone nods.

Clyde studies me and says, "We will agree upon a plan that we only feel is best for the entire town."

I tug at my collar as I walk into the office first. The orange carpet smells of dust mites and cinnamon bark—a huge box in the corner has Christmas decorations spilling down and wreaths propped up around the side. It's warm, and sweat collects around my neck as I put my pack on the office table.

Amelia grabs some food from the kitchen and sits down at the desk. I pull the iPad out. She picks up her sandwich and stuffs it into her mouth.

My eyes arch, and my mouth drops open a little. "Hungry already?"

She stops chewing. "I'm nervous."

I shake my head and hold up a napkin. "I'm here all day; no need to choke. Unless you're ready for me to perform mouth-to-mouth?"

She coughs; her half-chewed sandwich parts fly across the table. I snatch one of the unopened water bottles and open it for her.

"I'll take that as a yes." I lift my one eyebrow.

"Lucas Chernov!" she says after she takes a big drink, and her cheeks give her away.

I shake my head. "I'm trying to tell you to slow down. You're okay to eat slow." I look at her lips. "So I can show you I'm not a library killer. But I'll focus on pulling up the data we need to get started. You can nervous eat."

I pick up a purple dry-erase marker and write the words:

Keep library in current building—

Push library over to build apartments—

Option yet discovered—

I leave plenty of room for us to write everything out. I pull up the survey results on the iPad. I frown—it will ruin her day.

She finishes chewing, and I hold up the purple marker.

"You're purple; I'll be blue." She stands and squares her stance.

I smile as she sprawls out, scribbling all along the whiteboard and not leaving a spot for me.

I watch her write. *books to check out, educational classes for kids, story time, craft time, prevents another dark age, helps the underserved population of our town, internet access, educational resources, knitting club, passport help, holds AA every Thursday night, helps improve eyesight, a place to fall in love, and increase love of town.*

"Whoa, hold your marker, Pumpkin Spice. It'll improve eyesight?" She bats her eyes at me. I cross my arms. "How?"

She brings her nose up close to mine and looks into my eyes. Her green eyes light up like she knows all the secrets to my heart. "Have you, Lucas Chernov, ever looked out the window in the library at the view of our town and the mountains?"

I jut out my chin. "Yes."

"Staring at things far away is good for your eyes. Too many kids are on screens all day. That view from the window helps strengthen eyesight."

"You could just do that outside. And what is this, start another dark age?" She watches my lips as I speak.

"Don't you know your history, Lucas?" she pops her finger up like she has an idea. "I have a book or two that can help. Getting rid of libraries spreads ignorance."

"I know what you're referring to. We have the internet now. No dark ages are in the foreseeable Wi-Fi future."

She shakes her finger in my face. "What about those who don't have internet? You know there are lots in our community in that position. The library is the solution." She holds up her arms like she's cheering on a touchdown.

"And AA on Thursday? They could have that anywhere."

"No, they really can't. At least nowhere else that is available that doesn't charge a fee."

"No one goes to AA," I respond.

She barks a short laugh. "Where have you been living? Yes, they do, Lucas. All seats are full every week." She points at my chest and tightens her jaw.

I can't help it and grab her hand, flattening it out on my chest. I watch her pupils dilate and let a small smile take over my lips.

"And falling in love? Amelia Anderson, how can we prove that to the board?"

Our eyes lock, and I can see she is looking at my lips.

I look over her head and see the entire group outside the window with rows of chairs facing us, practically eating popcorn. Joe waves me on, motioning me to go for the kiss.

Stepping back, I shove a hand into my hair.

"Amelia," I say, facing the corner, "I believe you. The library is irreplaceable."

Turning to the table, I block the window. The audience is going nowhere until this is over. I have the graphs already pulled up on the iPad. Handing it to her, I say, "Don't think this means I want to get rid of the library. I've watched you for weeks now. Our town is a better place because of the library. It's a better place because of you, Amelia." I'm facing her again, and I lift her chin up.

"Let's make a third list."

She covers her mouth as she scrolls through the list. "Only 50 people used the library during the past six weeks?"

"Twenty-four were for the bat presentation. The other twenty-six came for resources in the library."

She sits down. "There is more, Lucas. I can show you. At least hundred patrons have checked out a book this year."

"How many during the past six weeks?"

She blanches. "Excluding yourself, Amelia."

"Ten," she says. "But the raffle is coming up, and so many people have signed up. It's better than it looks, I promise. At least, I just need more time to—"

I kneel by her. "I know." I touch her hair. "I want to help."

She blinks the moisture away. "Lucas? You really do?"

I nod. "Everything about you is resilient. I think with a little help, you can make the library shine."

She jumps up so fast her chair falls over. Her arms wrap around my neck before I can reach out my arms. "Do you mean that?" she breathes into my chest. Before I even give her an answer, she places a peck on my cheek.

I wrap my arms around her and let them rest in the small of her back. She ignites my heart, and a flame shoots up my body. I pull her back a little. "I think we can make both work. Do you believe it could be possible to keep the library *and* construct apartments?" It's the only way I can protect her from my brothers, from Kim and Mitchell Ricks. And most importantly, give Amelia her wish.

She wipes her eyes and hands me her purple marker. "Show me."

We hash it out for the next two hours—losing track of all time—every possible option we can think of that would please all sides: Noil Construction, Chernov Realty, and the library and patrons.

As I finish converting our plan from the whiteboard to typing it up on the iPad, Joe knocks on the window.

He talks through the window. “I need my siesta before the dance tonight. Pumpkin Spice, you’re still going to dance with me?”

She nods her head and opens the door. “We’re ready,” she announces.

Everyone on the board spreads their chairs back into a circle, out from the rows by our window.

“I think he and Amelia make a mighty fine couple,” I overhear a lady say. “I was hoping they’d seal it with a kiss.”

My heart agrees.

Chapter Twenty-Four

Lucas

Amelia runs to the bathroom, and I inhale a sandwich. Everyone on the board is anxious to see our final plan. They visit quietly as I walk to the front of the audience by a fireplace. My hands relax as I pull out an easel and a large white flip chart. I draw a quick rendition of the plan Amelia and I are thinking so the board can get a visual.

Amelia joins me and takes over the drawing—the room is silent.

"So, if I understand correctly," the bug trap lady says, "you're doing both: keeping the library and building apartments?"

Amelia responds, "Making substantial additions, with a connecting walkway full of natural light and bench seating, it will attract people from all around."

I add, "We will include all the essential updates needed for the library to be safe and up to code."

"What about parking?" Clyde tosses out.

Amelia responds, "Chernov Brothers Realty also owns the adjacent open lot. Lucas thinks converting that area for parking shouldn't be a problem."

Her smile is so wide her cheeks have to hurt.

"This isn't what we were expecting," Clyde says, eyeing me. He pauses and looks around. "I won't speak for the board, but I think it might be one of the best ideas and opportunities for our town."

Amelia jumps up and down and claps a little.

"Now, we know this still has to pass city officials. Rezoning still has to occur, and my brothers still have to vote on it. It's not a done deal, and there will be road bumps."

Everyone nods.

I rub my neck. "We love the idea of connecting people right into one of our best resources downtown. If my brothers are willing to fix up all the broken parts, build apartments, and connect both buildings together with an innovative hallway like Amelia described, they can charge higher rent prices having the additional resources plugged right into their building." I lift up both hands. "It's a win for everyone."

Amelia comes to my side like she's just been gifted a real unicorn for Christmas. She waves her hand in front of her face several times. "I might pass out, Lucas."

"Stay close, I'll catch you," I say. "Let's get air and let them talk."

We step outside and watch the staff set up lights along a dance floor just beyond a fire pit. They twinkle in the fresh air and reflect off the shiny dance platform.

Amelia takes several deep breaths. I can't help but laugh as she throws her arms around me.

"Thank you." Her voice vibrates through my chest.

The willowy camp director rounds the corner with his hat net down and runs us over.

"Oh, just the two I needed to talk to!" We take a step back. "I have to apologize. More cabins up here opened up. We can meet you at the big cabin by the lake right now and help you move your stuff over."

"Our stuff is in the small one," Amelia says.

He pulls his hat tighter. "Do not tell me you slept in the broken guest house?"

We stare at each other; her golden flecks are brighter.

Amelia answers while keeping her gaze tied to me. "I tried to open the door to the bigger cabin by the lake, but it was locked."

"The door sticks like molasses, honey. You gotta give it the onion and push with your liver." He puts his hand on his back. I nod at Amelia like that's the most normal way to open a door I've ever heard of.

She laughs. "I used no liver."

"We'll get you moved up into one of these cabins now. It's not safe for anyone to be in that thing. I'm so sorry you endured a night in that decrepit thing." He turns to flag down a golf cart driving by.

Clyde steps out and waves us close. "We just voted." His grin is wide. "We'll present your plan at the next city meeting, the rezoning committee will be there. It will be the meeting of the year, I think."

I lift my knuckles up to Amelia, and she pounds them.

"It's on Wednesday this week, the day after your Halloween thing. You'll have a busy week, Milly." Clyde says.

She smiles. "It will be worth it."

Dinner that evening is catered, and after some light dessert, music begins to play.

Joe hunts down Amelia, who's wearing the blue dress I'd purchased for her—it's hard to breathe every time I look at her.

Sandy finds me, and I hold her arm as she leaves the walker behind. The music is upbeat, and the lights glow as the sun starts to set.

The cool air hits fast, and Sandy doesn't last longer than two dances. "You've given me enough to daydream about for three years. I need to get to bed now." I smile and make sure Clyde is okay with helping her back to her cabin.

Amelia lingers on the dance floor; she's shivering again. I go for my pack and take out a jacket.

I place it over her shoulders. "Dance with me."

"I'm not that graceful."

I grin. "I know." The song is an old one I barely recognize, and no one else steps on the dance floor. I place her hands on my shoulders, and I lightly place both my hands around her and let my hands rest on the small of her back.

"You've done it, Lucas."

I shake my head. "We don't know that yet. There's a lot that could happen."

She lays her head down on my chest, and I let the vanilla and mint scent of her hair fill my nose. We move slowly, letting the twinkling lights and rhythm pulse through us both.

I pull one of her hands down from my shoulder and hold it gently in my hand.

"I don't know how it's going to work out, but thank you, Lucas." She's close, and I swallow.

"Today, you changed my mind about you," she says. "I don't believe you're a library killer anymore. And I have wanted to do this for a long time."

She leans up to me and waits for me, coming close enough that I can see the flecks in her eyes sparkle against the light. The sound of music makes everything shrink away, and I lift my hand up and trace her jawline, then move my hand to her neck and into her hair.

I let my hand slowly brush her skin at the back of her neck as my other hand places her hand on my chest, letting her feel the beat of my heart.

I gently place a kiss on both of her cheeks, then her chin. Her breath is heavy when I finally let my lips connect to her soft lips.

My breath swirls with hers, and all my thoughts fuzz away. All I can think of are the shape of her lips and the way my skin hums alive. I lean in, deepening our connection before I pull away—needing air and a moment for my heart to slow down.

The music mixed with cheers pulls me back to real-time.

She bites her lip, and her cheeks blush at the sound of more cheers.

After the dance, we separated into different cabins for the night, and I lay awake in my own bed, wishing upon every shooting star that she could be right—that I could pull this off and not be a library killer.

Chapter Twenty-Five

Lucas

Monday morning comes, and I'm at the bank building at 8 a.m. Amelia and I have been texting nonstop since we got home yesterday. Her first text pinged in at five Monday morning.

Amelia: *Oh no! I still have your jacket. Will you be coming to the library today?*

Me: *No, drop it off at the mansion tonight; I want to show you something. And I want my sleep. Who gets up this early?*

Amelia: *You do now. Does it involve a family dinner?*

Me: *Not this time.*

Amelia: *Oh! I will do the raffle on Tuesday, Halloween; you should stop by. Mikey would love to see you again.*

Me: *Do I have to dress up?*

Amelia: *Yes! That is if you want a treat.*

Me: *Not dressing up.*

Amelia: *If I like it, maybe your treat could be a kiss?*

Me: *Dressing up.*

Amelia hearts my message. I scroll through my text messages and find Atticus.

Me: *Where are you?*

Where is his cosplay stuff? I need Atticus's help.

I push the bank door open.

"Mr. Chernov, we missed you Friday and Saturday," the teller says loudly, smacking her gum and twisting her hair tight with a pencil.

"I went on a retreat," I say.

Her dimple sinks in. "Did you take a girl?"

I know some of my brothers love being flaunted over, but I can't stand it.

"Yes." I pull on my sleeves.

She leans in closer. "I'll give you a sucker if you tell me who the lucky girl was?"

As though it isn't already spreading like wildfire through town, I say, "Amelia Anderson."

She covers her mouth. "The librarian who hates you?"

I nod my head.

"Mr. Chernov, did you kiss her?"

My mouth cracks a smile. "Katie, do you ask everyone these personal questions?"

The woman in the booth beside her says, "Oh, this is nothing, Mr. Chernov."

Great, so they're all listening in. There are three other women in the back, two at the drive-in and one at the next desk.

"Yes," I say. All the women seem to work faster, pretending they can't hear me.

"Mr. Chernov, that's mighty fine confusing; I thought you wanted to push over the library. How does fraternizing with the librarian help you?"

I shake my head. "It doesn't, other than softening my stone-cold heart."

She offers me one of her business cards. "You give me a call if it doesn't work out with your stubborn librarian," she whispers and winks at me.

I don't take her card. "It will work out." I can hear several of the women sigh and exchange looks.

"Today's passcode tries are—" I hold up my phone and read from the list— "Rezone, reverse, receive."

She punches them into her computer system and gives me my usual response: "Rejected."

I walk out of the building, pulling up the spreadsheet on my phone and checking off those three words. I walk along Magnus Avenue, hoping I can find Nikola in his office.

I work up a small sweat as I rehearse what I'll propose to Nikola if he's in. I can't leave Amelia's heart on the line and up to chance.

My phone vibrates, and I open it up.

Atticus: *On the Appalachian Trail. What's up, bro?*

Me: *Can I borrow a costume of yours for Halloween?*

Atticus: *A photo of him wearing a small brown skirt, dirty and ripped. "Tarzan meets Atticus."*

Me: *lol, what year were you Tarzan?*

Atticus: *That's me right now, bro.*

Atticus: *Another photo of him staring at the camera, dirt-covered head to toe with no shirt on, and a person dressed up as a gorilla behind him.*

Me: *You need help.*

Atticus: *You do too, bro. It's all in my closet. Payment = selfie.*

Me: *k, Thxs.*

I walk into the office.

"Mr. Chernov!" The receptionist jumps like I'm a ghost; she moves several of her pencils around.

"Addy, it's nice to see you, too. Have you graduated yet?"

She nods her head up and down, her dark hair and eyes not meeting mine. "Yes, sir, I was able to graduate early."

"Hmm, good for you. Is Nikola in today?"

She nods and points to the hallway.

I haven't been in this building since before Dad died. I walk past my old office door, my name still on it.

Nikola's door is the only one open.

Our family office is in a new, sleek, and sterile building. Thanks to Addy, every piece of furniture is crisp, and even the carpet holds straight vacuum lines.

I knock on Nikola's door.

"Almost done..." he says as he finishes signing a stack of papers.

"Nikola," I say.

"Lucas?" He looks up, taking out his EarPods. "Wow, you're here."

I nod my head. "I need your help."

"What's up?" he points to the chair.

"I know I've been—"

"Emotionally distant?" he says.

"No." I pull back the skin around my healing cut.

"Incapable of dealing with grief?"

I square my eyes at him. "Nikola," I shake my head. "You're not making this easy." I rub my nose.

He holds up his hands as he swivels in his chair. "Just talk to us. We all know how you and Dad didn't get along. I think talking to someone would help."

I flex my hand and pick up a pencil to flip along my fingers, "What I was trying to say...I've been less than an ideal brother for a while now," I sigh. "That's why I'm here, actually."

"Well done." He holds up his hands in surrender. "How can I help you?"

I tap his desk. "I've got an idea."

His hand moves to his computer. "Yes," he says.

"I don't want the brothers to know."

Nikola's smile goes wide. "You know secrets are my specialty."

I nod my head. "That's why I came to you."

He nods, writes everything down, and promises to start working on my plan immediately.

Chapter Twenty-Six

Amelia

It's too easy to drive to his house, and before I know it, I'm ringing the doorbell at the Chernov mansion. I see several cars in the driveway, and a younger version of Lucas answers the door. His *Game is Never Over* T-shirt is on with a soda can in one hand and a VR headset in the other.

"Remington, right?" The youngest Chernov.

He smiles at me and doesn't say a word. I fidget with the jacket in my hand.

"I—" a loud group of people raises their voices; someone is losing. "I-I'm interrupting company," is the only thing that comes out.

The boy lifts a side of his lips into a smile. "There's always company here. Come in."

Hot wings and potatoes fill the air as men huddle together. Lucas is in the middle of the cluster.

He sees me and smiles, and I smile back. I should have never texted him about wearing a costume and getting a kiss for it. My brain has been fixated on that text all day and on the fact that I love Lucas Chernov.

I'll be a mess now that both sides of my brain know. I don't want to say anything until after the meeting, two nights away.

"Milly," a voice comes from the large gathering room.

"Dimitry," I nod and give him a tight smile that sends the message to stop dating your brother's ex-fiancé because that is against serious unwritten rules of brotherhood. His smile back at me tells me he doesn't get my message.

"We should get a burger sometime and get caught up," he says.

I nod my head. "Yeah, just let me know I'm—"

Lucas cuts in, "Goodbye, Dim."

"Everyone!" Baba yells from the back of the room.

"Nikola says the food is ready, but first—" she walks up to me— "make sure you say hello to Lucas's new girl if you didn't get a chance at the last family dinner!"

All eyes swing to me, and I shrink into an ant, trying to find the nearest crack to crawl into.

Lucas instantly pulls me behind him as he tugs me toward the front door. "Amelia isn't here for dinner; I'm showing her Olympus."

He pulls me hard toward the front door. I hold my breath until he slams the front door, stopping the followers. Several of his brothers look out the large picture window overlooking the front yard and entrance.

"Dimitry goes after any girl that's connected to me." He sets his jaw.

I nod my head. "Of course, but we are old friends. I'd love to catch up."

"Of course," he agrees. I walk to my car and let Neme jump out. He stays close by.

Lucas sits me down next to the fountain; the sound of flowing water is soothing, and the sun still has plenty of time before it lets cold air settle in.

I hear a whoosh next to my ear and swat at the bug, but it happens again. I get closer; orange foam darts, not bugs, are in the grass near me.

"Are we being watched?" Another dart makes its way to Lucas.

"Yes, I have grown men for brothers who still *act like boys!*" Lucas shouts the last three words loud so they can hear him.

My cheeks crease up. "You mean you've never shot anyone?" I let my finger dance across my collarbone. He drops his gaze and looks at my neck.

"That was..." He scratches his head.

"Very mature of you, wasn't it?" I add.

"Fine," he says. "The whole lot of us are terrible with girlfriends. That's why Baba thinks we're cursed."

My ears tilt up. "Do tell."

Several boys start to crawl out along the grass from behind the side of the house to a mound of landscaped shrubs closer to us.

"Real normal," he shouts out. Several boys chuckle. "You know we can see everything you're doing."

"We know," they shout back.

He leans close to me. "Is your car unlocked?" he asks as we dodge the incoming darts.

"Always," I say.

He grabs my hand, and we run to my car. Neme jumps into the back, and I get into the passenger seat. Lucas gets into the driver's seat and locks the door. His legs are jammed in tight, too tight. He can't even wiggle against the steering wheel. He tries to move a foot to the gas pedal, and I think I hear a rip in his jeans. My eyes go wide.

"Amelia, please tell me your seat can adjust." His brothers begin swarming the car. One even pulls out the pressure washer from the garage.

I cover my mouth. "This is normal?"

"Lever, Amelia, where is your seat adjuster lever?"

"It's gone."

"Gone? How is that possible?" he asks, feeling underneath the seat.

My neck and face bulge, keeping my laugh in. "It's an old car," I say, watching his brothers swarm and plot like sharks.

"Keys. Please tell me you have keys."

I feel my pockets.

"Here." I hand them to him. He starts the engine and pops the car in reverse.

"It gets stuck a little—" I grimace— "going from reverse to drive."

He tries to lift the gear up to drive, but it isn't going. I reach over, shove the stick forward, and it pops into gear.

He drives the car down the driveway, where two of his brothers seem to be waiting with the biggest squirt guns I've ever seen.

Lucas drives through a hurricane of water and down the winding path to the entrance of Snob Acres.

Lucas is packed into the driver's seat like a stuffed teddy bear in a small fanny pack. I'm laughing so hard I'm crying. He drives further before pulling over and asking me to help him get out. My feet hit the gravel on the side of the road, and I open his door and pull his hand.

I grunt as I grab his shoulder and jerk as hard as I can. He pops out as I tumble backward.

My body hums as I laugh, and I chase him into the forest. I have no intention of telling him about the rip by his inseam. He would be a blue underwear type of guy.

Leaves crunch, and he darts around fallen limbs. Neme gets ahead of Lucas, and I follow both as they keep us going in the right direction. He draws my attention to the spotted orange clouds that match the treetops.

Neme stays at my feet as I slow and close my eyes—memorizing the warmth in the autumn air, the chase of Lucas—and a surety that everything is working out.

When I look at him again, he's staring at my lips.

I gulp a breath. He meets my eyes, and I feel the crisp air buzz around me as he reaches

his hand out. "Almost there."

I slip my hand into his like it's my favorite book to reread again and again.

He points up into the woods. We come to the top ridge of a large hill, and my jaw falls open.

It's the biggest treehouse village I have ever seen in my imagination. It spans twenty or thirty trees with connecting rope bridges and zip lines. There are at least ten slides, rock walls, and pulley systems, not to mention multiple levels.

"I've died and gone to treehouse heaven."

"Olympus, actually."

My legs pull me forward, and Lucas starts chasing me. He reaches me without effort; he wraps his arms around me, and Neme whines. Lucas lets me go, and I start to climb up.

"There—" I point up. He follows me without a word. The sun starts to get closer to the ridgeline, and rays toss through our upward ascent.

"Are you sure?" he asks. It's the highest platform that I can see. Not only is it the highest part of the treehouse, but it's the highest part I've ever seen in Herasburg—the town, the library roof, and houses scattering up and along the base of the Blue Ridge Mountains.

Lucas touches the small of my back. "This platform was always my favorite."

"I can see why." I squint and point to a small roof underneath all the interconnection bridges. "Is that a fairy house?"

He smiles. "Here in the real world, small roofs could also be known as a 'wishing well.' Dad bought it long ago and we he built the tree house land up around it."

"So your father did all this?" I know Lucas has feelings about his dad, but wow. At least he had a dad. A dad who understood childhood to the tenth degree.

Lucas nods. "Yes..."

"Yes, what?" I ask.

He takes a deep breath and sits down. "He made this," Lucas says, like it's a bad thing. I sit by him, and our legs dangle together.

I reach up and touch his arm. "You want to forget your father?" I ask.

He swallows. "Yes. I guess so. It sounds terrible, doesn't it?"

"Yes, it does. Were you close to your Dad?" I ask.

He lets out a long sigh. "Yes, you could say that. I was his henchman."

I frown and lift one brow; I have been practicing, especially at night when I can't sleep.

"A glare that could kill," he chuckles. "I think you called me handsome henchman, too, according to Mikey's note. You read me like a book, Amelia." He looks at me. "I was called Zolt, Jr., for a couple of years. I did all his dirty work. I kicked people out who couldn't pay rent. I was the beast he'd send in to get his loans passed. I was the one who convinced everyone that Dad was doing what was for the best..." His jaw flexes, and his fingers reach for my hands; he takes both into his and places a soft kiss into them.

"I left," he says. "Five years ago, it was too much for me to handle. I loved him, but I was so angry at how much power he had over people, over me." He shakes his head. "I buried my hurt with my anger. Dad wasn't a dad at all. He was a businessman first before he was a father. And that's all I can focus on; I can't see any of his good parts."

I don't respond.

"I don't know how to let go, Amelia," he says. A tear drops from his face onto our hands. I push myself into his shoulder, nestle into his chest, and hold him.

Leaves crunch down below; Neme looks up and whines.

"Sorry, boy, this is too high up for you."

He lets out a small bark.

"How did you find that dog?"

I shake my head. "It wasn't me; it was my mom."

He moves his thumb back and forth over the top of my hand. "Did your mom pick him out?"

"Not exactly." I watch Neme pace back and forth, waiting for me to touch the ground again. "I told you how I didn't take the news about my mom well."

He nods his head.

"Mom had paid a farmer up north who had Newfoundland dogs. Their next litter was planned twenty months out. She orchestrated everything without telling me. She passed six months after she signed the contract with the farmer. Her speech and breathing were affected faster than the doctors could have imagined." I look down at Neme. "A kind woman and younger daughter showed up on my doorstep. I was a blubbery mess; it was the one-year anniversary of my mom's death. The woman and daughter had no idea that mom had passed. She had ironed out the details: payment, delivery, and all the minutiae months earlier." I tug my hands from him to wipe my eyes. "Mom had sent me a gift. A puppy. A best friend. She hadn't even been around to see how much it meant to me."

I pull up my legs and bend them behind me. "I always felt like Neme knew Mom in some way. Or maybe Mom would whisper to Neme the right time to lick my face awake. Or the right time to whine and demand a walk so I could get out of the house, get out of my head, and get some fresh air."

His slow hands pull through my hair, letting my hair surround his hand. The pulse of pleasure spreads as he inches closer to my lips. He gently traces my lips with his thumb and slowly moves closer toward me. His tenderness paralyzes me as his lips find mine. I fully intend to sink deeper into this kiss, and he's there to meet me. He wraps his arms around me and kisses me with a mixture of earnest softness that beats the romance section.

Lucas Chernov can love deeply; I feel that now.

I hear a ruffle of leaves, and Neme barks. I pull away, and our foreheads connect. I hear a click behind us, and then I see a dart fly.

"Amelia," his voice is grave as he pulls back and opens his eyes to meet mine. "Run!"

Chapter Twenty-Seven

Amelia

My orange zipper tugs on my hair. I pull my hair out of the stuffing that's all around my shoulders, chest, and torso.

"Miss Milly!" a cute little ladybug clings to my leg, one of the twins.

"Where's your sister?" I ask her. The hum of laughter and Monster Mash fills the air. Fake fog makers are placed at all the entrances of Magnus Avenue, and the streets crawl with creatures.

"Her tummy hurts. Mommy said no trick or treating."

"Oh, I'm so sad to hear that." I put two treats and two books inside her trick-or-treating bag.

"Will you tell her we missed her?" She nods, hugs me, and skips out the library's front door.

The entire town sits outside of their businesses or along the street, passing out treats, painting faces, playing corn-hole, or competing in potato sack races for the rest of the town members to enjoy.

I'm stationed where I belong: in the library, where I have propped the doors open to attract more new friends.

Mikey Edgewood runs up to me. "Guess what I am, Miss Milly?"

I scratch my head as I eye the flames, horns, and hooves he's wearing, "Fire goat!"

His broad bucktooth smile shows off his blue tongue. "How'd you know?"

I tap my nose, "Because that's your Chinese zodiac." I give him a wink and drop in two books and four treats. I hold up my finger to my mouth. "Shhh."

He runs off down the street to other businesses, and I watch Sandy turn her walker in circles, trying to keep up with him.

Today is the day of the raffle, and my final push is to get our numbers up before our meeting tomorrow. My face hurts from smiling as so many children have come.

Mr. Mettle is at a table out front, helping citizens get a library card and putting their names in for the raffle. The line has been constant, and everyone comments on his costume.

It's brown on half of the large circle around him and layered on the other. He's an onion. I smile at how well it fits him. The children don't like it as much as I do.

"What's the horrible smell?" one of the children asks. I see Mr. Mettle smile.

"It's my scented costume!"

The children plug their noses. My cheeks tighten; I guess he found a way to keep the chaos away after all. "Stop your prattle and go see Milly for your treat."

I hand out candy and books by the handful, and children pose for selfies with Nemean, the lion of Lionstone Library. Neme's large cloth mane and tail extension brush the ground. Children hug him and pat his head. He gives out paw shakes.

One of the children starts to cry when they look at Mr. Mettle, and the young mom brings her crying child into the children's section. The ebb and flow of citizens in the library brings me joy.

As if the sea of children is parting, I see Lucas coming.

He pushes the door open. "Pumpkin Spice!" he says as he bends down and lays a soft kiss on my cheek.

He eyes Neme. "He's a lion?"

I nod my head. "He's the library mascot!"

I take a step away from Lucas. "What are you?" my scowl turns into a smile.

"You're a worm," I say, covering my mouth.

His head has a wry tilt; he bends to my ear and whispers, "A bookworm."

I force my eyes to stay on his eyes, and not his lips—*Lucas Chernov is a bookworm for me.*

"You said you wanted to fall in love with a bookworm in your library." His eyes twinkle, and I lean up on my toes and sneak a kiss on his cheek.

"Trick or treat?" Lucas asks me. I tap my lips, contemplating which one he wants me to choose.

"Treat," I say.

He puts down the bag he's carrying and takes out a small bag. "I saw this and thought of you."

I pull off the wrapping paper. It's a mug with a lid that says, *Pumpkin Spice makes everything nice*, with several packets of pumpkin spice mix. A keychain is in the cup, too. I finger it. The keychain is a picture of a large-eyed raccoon poking his eyes through a pumpkin and a broom lying in front of the jack-o-lantern.

"Pumpkin Spice special," he whispers.

I toss my arms around his neck. "Thank you."

He tugs me further down a book aisle, where we can hide in a long shadow. He pulls me close, and our cheeks graze each other. "Amelia, I—"

I close my eyes, breathing in his soap and bookworm costume, and cut him off as I cover my mouth with his.

He pulls away. "Whatever happens tomorrow, I want you to know how much I admire you." He bends his neck, and our lips touch again, ever so softly. "You've helped me more than I know how to express."

"What if the library loses tomorrow?" I ask.

He touches my lips. "I think I'm making myself quite clear. I'm in this with you no matter what."

Our fingers intertwine, and my stomach swirls. And I want to walk Lucas down every single one of the library aisles and explore more of his lips in all the shadows.

I try to pull myself away. "I've got to make it back to the kids," I whisper against his lips.

I peel away using every ounce of self-control. I can't be around him without desire rising all the way from my toes back up through every tip of my hair.

I turn over my pumpkin stuffing shoulder. "I love you, my bookworm," I murmur.

Everything is falling together with our new proposal to combine apartments and Lionstone Library.

Tomorrow will be a day of the fates.

Chapter Twenty-Eight

Lucas

All day I stay away from Amelia.

Nikola is working hard to prepare my plans; my secret plan isn't ready yet, and I don't know how I'll keep it a surprise for much longer.

I keep my hands in my pockets. *This meeting will decide everything.* I still have napkins from my fried frog dinner with Amelia; I wore these same pants during the last meeting.

I had come early to the building, before the meeting. The council members, zoning board, library board, and citizens are finally filling in like a stream, and I feel hot bile in my throat. My fingers twist the napkins in my pockets. I'll take her back there on a real date when this is all over.

Several of my brothers file in. Dimitry is wearing his blackest suit; something is up his sleeve; that's how he plays this game. Nikola walks in and nods, a good sign that the trick up my sleeve is brewing behind the scenes.

I flex my jaw and rub my hands together.

Magnolia Grace and Andrei sit together; Vincent slips in too.

Tomorrow, I can share my surprise plan with Amelia—I close my eyes and take a deep breath.

I keep my eyes glued to the door; where is she? I thumb through the packet with the updated statistics I spent the day compiling.

The words *reimage*, *retire*, and *reshape* are checked off today after another rejected answer from the bank.

My nervous legs take me to the large window in the meeting room, and I stick my head against the window. *Where is she?* It will be standing room only again.

I see Amelia and her Grandpoppy park in her old car out front. I smile as she sees me in the window. It doesn't stop the tickle of a migraine from starting to touch behind my eyes as Amelia finally walks in with one minute to spare.

"Amelia, you really thought that was the best shirt to wear today?" I say.

Her lips twist up. "It's for luck." She brushes her hair off her shoulder, so everyone can see the words *I'm a librarian: I know everything.*

I bark out a tight laugh. Her hair is stunning, curled, and layered out like she knows what she's doing.

She takes a step back and takes me in. "Handsome henchman hair in place, shoulders tight, and..."

She pushes her cold fingers down my collar against my skin.

"Amelia—" my teeth clench— "we're in public."

"Your neck is sweaty. I've never seen you this nervous."

She has no idea how nervous I am.

We find our seats up front, and the meeting starts. The council discusses some business, including the cat population at the local trailer park, a footbridge that needs to be fixed, and, finally, rezoning.

"Now, it's time to hear from two friends of the library board."

I nod, and we both stand up.

Amelia is up first. Her introduction includes a heartfelt confession of having to learn to work together and the power of a compromise. We pass the data around and show the town what we have collected. A few of the council members ask follow-up questions. "More people use the internet connection in the library for job searching than people who have purchased the deep-fried frog legs at Franny Frys?" someone on the rezoning committee asks.

That brilliant comparison had been Amelia's idea.

Out of the corner of my eye, I see Kim and Mitchell Ricks walk in and stand up in the back. All my face muscles tense, my feet feel uneven, and I don't respond as well as I would have to the follow-up questions about the additional remodeling costs of the existing library; I'm thrown off. They shouldn't be here.

Amelia sees my stiff movements and lightly touches my arm. My throat is tight, and I want to growl Mitchell out of town. This is my assignment; why has he come?

"Is there anyone from the audience with anything else to add?"

Mitchell stands and approaches the public podium.

"To the town of Herasburg and its lovely citizens, I am the owner of Noil Construction. I assigned my most promising manager with the task of securing rezoning. I was surprised at the combined plan they shared, but I will point out that the need is still the same. We need that land rezoned. I—our company has the best interests of the citizens here and getting them closer to downtown will benefit everyone."

A zip of pain shoots through my forehead, and I push against it with my pointer finger.

Mitchell pulls out a file. "I also wanted to bring to everyone's attention something distressing recently brought to my attention."

He pulls out several photos of Amelia crawling into the Chernov mansion window with a cat mask on, wearing all black. Neme waits outside the window. And yes, a photo of her car in the area.

"I think it goes without saying that the reliability of collected data is directly influenced by the honesty of the data collector."

He passes the photos out, starting with the mayor, then walks to the back of the room and hands more copies to the officer.

"The Chernovs have state-of-the-art security systems just in case you ever try to break into their house; it's a bad idea. These photos are part of a backup camera and were provided to us by a concerned member of the family." His face is relaxed, and his dark eyes glow. "Somehow, the original video footage was deleted." The man doesn't even look at me or Amelia.

My blood begins to boil, "What is this?" I jolt up.

Mitchell pushes on. "Someone was trying to hide their tracks."

Amelia covers her mouth with both hands and lets out a whimper.

I feel the room spin, and if I had an arrow, I would shoot it through Mitchell's hand and then Dimitry's foot. He's behind this; I know it.

Amelia touches my shoulder; her eyes are wide, searching mine.

I point my lethal, sharp gaze at Dimitry. His eyes are wide, and he frowns at me. He tries to mouth something to me.

I move to the podium. "This is completely irrelevant to the library."

Someone shouts from the audience. "If she's a criminal, she has no right to work at the library."

James, one of the first patrons I met in the library, stands up and starts shouting. "If it wasn't for Miss Milly, I wouldn't have found a job. I think this is so unprofessional and totally inappropriate, sir." James walks up to the man and shoves his finger into his chest. "To go off talking about Miss Milly that way. She's the sweetest flower I've ever seen and is the best part of the library and this town for so many of us."

Several people murmur in the audience. Mr. Mettle is there, too, his shiny bald head turning red.

Rosabell stands up. "Ya'll are trying to cook a goose before you know what holiday it is!" She holds her Shih Tzu in her arms. She must have snuck it in. "Listening to this man is a mistake; we know our Milly Bean. She wouldn't do this."

"Well, she's a criminal." Mitchell lays his hands down on the podium.

"Mitchell, enough!" I shout, but it's too late.

Amelia stands up and walks out in front of the crowd.

Oh no, no, no. Amelia, no. I try to pull her hand to come back to the bench, but she shakes her head.

She speaks loud so everyone can hear. "Mitchell's right." She nods her head several times, eyes watering, "I did break into the Chernov home. I thought I could ruin a library deed document to help save the library."

The room erupts in yelling and pushing, and Amelia rounds her shoulders down, hugging herself and looking to the ground. My body is positioned between her and Mitchell. The mayor tries to speak, but no one listens. I watch Amelia wilt into a small ball, tears welling in her eyes, and she covers up her librarian shirt.

Several police officers walk around me and read Amelia her rights. "What are you doing?" I shout as I try to stop the mustache mullet officer.

"Sorry, sir. Evidence was submitted. We need to keep her in custody for now. She's coming with us."

I ball my hands into fists.

James swings an arm before me, and Amelia follows the mustache-mullet officer to the back of the room. Several officers lunge toward James and pull his arms behind his back. I think I see Sandy pull out a popcorn bag from her purse; she gives me a wink.

An officer pulls James out of the room and out of the building. I glance out the window; he is in a police car.

Several people shuffle and barricade the doors in front of the mullet officer and Amelia.

"Let the officers go." The mayor's voice is a steel rod.

I don't know what to do, and one feeling I know all too well flares up: Dimitry is behind this, and my rage burns.

Mr. Mettle stands up. "If I may say something..."

The room simmers.

The small, old man walks over to where Amelia is and clears his throat. "She's late. She's loud—" he wipes his bald head with his hand— "And she makes things bright and kids smile. She cares more about that library than most of us in here combined. She's put her heart into the library and into every person who has ever known her." The blotches on his skin turn a purplish hue. "I think you are making a terrible mistake." He stomps his foot, and I can see a spray of saliva projected onto the officer as he enunciates his anger with every word.

The young officer takes out a handkerchief from his pocket and wipes the spray.

The onion has spoken, and Amelia has tears streaming down her.

A different officer takes over long enough for me to make it to the doorway and follow them out of the room. I follow them outside, Andrei and Grace on my heels.

"Who submitted the evidence? You're not telling me just from that right now you are making this arrest?" I sneer.

"That's confidential information only the Chernov family needs to know right now," the officer replies.

"I am a Chernov!" I shout.

The man scratches his chin and looks me up and down. "A young lady submitted everything to us over the weekend. We didn't want to ruin Halloween for the kids and were asked not to make an arrest until now."

Kim.

I growl. "Amelia, look at me." I place my hands on her shoulders as the officer opens the back door of the same patrol car where James is now detained.

She shakes her head. "I trust you, but I deserve this," her small voice says as her soul lets out a sob. It cuts through my skin and ribs and straight through my beating heart.

She steps in; he closes the door and pulls out.

I run back into the meeting; Andrei tries to grab my arm, but I rip him off.

Come heaven or Hades; I will get Amelia Anderson her library because I love her, and my heart is shattering into pieces.

I'll start by giving Mitchell Ricks a piece of my mind.

Chapter Twenty-Nine

Amelia

James rides with me in the car. I hug myself and let my tears fall.

James reaches out and pats my leg. "Look on the bright side. At least Neme didn't get stuck coming along with you."

Yes—that is a good thing, but it makes me cry more. Neme has licked up so many of my salty tears over the years.

"Maybe it's just the salt," I say out loud. I shake my head. Maybe he just likes the taste of my tears, not actually comforting me.

The tears come faster now. No, Neme knows me. I know he does.

If he was here, he would jump up on the extra seat between us and try to sit on my lap. Maybe he'd even whine a little for me.

I've never been to jail; no book has prepared me for this.

Criminals go to jail. I hide my face in my hands and weep. I feel James pat my back as he lets me howl.

I failed Mom.

I failed the library.

I failed Neme.

But the worst part of all, I love Lucas. My heart rips open, and it feels like a meat mallet is pulverizing it. I'm trying my hardest not to believe that he's betrayed me. The thought has crossed my mind several times now, and I push it out. I trust Lucas.

I'm angry at myself for being a criminal and letting my determination cloud my judgment.

I can't save the library if I am in jail. Craft time is tomorrow, and I have plans to use the pinecones I collected on the retreat. I hope Mr. Mettle won't leave for bingo. Those kids depend on craft time.

I won't be there for Evee, the twins, and Charlie Roo.

My flood of tears flow without relief as I'm now alone in a jail cell. The officer is kind and doesn't handcuff me, but I overhear them talking about me. "Remember that alarm we checked on a while back at the Chernov's mansion?"

I don't eavesdrop anymore, and my arms wrap around my waist again.

The corner of the cell is farthest away from the echo of the hallway, and I crouch down.

No loud tears come. Only the silent ones. The ones that make a permanent mark.

"Milly," James yells out. "Hang in there. Don't give up. This has happened to me before; it goes by quick."

I close my eyes and wish Mom was here, pushing back my hair.

She'd whisper, "Shh, shhh. Don't be sad. It will work out. You seem to have a way of making things harder than they need to be." She'd let out a soft sigh. "But the light you share along the way is worth every extra hurdle you put up for us, sweetheart. There, there now."

I can feel Neme licking my tears and Mom kissing my forehead. I don't let myself think about Lucas holding my hand, not yet.

"The sun is always up somewhere. It will come out again; you just wait and see," Mom had always said.

I let myself try to fall asleep to that thought, and I fade in and out for a few hours.

I hear the cell door open. "Milly, you've got a visitor." I don't recognize this officer.

My hair is slick and crusted against my cheek. I blink my eyes open and shake my head. "No, sir. Please, no." I can't hide the quiver in my voice.

"He's a handsome fellow; you sure?"

I am. I can't while my heart is still bleeding out.

"Please, sir." I wipe my nose. I didn't even know the silent tears started again.

I know I can't afford a lawyer, and I don't have any friends in law—except one. "Can I have a phone call?" I call out after him.

He nods his head and takes a few steps back toward me. "You'll have to wait, though. Public calls don't start until our secretary opens her office. She's out until tomorrow."

"You don't have a key to her office?"

"Nope, she's protective of her plants."

I nod my head, slip in and out of sleep, and pace the jail cell until an officer comes to unlock the door.

My legs are stiff, and I feel a new kink in my neck when the officer walks me to the phone booth inside the secretary's office. Sun rays plaster light across the leaves of the plants that take up every free space by the window.

"You've got a green thumb," I say as the phone rings and rings.

The younger-looking woman bends back the newspaper. "Two, actually," she says over her glasses. "Milly, right?" The woman doesn't look familiar.

The call connects, and I hear my friend's voice—I hope with all my heart that taking the time to care about his speedometer goal will pay off.

"Simon! It's me. Amelia. I'm—"

"Milly, I've been as worried as a cat on a hot tin roof. You wouldn't believe how cattywampus things are right now."

"Simon, I just...What are you talking about?"

"Just come down to the library, you'll see."

I squeeze my eyes shut and tap on the glass surrounding the phone booth. I don't know how to ask this. "I made a bad choice, Simon, and now they've locked me up, and I need someone."

"You're in jail?" He laughs into the phone. "Who's dumb enough to arrest you?" I swallow and no words come. "No matter. What's done is done. I'll suit up and be there in no time. Does your Granddaddy know?"

I whisper, "Yes, he was there."

He doesn't even say goodbye; the line just goes dead. I hang up, squint at the newspaper, and use my backward reading skills.

Librarian Thief and Demolition Effective Immediately

"May I?" I point to the paper.

"Oh honey, not in a million years. It will ruin your day, trust me."

A web of despair spins in my stomach, and tears burn like lava again. The officer escorts me back to my cell. It's just a matter of time now.

Later that afternoon, I hear loud voices—it's Simon, I'm sure.

I use my shirt to wipe my face off as best as possible. More loud voices come from the front. I hear, "Citizen rights," "I'm older than your grandpa," and "Son, who even taught you how to dress?"

Yep, it's Simon.

"Sir, you can't go back there!"

I hear a shuffle of feet. "Just let me talk to her, kay?"

Simon is a friend, even when I am here. I see him round the corner.

"Simon," I say, "you came!" He lifts his hat and nods.

His uniform is starched, and he looks like an officer from thirty years ago. "You even wore your badge." I point to the star on his shirt.

"This old thing?" He looks down, and his reflection in the badge smiles. "Of course I did. I haven't seen this much excitement since the year the knitting grandma's float got a flat tire in the Christmas parade!"

"What's happening out there?" I beg.

He pulls out some sunflower seeds from his pocket. "Let's get you out of here. You can see for yourself."

I close my eyes. "Are they really demolishing the library already? How could they? That's impossible; all the books..."

He nods. "The boss of some company already had his crew ready. They worked through the entire night long, straight through. Let's be honest, Milly. You didn't have a lot of books in that building to begin with."

I want to fight back and tell him about all the books upstairs. Or all the storage we had hidden somewhere. But that wasn't true, I'd donated everything the library didn't keep on the shelves.

"Something about a deadline they had to meet, or the deal was off. That part is still fuzzy, but they've packed everything inside white trailers and worked nonstop since the meeting. It's cleared out by now; their highfalutin boss thinks the sun comes up just to hear him crow."

I shake my head. "I don't like him."

More commotion and shuffling of feet bounce down the hallway.

The officer appears again. "Another visitor." He points to Simon. "You promised you'd be one minute, sir."

Simon narrows his eyes. "You ain't got the good sense God gave a rock if you think I'm leaving here before Milly does."

The officer pulls out the keys and twists the lock. "That's right now." He unlocks both cells.

James and I are free.

We round the corner back to the secretary's office; does everything happen in her office? She pretends to file in the corner as we all go into her office. I cover my mouth as Grandpoppy, Andrei, and Magnolia Grace round the corner. I met the woman briefly at the disastrous family dinner night.

"Grandpoppy?" His cane hits the ground lightly.

"Amelia." He reaches his hand outward and holds my hand. "You look like you slept in a lion's den. You okay, Mil?"

I try to build an emergency dam around my tear ducts and forbid them to overflow. They don't listen. "I'm fine, the library?"

"I know, Pumpkin. At least it will happen fast."

Magnolia Grace steps where I can see her.

"What do you mean?" I rub my eyes.

"Construction equipment rained in on us. There are some people out by the library protesting. I think they are starting demolition today."

Dark specks start to crowd my vision. "That's impossible," I say.

Grace touches my elbow lightly. "We'll fill you in on the drive. Let's get you home and cleaned up. All charges have been dropped."

The car ride home is a blur. Grace and Andrei take turns getting me caught up.

"Lucas has stayed up all night reading over Noil Construction's legal agreement with the Chernov firm. Apparently, there is a clause requirement and a deadline for demolition, or else the partnership will be dissolved," Andrei says.

"Mitchell panicked. Kim heard about Dimitry's suspicions and knew about Amelia charming you." She nods. "And she found a way to get the break-in photos," Grace says. "We contacted the security system management team, the main database keeps all footage for seven years. Even though Lucas deleted that night's footage, it would have been easy to get it by contacting the company."

Lucas deleted the security recording? "When was the security film deleted?" I ask.

"That same night," she says. "You could get recordings or photos back from their archive database. They make it difficult but not impossible."

My heart shoots up to my throat. I stare out the window. Lucas deleted my break-in that night. He never had any intention of turning me in when he could have from the very beginning. The first smile all day touches my face.

"Dimitry admitted to threatening Lucas. Kim somehow found out and stole the information from Dimitry."

"Is there any way we can stop what's happening to the library?" I ask.

She shakes her head. "I don't think so. All the legal documentation has been put into place, and he's moving fast, so we don't have time to find any loopholes."

Grace touches my hand. "Lucas hasn't slept a wink; he's there now, doing all he can. I hope you know how much he cares."

My hands stay fisted up in my pockets, hiding my shakes. My library is dying today, and a part of me with it.

I step out of the car into our house, hoping a shower and a meal will help me face the rest of the day.

The front door is slightly open when I arrive.

"Neme?" The house is still. I yell again, "Neme!" No hint of paws on the floor. No bark and no sound of nails hitting against the linoleum.

"Neme!" I run to my room. Next to Grandpoppy's and look underneath his bed. I run back to Grandpoppy, "Did you bring Neme somewhere?" I ask, panting.

He scowls. "No, he was here when I left earlier today."

Neme is gone, and a sinking fear takes hold.

I do the only thing I can think of—I call Lucas.

Chapter Thirty

Lucas

My shirt is rumpled, and I don't try to tuck it back in as I pace outside the library. Orange cones and yellow caution tape block off the road and the land the library sits on. Mitchell hasn't shown his face since yesterday.

I hold my phone in my hand in case Andrei needs me. I'm furious, but thankfully, Andrei was by my side all last night, so I didn't hit Mitchell in front of the town.

I'll do that today.

After Amelia was taken from the meeting, it was like a giant spiraling funnel of a bad deal gone doomsday.

Mayor Davis finally boomed his voice loud enough to gain control of the room, but Mitchell had come prepared with all the cunning flatteries to sway the decision in his favor, and I felt helpless.

I feel tricked and angry. At myself. And Mitchell. Everyone, except Amelia. I didn't know about the clause in the agreement about starting demolishing by a certain date, and that was my job to know. We had a demo date picked, but we still had time, or so I thought. The very thing I had spent months constructing, is now my enemy. Amelia and I created the perfect solution together—the perfect team—and now everything I thought I wanted before is unraveling right into my hands.

Have I always been this blind?

Mitchell brought the entire team down earlier that week so he could start demolition immediately after the meeting, and I had no idea he was planning this the entire time.

I guess it's my fate, my curse, to labor under cruelty—maybe that's my inheritance.

The officials say the library will relocate in "some unforeseeable future." My knuckles are so white I can see the nail marks on my palms.

Amelia's words stabbed me all night. "I trust you."

I had to see her, but the officer at the jail pointed toward the exit sign. "She doesn't want any visitors."

I have to fix this—I refuse to be like Dad.

Mitchell and Kim finally pull up in the late afternoon. The swarm of workers is on the tail end of bringing out furniture from the library. None of them has listened to me, even though I've demanded that they stop.

"Mitchell," I growl. The large excavator and loader have been unloaded out front, ripping up the grass and knocking down one of the lion statues as they park inside the yellow caution tape. "What do you think you're doing?" I should have brought a bodyguard. I need restraining.

"Well, well, well." He brushes his hands together and puts his hands inside his designer jean pockets, the kind that no old man should ever wear. "Look who shows up when the work is done."

I flare my nostrils. "You didn't have to go about it like this!" I point to some bystanders holding up homemade signs saying *I heart the library.* If everyone in town hadn't heard about last night's meeting, the morning newspaper would make sure to change that. The audience appeared first thing in the morning and was still growing.

"You humiliated Amelia and tossed one of the kindest people in jail." She is so much more than that to me. She has become my sun, moon, and stars. The part of me that makes sense—the part that makes being not normal worth it. "Just to start on the project earlier? The library is going nowhere. There was a better way, Mitchell."

Dad wouldn't have hit anyone, and I am glad I am not Dad. I take a step back and swing at him.

He takes a step back, missing the bulk of my swing.

He laughs. "Lucas, you've been so dedicated. You've helped the company stay alive." He wipes his lip. I haven't broken the skin yet. I'll have to swing harder.

"Your father was right," he takes a step back, "you were the best asset to my company."

"My father?" How does Mitchell know Dad?

Mitchell tips his head to the side. "You didn't know?" He laughs, "Your father and I go way back." He draws an arch with his hands. "He said you'd be a bull, just like he was, and you'd save my company, dominate, really. And this project will finally bring it all together. He was right about you."

I am going to make him bleed.

"It's a shame I'll have to fire you." He backs up toward the library door.

He keeps moving backward, and I spit out, "I quit—" and turn to walk away, but Kim pops out from around the corner, stopping my path.

"Lucas! I wanted to ask how your girlfriend's night was." She widens her eyes like she cares. "She looked really scared when all the police officers came in to take her away," she pouts.

My organs bake. "She's one of the bravest women I know, Kim."

She pulls her lips to the side of her face. "Well, she won't be interested in you anymore; you're letting her library go bye-bye." She waves her hand.

"Please," I say through my teeth, "push the demo date back until she has a chance to be here herself? Or until all the Chernovs have a chance to evaluate their positions?"

I need to buy time, even just one day; that's all I need.

She shakes her finger. "You made it perfectly clear where our relationship stood when you called off our engagement, Lucas." She leans in close, and I cringe at the thought of how many times

I kissed her lips. "You can't offer me anything that Dimitry isn't giving me. This project will be a good thing." She points to the people. "You should use your energy to make sure everyone stays safe. The building is almost empty. We'll start tearing it down before the sun goes down."

She pats my cheek like I am her dog, and my skin curls—she is a witch in sheep's clothing. My phone lights up the same moment the large loader engine roars alive.

It's Amelia—I run back to my truck so I can hear over the rumble of the engine. "Amelia, are you okay?"

"Is Neme with you?"

"No, I—I haven't seen him since Halloween. Are you safe?" I ask.

"I'm home," her voice cracks. "Lucas, I need your help."

I won't fail her this time.

"Neme's gone."

"What can I do?" I ask.

Her voice is higher than normal. "I'll look along, Magnus. Will you take the flood wall? I'll drive there, too; maybe he's along the way."

"We'll find him," I say. "Amelia, I'll make this up to you," is the only thing I can think of saying. She clicks the phone.

Reinforcements are needed—so I call Baba.

My voice hurts from calling Neme's name so much.

I round the corner to get back to the library—more and more people are gathering on the street, and Mitchell paces the property line like a territorial hawk.

I text out the group, *"Any luck?"*

Baba lays down the grandma card, and every single one of my siblings drops everything they are doing and starts looking for Neme.

Except for Nikola.

Their replies come back almost instantly, all saying the same thing: *no*.

I round the corner and see two of my brothers, Apollo and Max, at the library. They are inside the yellow tape, wearing hard hats, watching the building start to come down.

I feel like a villain—it's really happening.

The excavator hasn't gotten very far; they stop to confirm all power and gas has been turned off. The engine starts up again, and I see Amelia running down the street and through the small crowd.

She doesn't look like herself. "No, *no*!" I hear her yell and burst through the tape. The police are helping patrol the streets now, and Amelia slips through them. Blood rushes through my legs as they pound fast to stop her.

Amelia should not be watching this. She deserves to be taken far away and to have her own private library built for her. But that's the thing about Amelia: She doesn't want the library for herself. She wants it for the community and for her mother's legacy.

I run as fast as I can. "Whoa, there!"

I can barely hear Max over the loader and the crush of bricks.

She starts swinging her fist. Apollo holds both of her wrists. "Amelia, it's over," Apollo yells over the engine.

I step up next to her; she lurches into my chest. "He's in there. Lucas, I know he's in there! My Nemean is in there!"

"What are you—" I don't finish talking and run toward the loader and yell for him to stop. All workers must have been ordered to ignore me. So I turn and embrace my inner Amelia—I don't think.

I run through the door and dart to the children's area; dust fills the air. I cough and squint. The building is bare, and I hear some bricks tumbling down.

The loader crunches through the building again, in the same corner. My thighs burn as I bend and check every possible small nook he can hide in, shouting.

I hear a loud siren, and the loader finally turns off. Voices are yelling outside, and I hear it—a very small whimper.

Neme.

"Neme?" I wheeze. He whimpers again, and I approach the crushed corner. A part of the bookshelf has popped off the wall, and there is a half doorway opening hole that looks like it is just big enough for Neme to get through. I whip out my phone, turn on the light, and hold it in my teeth as I crawl along the floor.

"Emean," I try to call through my teeth—I am getting closer to the whimper. The crawl space is tight, and I have to force myself through, metal mesh and nails ripping through my jeans and shirt, reaching my skin. I feel a cool, damp flooring as the room opens, and I stand up.

Neme's whines are loud.

I hold the flashlight around the room, and I spot Neme. His paw is stuck between the wall and the floor. The floor must have separated from the wall over time, and the excavator compressed them back together, trapping Neme's paw.

I grip a metal pole on the ground and smack the wall with all my might, but it doesn't budge. I hear a few more bricks from the third and second floors hit the top of this room. I flash the light around. It has bars for a window, and it looks like all the walls are metal.

With all my might, I shove the bar into the crevice and pry with every muscle of my body. I feel a pop in my shoulder, and a searing pain bursts through my back muscles. I use the adrenaline pumping through my veins, and I scream.

I let the scream come from deep within, from all my failures, and for better versions of myself I want to be. A small movement in the metal wall finally gives in, and Neme pulls his paw out. I nearly tumble to the ground out of strain.

Neme whines as I rush to the small entrance. Neme only moves enough to lie down.

"Come on, she needs you."

He whines softly as he licks his paw.

"Neme, stay focused." I bend down and push him up. "We need to get you out; Joe will be so happy to hear what you found," I say as the pain shoots through my back. I have to focus on breathing. I moan out, "Remember the first time we met?" I say, crawling through the small entranceway. I am trying my best to push him forward. "You left lots of your slobber in my house, remember that?" I smile, remembering how sticky it is. "Amelia still needs your slobber, boy. She needs you. Just like I need her," I say through the strain. My arm is going to fall off.

She is worth it.

I see a flashlight peer through the small pathway—his silhouette fills the small entrance. Dimitry.

"What are you doing in here?" I cough.

The dust is so thick I can barely see his face. I cough again, and Neme doesn't even flinch.

"I run into falling buildings just for fun. If I see my older brother do it, then I think I have to try it too."

"You know you shouldn't follow his example; he's just trying to find his own way in the world." I moan with every movement.

"That's what he doesn't get; so are we all. And we admire every effort he makes."

He puts the light on the ground and crawls in. The light bounces off the small tunnel the bookshelf and metal wall form. He pulls Neme through the hole.

I can't move; he slips back in and pulls my good arm out. I yell out.

"Plus, someone has to save the hero," he says.

I almost let out a laugh, but it would hurt too much, and I slump more to the ground.

"And just to warn you—" his face frowns, but his eyes are bright— "you'll probably get arrested for dashing into a building being demolished. Or Baba might drag you to the jail herself."

"I don't think he can walk, Dimitry," I say, looking at Neme.

"Here." He hoists me up. "I'll get you. Can you help carry him?" I nod as we both bend down. Dimitry is keeping the balance for both of us. The hundred and fifty-pound dog lets us pick him up as we make it toward the door.

"I'm sorry for everything," he says.

"I know. I am, too."

He pushes both the doors open, and several police officers are at the entrance to help us with Neme.

Amelia charges at me and hoists up my other side. "Thank you," she whispers as her warm body holds me up.

Baba, my brothers, and a few library board members gather around me as the emergency team sits me on the bench and begins to clean me up. Blood, dust, and sweat itch my face, but I keep my eyes on Neme.

"Neme's going to be okay," Andrei says, trying to distract me. The emergency response team steps away to get more supplies.

Mitchell walks over to my first-aid circle. "Don't think sabotaging today will stop the building being demolished, Lucas." He holds up the keys to the loader. "We'll get the police to clear this lot and work through the night until this building is flattened."

Amelia's face turns white.

"Not so fast, Mitchell." I see Nikola running up to our circle. I stand up to face him. "Neme found something in there that will buy me time."

He shakes his head. "You're fibbing."

"No, I'm not. And the National Historical Society will do whatever they can to protect what Neme found. That is—until the building's new owner takes over."

"What are you talking about?" he asks.

I turn, letting my arm hang limply at my side.

Nikola steps in. "In two weeks' time, Lucas will be the new sole owner of this lot and building. He's in the process of selling other investment properties and apartments. He's offered Chernov Realty the future market value. We are proceeding with the sale on the contingency that all his capital comes through. I would have stopped everything last night, but I hadn't finalized the contract."

Mitchell stumbles backward. "I'm calling my lawyer." He fumbles with his pocket. "I'll find a way to get to you, Lucas!" He scans the crowd for Kim and fumes off.

Amelia jumps to the undamaged side of my body. Her skin soothes the pain. "I just..." she says, eyes wide, "you bought the library?" The beam of joy from her face is blinding.

Her lips touch my cheek.

"Remember the pumpkin and raccoon keychain I bought you?" I ask. "It's for the key to—" her lips cut off my words. And just like that, I know what the passcode is.

At least I have an idea of what word Dad wants me to know because I can feel it in my proverbial invisible scar: the need to make things better than they once were.

Baba reaches for me and grabs my hand. She looks at the demolished lion statue. "I was wrong." She shakes her head. "You didn't have to slay a lion to start breaking our family curse." She points back to Neme. "You needed to save one."

My eyes blink back tears as my brothers nod in approval at me—all that time I spent running away, swimming in my own anger and grief, with a nod of a head and a blink, they forgive me.

My selfishness is forgiven and swallowed up.

I wipe my wet face and hold my arm still. "Joe, can you hear me?" I holler.

A few of my brothers step out of the way, and I see his feathered hat bobbing. "It depends on who's asking," he hollers. "I ain't the type to break up a family reunion." He takes a step closer.

I let one corner of my mouth smile. "Guess what Neme found in the library?" He takes off his hat and holds it against his chest. "The lost jailhouse."

Joe smiles and small airy laughs bubble out. He shakes his head and puts his hat back on. "Pumpkin Spice, you were hiding treasures in there after all."

Chapter Thirty-One

Lucas

Six weeks later

The room is crowded; hot cinnamon and pumpkin fill my nose. The long table in Grace's office has mini poinsettias and juniper sprigs along the middle. The lights that hang around the edges of the room pop more as the sun goes down.

My inheritance box sits on the table in front of where I am sitting. I decide to wait to open it until Mom is back in town. Waiting is easy; I am plenty busy gathering data for what patrons want to see in the updated library.

The brothers are okay waiting for me to open the box, too. I promise them that I'll attend every family function for the next five years. Andrei keeps himself busy and seems somber.

It gives my arm time to heal and time to contact historical societies. They've speculated that the old jail cell was sealed, hidden, and blocked off not long after the building was built, over a hundred years ago. Documentation was lost, and only local lore kept the story alive that a jail cell existed and was sealed up somewhere in town.

Several local historians are on the trail to discover the mystery behind the jail cell, who was incarcerated there, and why no one other than local lore knew about it.

The plan is to convert that part of the library into a museum and gift shop with two apartments on the upper floors, keeping the front portion for the town library. After all the feedback from the town, Mikey Edgewood suggestion won out. The demolished back corner will become a three-story-long slide.

I'm happy to oblige.

When Mom returns to town, one of the first things she does is talk to Mitchell Ricks. Shortly after, he closes his construction business. I don't ask, and I know in the back of my mind I don't even want to touch that can of worms.

Each of Dad's past wives are sitting at the end of the table. I give them all a hug. Baba is sampling the bursting hors d'oeuvre table: cheeses, crackers, grapes, salamis of all sizes, fruit in all colors, and several pies.

All my brothers are there, and Atticus is wearing Christmas lights, with pants—it's a miracle.

I roll my eyes still; he now has a mullet with a mustache.

We are waiting for Amelia and her grandfather. I look at my watch. *Running late, be there in five!* her message flashes.

I feel the small box inside my pocket. I want to offer her forever if she'll have me. Everyone knows I am planning on proposing, except Amelia.

The passcode, *restore*, is constantly on my mind now.

That one word takes an entire spreadsheet and library debacle to find—and an Amelia to really help me understand.

She pulls up outside, and soft snow starts to fall. She is wearing one of her favorite T-shirts, *Hug a Librarian for Luck*. She helps her grandfather and Neme inside.

The vet says Neme will have a limp for the rest of his life; Amelia takes the news well. Mr. Mettle officially retires from the library, and Amelia fills the director role. She'll bring Neme any day he's up for it.

I can see her soft, curly hair through the window.

"Can a speech wait until after you open it?" Vincent asks.

Everyone starts to settle around the table, and I nod in agreement.

Amelia and Neme walk up to the front near me. I bend low and kiss her cheek. "You're late."

"Like always."

I reach my arm down and pinch her bum. She yelps, and Baba frowns at her. She pretends that she finds something in her hair and steps on my toe.

"I deserve that," I whisper in her ear. My stomach clamps.

"It's time, you ready?" she asks

"As I'll ever be."

I pull the box toward me. "Vincent has requested no speech." Everyone sits down, and the room feels as still as ice. "I just have to say thank you for everyone being here."

My sweaty palms lift the box lid up. It's made of cedar, with the Chernov seal as a crest on top. I pull out a manila envelope. Andrei's name is across the top, and I place it in his hand.

I don't look at the other folders in it; they seem legal enough, and I'll unpack everything after I propose to Amelia.

The smaller white envelope is easy to find; my heart pounds in my ears.

There is no dog saliva or holes, and I smile, clear my throat, and read out loud:

Lucas,

I can imagine how you might feel about my inheritance hunt, which I'm putting everyone on. It was the only thing I could think of that could hopefully bring you closer together.

I know how much pressure I put on you and how hurtful some of my demands were to you. I want you to know it's one of the biggest regrets of my life: forcing my will onto you, forcing it on any of your brothers. I didn't want to ask for forgiveness on my deathbed; I didn't want your pity.

But I do still want your forgiveness.

Not for me anymore, but for you. I want you to learn from me. Holding onto hate becomes heavy and selfish. I don't want to leave that for you.

Forgive me for you, *Lucas.*

Despite my big handful of regrets, I also have so many things I did right. Having each one of my children was my greatest accomplishment. I don't know what path in life you will take, and I'm sorry I forced you away from the family.

My gift to you reflects one word that I want for you.

Restore.

I want to gift my "restore" projects. You will have access to a five million dollar trust fund. It never goes as far as you think; you know this by now. But I trust you will find projects, hopefully in Herasburg, that can have the biggest impact on our family, the community, and your future family. Please see attached the current projects I was working on before I was diagnosed.

Please accept your inheritance and help me restore things of the past. Start by forgiving your dad.

Your ever-loving father,

Zolton Chernov.

A QR code is underneath his name.

I wipe my eyes. Nikola and Dimitry snatch the letter away from me as I let the letter circulate the room.

I pull Amelia close and know—I want to forgive him for myself, her, and for my brothers.

"I love you," I whisper into her hair. "Follow me..."

Amelia

Lucas rests his jacket over my shoulders. The small flakes fall, and my goosebumps make my teeth chatter. Large bright ornaments decorate the city lamp posts—Neme stays inside; I don't know how long of a walk it will be. His steps have been slow ever since his paw was wedged in the side of a collapsing library. No more jogs.

Lucas, he'll go on long jogs with me—he pulls my arm along Magnus Avenue.

The town Christmas tree is especially large this year. All the children place small red bows on the tree, and city employees finish the top half. The tree has perfect proportions on top and is clumped up and sporadic on the bottom.

"It looks like me and you," I say. His warm hand stops the cold from reaching my bones.

He laughs. "You complement me perfectly." He kisses my forehead.

"Spontaneous and fun-loving. Maybe a little more complicated than necessary?" I'm glad he doesn't answer. I cling to his arm, and he embraces me as we make it to the library lot.

"Bartholomew the Boastful was a noble guardian of the library. I'm sad for Gertrude. She doesn't have her friend anymore."

"Are you talking about the statues?"

My mouth cracks open; does he need to know I named the statues? My eyes wrinkle. "I gave at least one a kiss most days. They've done their duty better than I could have ever wished for."

Lucas reaches behind me, positioning himself into a back bear hug, his warm chest blanketing me. "What if we have a replacement statue?"

I smile. "I would love that. Could it be a lion?"

"What do you think if it's Nemean? The lion dog, watching over the library?"

I cover my mouth and then give Lucas a kiss, deep and full. "That would be so special. The children would love that. So would I," I say after I pull away.

"Let's put it on the ground so the kids can climb on him." He runs his hand through his hair. "I can see Mikey riding him like a bull."

We both laugh. His warm breath warms the air between us. He looks over to the window where Magnolia Grace's office is at. Anton, one of his brothers, waves at us from the window—Lucas gives him a thumbs up.

"I want to ask you something, Amelia Anderson, then I'll take you back inside."

I twist in his arms and several flakes land on my cheeks. I turn back around, and words light up along the entire front building of the library.

Will you Ma__y me? Two R's flicker in and out until they pop and go dark.

"Will you Ma__y me?" I crunch up my nose and twist my head. Lucas looks back at the lawyer's window. He frowns.

"No, no—it's supposed to say..."

I pull his warm cheeks into my cold hands and look into his eyes. "I love it."

His soft eyes meet my lips. "Will you May me?"

"Yes," my smile is wide. "I want to May you. I'll May you forever."

We seal our promise with a long exploring kiss, an expression of the commitment we forge together—the kind of kiss that reaches beyond the end of a book and into the part of my heart that will never forget.

We look over at the party window. Neme is sitting in a chair, and everyone is cheering, arms raised.

"I have most of my assets tied up in the library. How do you feel if we live in one of the apartments planned for upstairs?" His tender lips haven't lingered far from my skin.

I imagine Mom smiling down, shaking her head. *See, baby girl? It always works out.* I imagine her saying, and I know that I will never forget how many dreams have come true.

My love story has been about the library all along.

Historical Note

The Buena Vista Public Library in Buena Vista, Virginia inspired this book. Originally built as a courthouse, it was transformed into the library for the city of Buena Vista in 1971. Though hidden from patrons, the jail cells from its courthouse days still remain.

Libraries are pillars of local resources, and I'm over the moon about everything our small-town library does—it's truly a bright spot in our community. This story was conceived out of love for our local library. I wanted to pay tribute to it and raise awareness of the vital role small-town libraries play in supporting their communities.

Acknowledgments

Jason F. Wright's writing classes at Southern Virginia University: You changed my life.

Classmates and writers' group: Each of you have also changed my life.

Neil: The love and support you showed when reading a draft of this manuscript was monumental. I love everything about you, even the part where you dislike fiction.

Camden Cooper: Thank you so much for your help and support as a friend and editor!

Ally Haney: Your creativity, diligence, and attention to detail are truly a gift. Thank you so much for all your work on the cover and for being you!

Joy Hensley: You are ridiculously talented, and I'm so grateful for you. I can't wait for your romcoms! Thank you for your vital role in helping me make my self imposed deadline.

To all of my beta readers: You were pivotal in shaping this book, and I cannot thank you enough for looking past the typos and providing essential feedback!

Lastly, and firstly, I want to thank God for giving me the strength to perform gymnastic time management skills, for the ideas, and for the stamina to grow through all that's required when you decide to pick up writing as a hobby and you're terrible at all things English. It's a lot. I'm so grateful for the team of support I know He has placed in my path.

If you've ever wanted to write a book, I need you to know that I believe in you.

Cast

Amelia Anderson – Librarian

Lucas Chernov– Oldest son and Head Contractor at Noil Construction

Nemean (Neme) – Newfoundland Dog

Grandpoppy – Amelia's Grandfather

Baba (Babushka) – Lucas's Grandmother

Mikey Edgewood – Library Patron

Sandy – Library Board Member, Patron, Grandmother of Mikey

Simon – Retired police officer with speedometer.

Magnolia Grace (Lawyer)

Mitchell Ricks - Noil Construction CEO

Kim Ricks - Daughter or Mitchell and ex-fiancé of Lucas

Mayor Davis – Mayor of Herasburg

Marcus Mettle – Library Director

Anya – Lap dog

James Hodd – Library Patron

Evee – Library Patron

Charlie Roo – Library Patron

Twins – Library Patron

Georgy – Son Library Patron

Rosabell – Library Patron

Bob – Security system creator

New Officer – Mullet and mustache ambassador

George – Police Officer

Sally Carter – Secretary of Lawyer

Betty Sue Tate – Substitute town recorder

Aaron – Carries Fiancé

Clyde – Executive Director of Library Board

Gertrude of Goodness and Bartholomew the Boastful – Lion Statues

Mrs. Licket – Library Board Member

Joe – Library Board Member and treasure hunter

Mev – Treasure hunter enthusiasts

Mary and Maryanne – Daughter and Mother on Library Board

Savanna – Works at Holy Sheep

Gemma – Library Board member

Brenton Hill – BAT representative

Char Char and Benzie – Bats

Camden (Cams) and Devin (Dev) – Apollos best friends

Patty – Rosabell's shih tzu

Brian – Kind barber

Addy – Secretary for Blackwall Sons Brokerage Firm

Katie Dale – Bank Teller and Town Gossip

Leroy – James Nephew

Loretta – Town recorder on vacation

Luna Prosa – Works at Amora Comida

Karol – Engineer

Sydney – Worker at Fannie's Fry

Linda Anderson – Amelia's late Mother

Zolton Blackwall (Late Father)

Harriet (First and Last marriage)

Felicity (Second marriage)

Leah Road (Third marriage)

Alydia (Fourth marriage)

Brothers in order

Zolton and Harriet

1)Lucas

2)Andrei (Drew)

3)Nikola (Nik)

4)Dimitry (Dim)

Zolton and Felicity

5)Atticus (Att)

6)Anton

7)Maximillian (Max)

Zolton and Leah

8)Vincent (Vin)

9)Apollo (AP)

Zolton and Alydia

10)Remington (Rem)

www.ingramcontent.com/pod-product-compliance
Ingram Content Group UK Ltd.
Pitfield, Milton Keynes, MK11 3LW, UK
UKHW012251290726
14090UKWH00016B/595

9 798218 524524